ROSE OF ANZIO

Book One ~ Moonlight

Alexa Kang

For Maria Ting

Acknowledgements

Rose of Anzio began as a personal challenge for me, but over the course of last year, I discovered that writing a full-length novel (four novels, in fact) is a group project. Words alone cannot express my gratitude to everyone who had encouraged me and helped me bring this series to its completion. I am still amazed at the time and efforts of those who volunteered to help me make this story stronger and better.

Thanks to Anneth White, who first encouraged me to write this story and continuing to inspire me by following it faithfully throughout. Thank you to Pamela Ann Savoy, who gave me great feedback on story ideas and development along the way, and took time out of her super busy schedule to proofread my work as I wrote. Thanks to Eleanna Sakka, whose shoulder was always available for me to lean on every time I hit the wall. My utmost gratitude to Brandon Bjorklund, a fellow writer and good friend who reached out to teach me the ropes of self-publishing, and gave me valuable advice and support throughout the process. Also, a very special thank you to Ms. CandyTerry, who gave me a huge amount of moral support, as well as the first platform for me to introduce this story.

My heartfelt thank you to both Kristen Tate, my content editor, whose suggestions and insights helped me improve my story significantly, and

Geoff Byers, for his tremendous help and advice on how to create and construct my battle scenes throughout the entire series so I could keep the story as realistic as possible. Thanks to Stephen Reid, for making sure Tessa speaks proper British English. Thanks also to my copy editor Fiona Hallowell, and proofreaders Margaret Dean and T.J. Moore, for making my story a truly polished piece of work.

Last but not least, thanks to my husband, Dan, for his unending amount of patience and support.

PART ONE
The Rose Garden

Chapter 1

It all began in the rose garden.

A dark blue Buick convertible pulled up to the entrance of the driveway leading to a limestone mansion. The mansion itself was barely visible from the street, but from there, the passersby could catch glimpses of the magnificent rose garden in front of the house.

Anthony Ardley got out of the car, said goodbye to his friend who had driven him, and walked toward his home. It was only the end of May, still early in the summer, but the Chicago heat had already started to swell. He didn't mind though. With the heat, his summer vacation had begun.

Home at last.

Exams, over. No more term papers. No more endless debate team meetings. His first year at the University of Chicago, finished.

He slung his duffle bag over his shoulder. In the familiar front yard ahead, the roses in the garden should be in full bloom.

Indeed, the blossoms were as spectacular as he expected. What he didn't expect was a teenage girl kneeling on the ground, chopping away at the flowers surrounding the tiered water fountain. Her brown hair, cut just below her shoulders, fell forward down her neck. Her arms were lithe and quick as she gathered the cut roses. He had never seen her before.

Vandal! He walked closer. She was an unusual-looking girl. She wore her hair straight. Girls didn't usually wear their hair straight. Her bangs were dampened by perspiration and her hands and slender fingers were covered in soil. She wiped the sweat dripping down the side of her face, leaving a dirt mark on her left cheek. So immersed in her task of ravaging the roses, she didn't look up when he approached.

"Who are you?" he demanded to know. "You're trespassing."

"Who are you?" she asked him back, surprising him with her British accent. "Why do I have to answer to you?"

"Because this is my home," he said. A large patch of the flowerbed was now in disarray. "What have you done? You're destroying private property."

The girl barely raised an eyebrow. Without answering him, she picked up the cut flowers and put them into a bag next to her, then got up and walked away.

"Hey!" he called out after her. "Come back here! I'm not done talking to you."

Ignoring him, she disappeared onto the street, leaving him with no answer except the gurgles of water flowing down the fountain.

He looked at the ravaged scene she left behind. His family had set aside this part of the garden as a dedication. They had planted the most beautiful species of roses here. Several home and gardening magazines had even printed feature articles about it. Now, patches of leaves and shrubs were crushed. Headless stems stuck out from what was once an enchanting arrangement of flowers. The garden's beauty was ruined.

Their gardener would surely have a fit tomorrow.

He crouched down and removed the leaves that covered the small memorial plaque on the ground. Designed in the shape of a rock, the plaque was placed in an inconspicuous spot of the flowerbed to naturally blend into the garden's landscape. Engraved on the plaque were the words, "Anthony Browning, 1903–1919 ~ Gone but not forgotten." He had never met the person named on the plaque. He did, however, feel a special kinship with the deceased. Anthony Browning was his father's cousin and had passed away before he was born. His father had named him in memory of Browning. Growing up, many people had said he and Browning looked alike, with the same blond hair and athletic built.

The memorial garden. What a mess it had become. Who was that girl? Was she a neighbor's kid? Perhaps a British family had moved into the neighborhood? He needed to tell his mother and ask her if she knew the girl. They should tell the girl's parents what she had done. He hurried up the lane toward the circular driveway in front of the house.

Inside his home, his Uncle Leon was visiting with his parents in the parlor. Actually, Leon Caldwell was his father's other cousin. But as far back as he could remember, he had always called him Uncle Leon.

His mother, Sophia, rose from her seat when he walked in. "Anthony! You're home."

"Mother." He threw down his duffle bag and gave her a hug. "Father," he said to his father.

His father, William, also got up to greet him. "Welcome home."

"Did you see what happened outside? A girl stole roses from the memorial garden. She made a total mess of it. Do you know who she is? Is she a neighbor's kid?"

"She's not a neighbor." Sophia took his arm and walked him into the room. "That was Tessa. Tessa Graham. She's staying with us."

"Staying with us?"

"Come. Take a seat," William said. "We'll tell you all about her later."

Anthony sat down next to his mother. "Uncle Leon, what brought you here today?"

"Came to talk to your father about trade opportunities in Latin America," Leon said. "Europe is having widespread shortages of everything with that war they got themselves into. Oil, metals, sugar, everything. If all I care about are profits, we should absolutely invest more in South America, for access to raw materials if nothing else. As it is, though," he said and rubbed his chin, "I have a lot of misgivings about putting my money into anything that might get us more involved with that pot of trouble in Europe. A lot."

"What's happening with the war?" Anthony asked. "I haven't kept up with the news. Been buried with exams the last few weeks."

"Things aren't looking good," William said. "The war, it's spreading like a disease through the Continent."

"Tell me about it," Leon said. "It's a plague. They better keep their sickness in quarantine. Don't let us catch a whiff and infect us with it." He finished the last drop of his brandy. "I don't understand those people. Wasn't the last time bad enough? Wasn't it supposed to be the war to end all wars? But no, they're at it all over again. Well I say, let them stew in their own juice this time. Keep us out of it."

Neither William nor Anthony disputed him. They knew well how vocal Leon could be with his anti-intervention views. Few people were as well-versed as he when it came to the political and economic arguments against American involvement, and he would be the first to debate anyone on the subject. As his family, though, they knew the real reason why he felt this way. His brother, Lex, had been an air force pilot. Lex died in the Great War twenty-two years ago. Before he died, they had been close.

William Ardley, Leon and Lex Caldwell, and Anthony Browning. The four cousins had grown up together and were very close.

"But Juliet and Dean are over there in London," Sophia said. Her mention of Juliet piqued Anthony's attention. Juliet was an unspoken taboo in the Ardley household. He didn't know all the details as to why.

Juliet had left the family before he was born and he had never met her. All he knew was, Anthony Browning's father had adopted her after his son passed away, and as a result, she became part of their extended family. Something happened afterward and led to a fall-out. The fall-out was so bad that his late grandmother Helen Ardley had absolutely forbidden anyone from mentioning Juliet in her presence when she was alive. Even now, with his grandmother no longer here, his parents and uncle became somber at the mere mention of Juliet's name.

"Since we're on the subject, Anthony. The girl you asked about before, Tessa, she's Dean and Juliet's daughter," William said.

"Dean and Juliet's daughter? Are you serious?"

"We didn't tell you earlier because you were busy with exams and there was no reason to disturb you. I went to London last month to see Juliet and Dean. London's unsafe. I invited them to come back with me but they didn't want to. They did agree Tessa should come live with us until they're sure England is safe."

"Oh." He couldn't believe his father had gone to London. No one in the family had spoken to Juliet in years.

"It must be tough for Tessa," Sophia said. "She's young. She's in a foreign country away from her parents, living with people she never met before she came."

"I don't know about that, Sophie," William smiled at his wife. He always called her "Sophie" as a term of affection. "If she's anything like her mother, she won't be fazed by any of this." He spoke with the tone of fondness he used whenever he talked about Anthony Browning and Lex. Anthony had never heard his father speak this way about Juliet before. It seemed his trip to London had brought them closer again.

"She's been good with Alexander," Leon said, referring to his ten-year-old son. "I wish she and Katherine could be friends though. They're the same age. I thought they would become best friends." Katherine was Leon's fourteen-year-old daughter.

"You want them to be the way we used to be with Juliet," William said. Leon smiled and didn't deny it.

"Sometimes, you just can't go back." William looked over at a framed photo on the display cabinet. In the photo, he, Leon, Lex, and Anthony Browning were still teenagers. They had their arms around each other's shoulders.

"At least Juliet is back on speaking terms with us," Sophia said. "Anthony?"

"Yes, Mother?"

"Try to make Tessa feel welcome and at home, will you? We must all try."

"Of course." Feeling a little ashamed, he shifted his eyes away from her. Maybe he shouldn't have been so confrontational with the girl earlier. He would have to properly introduce himself and make it up to her later. "But why was she picking the flowers in the rose garden?"

"She takes them to the hospital. Apparently, Juliet planted a rose garden in London in memory of your uncle Anthony too. Juliet's a nurse now. When the flowers bloom, she brings them to her patients. In the summer, she always took Tessa with her." Sophia took a sip of her tea. "Tessa asked us if she could take our roses to the hospital and I told her yes. I guess it's a way for her to keep something consistent in her life."

"Isn't it strange to take flowers away from a memorial garden?"

"Not for Juliet," William said. "Anthony and Juliet used to bring roses to the hospitals every week for the Great War veterans. They started doing that after Lex died. As for taking roses from the memorial garden…" He glanced at Leon. "She said that's what Anthony would've wanted." He turned back to his son, "You know, our rose garden was originally her idea."

That their rose garden was Juliet's idea was news to Anthony. The garden had been there since before he was born. He had never thought to ask how it came about.

"Leon, why don't you and Anna bring Katherine and Alexander over this Sunday?" Sophia asked. "Now that Anthony's home, we can have a nice family reunion and Tessa can get to know everyone better."

"Sure. I'll tell Anna."

"How about we make it a pool party?" Anthony said. "Katherine and Alexander can invite their friends."

"That's a wonderful idea," Sophia said. "Tessa can meet some new friends. What do you think, Leon?"

"I'm all for it."

"It's settled then." She sat back into her seat. A gush of admiration rose in Anthony's heart. His mother was always so thoughtful and considerate. She knew exactly how to make everyone around her feel important. His father's success owed no small part to her ability to make his clients feel special when she accompanied him to social functions.

"What?" she asked, noticing her son staring at her.

"Nothing," he said. "Just, it's good to be home."

# # #

When Leon left in the late afternoon, Anthony finally had time for the swim he had been looking forward to all day. Back in high school, he had been a swimming champion and the captain of his academy's swim team. He competed at the university level now, usually with excellent results.

He couldn't wait to dive into the pool. His parents had built this swimming pool especially for him. In the water, he could move around with the kind of freedom he had nowhere else. For him, swimming felt like flying in the air.

On his way to the pool, he saw Tessa lying under a tree. The girl didn't tell anyone she had come back and no one knew she had returned. *So aloof*, he thought.

Remembering what his mother had said, he decided to take a detour to reintroduce himself. Beneath the tree, she lay with her eyes closed and a book by her side. He couldn't tell if she was asleep or if she had heard him coming.

"Hello, Tessa?"

She opened her eyes. Standing under the tree, he towered over her. He thought she would get up but she didn't. Without acknowledging him, she closed her eyes again.

"I'm Anthony." He crouched down to be closer to her level. She opened her eyes again. He smiled and made an effort to be friendly.

"You're Uncle William and Aunt Sophia's son."

"Yes. I heard you'll be living with us for a while."

"Apparently so."

"Sorry about before. I thought you were one of the neighbors' kids vandalizing our property."

"Apology accepted."

Her answer put him off. He didn't expect her to say that. He wasn't really apologizing to her. It was only a polite way to break the ice. She ought to know that. After all, he hadn't known who she was and she had made a mess of the garden. And now, it was as if he had done something wrong and he was apologizing to a kid.

"You should talk to Mr. Miller. He's our gardener. He can teach you how to handle the roses properly."

She didn't answer him, only frowned. She closed her eyes again. Her attitude was beginning to annoy him. Still, he held his tongue. "What are you reading?"

"A book."

He might as well be talking to a wall. He picked up the book next to her. *Damian*, by Herman Hesse. An unusual read for a girl, he thought. Definitely not a book of choice for any girl he knew. Not even for the older girls at his school. More popular with them would be something by Jane Austen or Edith Wharton. Maybe poetry by Wordsworth or Emerson, or Charles Dickens if they liked something deeper.

"I prefer to be left alone if you don't mind," she said.

She preferred to be alone? Did she think he didn't have better things to do? He tried to be nice, and all she did was give him a bad attitude.

"All right. Suit yourself." He put the book back on the ground and walked away. He had told his mother he would welcome her. He tried. It was not his concern to waste time befriending a sulking teenage girl.

He walked to the pool and jumped in. In the cool refreshing water, he gave no more thought to the girl under the tree.

PART TWO
The Pool Party

Chapter 2

It was a festive Sunday afternoon at the Ardley residence. Leon Caldwell, along with his wife Anna and his children Katherine and Alexander, had come for the pool party as planned. The Ardleys had invited the Lowes, their long-time neighbors. Their son, Brandon Lowe, was Anthony's friend and university classmate who had driven him home several days ago when the school year ended.

As much as Tessa would have rather spent the day by herself instead of being with a group of strangers, she had no choice but to come down and meet everyone. The men didn't trouble her. They withdrew into the library soon after their arrival to enjoy their brandies. Their wives, eager to hear from Anthony and Brandon about their past year's studies at school, remained outside, enjoying cold summer drinks at a patio table. Alexander and his best friend Robbie were the only ones frolicking in the water. They had been in there since the moment they arrived. Tessa almost wished she could join them, but Aunt Anna wanted her to meet Katherine's friends.

Katherine had invited two schoolmates, Lilith and Isabelle. They were both juniors two years above Katherine. When Aunt Anna introduced them, Lilith and Isabelle had greeted Tessa with all the proper pleasantries, but Tessa knew right then Aunt Anna's efforts were hopeless. Katherine and her friends, in their expensive designer swimming suits, looked to her like dolls on display. Isabelle's bright pink and white checkerboard one-piece cried out for attention. Lilith's forest green two-piece, which exposed her midriff, showed off her body too much considering the number of adults here. Katherine's blue and white bathing suit with a bow in the front, though more conservative, was too cute.

When they got to the pool, Tessa decided not to put on a bathing suit. Keeping up with these girls would be too tiresome, and competing with them too boring. She kept what she had on, a light off-the-shoulder top and a soft, flowing skirt with a small floral print. Her clothes hung loosely on her body. "Like a bohemian," as her mother would say. That was how she normally dressed. Next to the dressy threesome, she looked strange and out of place.

No matter. The girls weren't much interested in her anyway. They had more pressing concerns on their minds. Whenever Anthony or Brandon came near, Lilith and Isabelle would become self-conscious. They would talk just a bit louder, and laugh just a bit harder. They shifted their bodies this way and that way while trying hard to act natural. Tessa felt embarrassed for them, the way they acted. Meanwhile, Katherine paid no attention to Anthony and Brandon. She was too busy trying to please her friends, following them around and laughing at their every joke.

Tessa stayed with them only to please Aunt Anna. Once outside, Katherine and her friends decided to lounge by the pool, preferring not to get their hair wet. They began blathering on about the recent trips they had taken on holiday and the grand places where their classmates were spending their summer. Next to them, Tessa lay on a lounge chair and pretended to be asleep. She had no idea who or what they were talking about and they didn't try to talk to her or ask her anything. That was all right. She never enjoyed crowds and she didn't like talking. All was fine as long as everyone left her alone. She closed her eyes and let her mind wander. The warmth of the summer sun soothed her. The voices of everyone around her became background noises. In the heat, her surrounding faded from her consciousness and she drifted off into sleep.

A loud splash jolted her awake. Screechy yells and screams followed. Startled, she woke up and saw Anthony swimming across the pool.

While she dozed off, Anthony had decided to take a swim. As he stood on the edge of the pool, Katherine's friends took notice of the young man whose golden hair shone in the sun. His tall, toned physique was as beautiful as if Adonis had come to life. They knew his record as a swimming champion, and he didn't disappoint. He dove in and swam several laps with flying speed. Lilith and Isabelle screamed in delight, cheering him on.

As he climbed out of the pool, his body still halfway in the water, he turned to the girls. Seeing them watching him, he pulled himself all the way out, waved, and walked to the other side of the pool to join Brandon.

Afterward, Katherine's friends would not stop talking about him.

"He's such a dream!" Lilith swooned. "Katherine, do you know if he has a girlfriend?"

"I don't think so," Katherine said. "If he does, she can't be that important because he hasn't introduced her to the family."

"He's so good-looking, and such an amazing athlete." Isabelle stole glances at Anthony while pretending she wasn't staring at the same time. "Katherine, can't you get him to come over and talk to us? Oh no. Wait! Don't do that. If he comes over, I won't know what to say to him. I'll make a fool of myself!"

Lying on her back with her hands clasped behind her head, Tessa stared up at the sky. She thought she would go crazy if she had to listen to any more of this. They sounded like all the silly women who fancied

17

her father, the ones who shamelessly schemed to meet him and sought his attention. At least her father was one of the most admired actors in the West End. What were these girls fawning over? She glanced at Anthony, this man-child who got all riled up over flowers in the rose garden. She had seen so many similarly good-looking young men come and go on the London stages. There were plenty of them everywhere. Why all the fuss? Katherine and her friends were laughably shallow.

Over by the gazebo, Alexander and Robbie were playing marbles. They had finally gotten out of the water. She decided to get up and join them.

On the other side of the pool, Anthony dried himself with a towel and sat down next to Brandon, who was reading a magazine on a lounge chair near the ladies at the patio table.

"She doesn't seem to mix well with the girls." Anthony overheard his mother say to the ladies behind him. He looked across the pool. Tessa had left the girls to join Alexander and Robbie.

"Maybe she's a late bloomer," Aunt Anna said.

"Perhaps the other girls are a little more mature," said Mrs. Lowe. "Give her time. She'll lose interest in playing games with children soon enough."

"I'm not sure it'll be that simple." Sophia said. "She's different from what I expected."

His mother sounded slightly distressed. He looked over at Tessa again. She had just said something that made Alexander and Robbie laugh.

"How'd she come to live with you anyway?" Mrs. Lowe asked.

"It's a long story. It goes back many years, starting with Tessa's mother," Sophia said.

The mention of Tessa's mother roused Anthony's curiosity. No one had ever told him the whole story about Juliet and why she had left. Vaguely, he got the impression that she left under a cloud of disgrace, but a scandal that happened years before he was born didn't interest him and he had never thought to ask anyone about it. With Tessa living with them now, though, he had begun to wonder. Discreetly, he turned toward his mother to listen.

Sophia put down her glass of iced tea. "Tessa's mother, Juliet, grew up with William and Leon."

"And Lex, Leon's older brother," Aunt Anna added.

"That's right. Lex too. And their cousin Anthony Browning. Anthony's mother was William's aunt. She gave Juliet's mother a job as her personal maid when Juliet's father died from measles. Juliet was still a baby back then. The Brownings treated them like family and Juliet grew up with the boys. William said she was a precocious child. Outgoing, always knew the right things to say. Everybody adored her, but the good times didn't last." Sophia stopped. Mrs. Lowe leaned closer to the table, waiting for her to go on.

"When Juliet was fifteen, Mrs. Browning and Anthony died in a car accident," Sophia said. "Juliet's mother was in the car with them and she died too."

"My goodness." Mrs. Lowe put her hand to her mouth.

This was news to Anthony. He didn't know Juliet's mother had died in that same car accident.

"It was a sad time for everyone. Juliet became an orphan. In the grieving process, Mr. Browning adopted Juliet because she had no place to go. It was the only good thing that came out of that tragedy."

Interesting, Anthony thought. So that was how Juliet became part of the family.

"Until Dean came along," Aunt Anna said.

"Yes. Dean Graham. Tessa's father," Sophia said.

19

"Dean Graham? The British actor? Dean Graham is Tessa's father?"

"Yes." Anna looked over at Tessa. "It was big scandal back then."

"Why? What happened?"

Sophia shook her head lightly at Anna. "That was a long time ago. Old news. Not worth bringing up anymore." She turned around and signaled their housekeeper to serve them another round of drinks. The other two women took the hint and dropped the subject.

Anthony shifted back toward the pool. Too bad his mother decided not to go on. He wanted to know what happened too.

"Look at her," Mrs. Lowe said while watching Tessa. "What a remarkable resemblance between her and her father."

He glanced at Tessa. For a kid, her expressions were hard to read. He couldn't tell just by looking at her what she was thinking. When she smiled, there seemed to be layers of meaning behind her smile. He wondered if she had picked up some of her father's acting habits.

"I'm a huge fan of Dean Graham," Mrs. Lowe continued. "I saw him in Henry V on stage when I went to London four years ago. He's a wonderful Shakespearean actor."

"Yes. He made quite a name for himself after he married Juliet. Anyway, after they met, Juliet left with him for London and that was where Tessa was born. With the way the war's going, William had been worried about them. He went to London last month and invited them all to come back to America, but Juliet and Dean decided to stay. They did agree it would be best for Tessa to go away until they're sure England is safe."

"It hasn't been easy for you, has it?" Aunt Anna asked.

"No," Sophia admitted. "She's not an easy child. I had hoped it would be like having a daughter in the house. It's been so quiet since Anthony went off to college. I thought she and I could do a lot of things together. Go out for tea and shopping. I wanted to bring her into the

Junior League. But," Sophia paused, trying to find the right words, "Tessa has other interests."

Other interests? Anthony thought. She was only a girl. What other interests could she possibly have that was so important? His mother wanted to make her feel at home with them. She shouldn't have turned down his mother's good intentions. If he were living in someone else's home, he would be definitely make a sincere effort to show his appreciation.

"Leon was thrilled when he heard Tessa was coming. He thought she'd be a mini-Juliet and it would be like old times for him again," Aunt Anna said. "He was surprised at how quiet and aloof she is. She's nothing like how he remembered Juliet. Tessa's more like her father."

"Be that as it may. She's here now and William and I intend to do everything we can for her. It's harder on her than on anyone. She's in a new country. She's far away from her parents. England might be attacked and her parents might be in danger. It's a lot to take for a fourteen-year-old."

Anthony looked toward Tessa one more time. Katherine had now joined her and the younger boys. At least Katherine knew how to be nice. Since Aunt Anna and Mrs. Lowe said Tessa was immature, maybe he should try to be a good role model to her like he was with Katherine and Alexander. He could give her some guidance now and then. Maybe that would make things easier for his mother.

"Tessa, can we talk?" Katherine approached her, her voice unduly warm and inviting.

"Of course," Tessa said. Mistaking Katherine's warmth as an attempt to befriend her, she tried to be amiable in return. "What about?"

"My mother and Aunt Sophia said you'll be coming to my school in the fall."

"I suppose. If that's what they decided."

"St. Mary's is a great place. The daughters of all the important people in Chicago go there."

Tessa didn't say anything. She didn't like the tone of Katherine's voice. It sounded too haughty for her taste.

"Everyone at school likes Lilith and Isabelle." Katherine turned to her friends, her eyes full of admiration. "Lilith's father is a senator. Isabelle's family owns the biggest furniture production company in Illinois."

"That's nice for them." Tessa said, unimpressed.

Not noticing Tessa's indifference, Katherine continued, "They really like Anthony." She sidled up to Tessa and lowered her voice. Tessa wasn't sure what all this had to do with her.

"They want to know if you can invite them over whenever Anthony's home."

For a minute, Tessa thought she had heard wrong, but Katherine was serious. "If you do that, they'll appreciate you and we can become good friends with them."

Tessa looked over at Lilith and Isabelle. They were smiling at her like they were her best friends.

"No."

Katherine stared at her, speechless. No one ever said no to Lilith and Isabelle. "Tessa, please! Do it as a favor to me?"

"I am sorry. I cannot help you with anything this ridiculous." Tessa got up and walked back into the house. At her abrupt departure, Alexander and Robbie stopped their game and made a face at each other. Katherine returned to the older girls, miffed.

"Oh, that's not good," Sophia said.

Anthony looked up and followed the direction of his mother's eyes. Across the pool, Tessa stood up and went back into the house, leaving poor Katherine looking upset and rejected.

"Anthony," she called out to her son, who was sitting with Brandon near them by the pool. "Could you please go check on Tessa? I think she's upset."

"Sure, Mother." He grabbed his shorts and shirt from the lounge chair behind him and threw them on. His shirt still unbuttoned, he went inside the house and saw Tessa heading out the front door. Quickly, he went after her. In the circular driveway in front of their house, Tessa mounted a bike, getting ready to leave.

"Tessa!" he yelled out to her. She halted.

"Is everything okay?" He ran up to her, his voice genuinely concerned.

"Yes. Everything's fine. Why?"

"Mother thought you looked upset."

"No. I'm fine." She blinked and looked blankly back at him. He couldn't tell if she was happy or troubled.

"Where are you going?"

"I'm heading out."

"You can't leave. This party was planned for you."

"Was it now, really?" She gave him a sarcastic smile. "I thought it was planned for you to show off."

"What are you talking about?"

"Don't deny it, swimming champ." She eyed his open shirt. "You want everyone to cheer and rave about how good you are." Her smile widened with a spark of mischief in her eye.

"I do not," he said. "And you can't talk to me that way."

"Why not?"

23

"Because it's rude. And because…because I'm older than you and you should do what I tell you."

She laughed. "That's the dumbest thing I've ever heard. How old do you think you are?"

He stood there, lost for words. His face turned several shades of red.

"Don't pull rank with me." She stopped laughing. "I'm not a little child. I don't have to listen to you." She stared him in the eye. For the first time since they met, he heard vulnerability in her voice.

"I…" He didn't know what to say. She sounded like she was all alone, fighting against the whole world.

Before he could respond, her demeanor changed again and her mischievous smile returned. "By the way, you look funny when you're all riled up."

Her rapid change of moods left him dumbfounded.

"Bye!" She rolled away before he could answer. He watched her bike go down the driveway until she disappeared out of his sight. He had never met any girl so rude and arrogant and so difficult to handle. The thought of being in the same house with her all summer long was starting to give him a headache.

Chapter 3

Tessa pedaled her bike faster and faster until she reached maximum speed. She wanted the wind to blow away everything unpleasant around her. She pedaled until her legs burned. When she came to a small beach by the shore of the lake, she slowed down and coasted along the path.

She got off her bike and rolled it to the side of the road. Alone, she walked to a secluded spot on the beach where she could hide under the trees. She had discovered this place two weeks ago. Here, she could enjoy her solitude.

Sunlight glittered across the expanse of Lake Michigan. She had never seen a lake this large and wide. It went out to the horizon like the ocean. She wished it really were the ocean and the sailboats out there could take her home.

She wondered what her parents and friends were doing back in London. Normally, the theater season would end now and summer training would begin. The summer training programs always brought in new young aspiring actors and actresses to her father's theater troupe. When the school term ended, they would invite her and the other sons and daughters of the troupe's members to join them for parties. They did so partly in the hope of gaining inside knowledge about the troupe members and partly to curry favor with influential actors and directors.

She didn't mind them though. Because of them, she and her friends often got to spend time at the homes of young actors, artists, and musicians. Their creative minds fascinated her.

If she could, she would go back to all of them without a second thought. She feared what could happen to them and wished she could be there with them. Every day, the newspapers brought more dreadful news about the war and more photos of places under attack. She told no one about her nightmares of her parents trapped in London facing a row of German tanks.

Everyone treated her like a child. No one would talk honestly with her about the war. Her mother never mentioned the war in her letters and telegrams. The Ardleys and the Caldwells avoided the subject around her. Her father was the only one who was forthright with her. In his last letter, he admitted that it might be a long while before she could go home.

Alone, she lost track of time. She didn't want to return to the Ardleys' house. It wasn't that she was ungrateful. Aunt Sophia and Uncle William had tried hard to make her feel welcome and so did the Caldwells, but their lives were so different from hers. She missed following her father to rehearsals and watching him act on stage. She missed going to the hospital with her mother and visiting her patients. Her mother had a gift for making people happy. She could magically cheer up even the saddest and most decrepit people with ease. Too bad that gift didn't pass on to her daughter. Tessa was never very good at talking to people.

The sun began to descend and the sky turned to a luminescent yellow and gray hue. She felt someone approaching her. It was Uncle William.

"Beautiful sunset, isn't it?" He sat down next to her.

"How'd you find me?"

"You forget I've lived in this area for many years. There's no corner within a ten-mile radius of where we live that I don't know."

She turned to stare out at the lake again.

"But, you are your mother's daughter. Juliet used to come here too when she wanted to be alone. Especially after your grandmother and Anthony Browning died."

How strange to hear him talk about her mother. Until a month ago, she had never heard of the Ardleys or the Caldwells. She found out her mother was part of their families only when her parents told her they were sending her to Chicago, and it was only now that she realized her mother had once been very close to them. They knew things about her mother she had never known before.

"Why didn't you ever contact or visit us? Why didn't Mother ever speak of you?"

"That was my fault," William said with an apologetic smile. "I take full responsibility for that. I should've reached out much sooner."

She waited for him to explain.

"Did your mother ever tell you? When she and your father met, it was a huge scandal in Chicago."

"No. I don't know anything about what happened in Chicago. I know there was a scandal with an actress. It's still a scandal. She tells lies about my mother in the papers all the time."

"Alina Fey."

"You know about her?"

William gave her a sympathetic look. "Is she still going around saying Juliet stole your father away from her?"

Tessa wrapped her arms around her legs and looked down.

"Your father and she were together once. She brought him out of obscurity. She was already an established actress on Broadway when they met. Your father was a young actor starting out. It didn't last because she held that over him like he owed her. Maybe you're too young to understand."

"I understand," she said. "But that was a long time ago. She still says a lot of vile things about Mother in magazines and people believe her. She does it to get attention. She wants people to feel sorry for her."

"I'm sorry to hear that."

"People think Mother is a shameless woman. A temptress. And she can't defend herself because she isn't famous. No one ever asked for her side of the story. It's so unfair."

William's eyes softened. "Did your parents ever tell you how they met?"

"They met and fell in love when Father was on tour in Chicago. People thought he and Alina Fey were engaged because his troupe spread that rumor, but they were not. Mother and Father eloped to get away to start over in London."

"That was true, but they left to get away from my family too."

"Why?" Tessa couldn't see what would make her mother turn her back on the Ardleys.

"Your parents met because my family was a patron for your father's troupe at the time. In fact, my mother was the one who brought them on tour to Chicago. She didn't have any daughters or nieces, so she took Juliet with her to all the social receptions for promoting their shows, and,"—he rubbed his nose, hiding a smirk—"that was how all the troubles started. Juliet and Dean fell in love."

"But why did she have to leave your family?"

"Because your father's breakup with Alina Fey and your mother being the other woman drew our family into the scandal. Alina Fey wouldn't stop talking to the press about it. My mother was very sensitive about our family's good name. She demanded Juliet break things off with your father. Instead, they eloped."

Tessa listened, trying to absorb all she heard. Her mother had never told her anything about this. "Mother said she had no other relatives after Grandma died. I always thought the Brownings were just people Grandma had worked for. They didn't even tell me Mr. Browning had adopted her until they told me they wanted me to come to Chicago. Why didn't Mother ever talk about any of you?"

"Maybe she felt bad for leaving us the way she did. Some people thought she was ungrateful to us. I think she didn't want to bring any more scandal to our family. In any case, Leon and I were very sad when she left. She was practically a sister to us, but my mother was furious with her and there was nothing we could do."

"What about Mr. Browning? Why didn't he do anything to help her?"

"He adopted her, but my mother was the one who took her under her wing. She wanted to turn Juliet into a lady. People warned her back then. They said a maid's daughter couldn't be trusted. My mother meant to prove them wrong. Of course, when the scandal broke, everyone who'd warned her was delighted to see things turn out that way. My mother felt humiliated." He looked apologetic. "Anyway, Charles Browning worked for my father. He owed his career to my parents. He wasn't in a position to cross my mother. Besides, your mother was an adult by then. She made the decision to elope. None of us could've stopped her from doing what she wanted."

Tessa never knew so many people had opposed her mother. Feeling defensive, she wrapped her arms tighter around her legs and held up her head. "She loves my father."

William didn't comment, but smiled to let her know he understood. "My mother never forgave Juliet, not that there was anything to forgive. Juliet followed her heart. Later on, the scandal died down, but my mother's health started failing. I couldn't risk upsetting her to reach out to your parents. When she finally passed away, so much time had passed, I didn't know if Juliet would want to hear from us. I didn't know if she would ever forgive us."

Tessa thought for a while, then loosened her arms and turned to him. "There's nothing to forgive."

William relaxed. "Your Aunt Sophia, and Leon and Anna, they mean well." He leaned back on his elbows and stretched out his legs. Amused to see him sitting so casually this way, Tessa lowered her eyes to hide her smile. In the short time that she had been with the Ardleys, she had discovered that her Uncle William, revered patriarch of one of Chicago's oldest and wealthiest families, was at heart a mellow man who eschewed formalities whenever he was out of public sight. "When you get to know them better, you'll find out for yourself they are kind, wonderful people."

"I know. I like Alexander. He's a fun child."

"But not Katherine?"

She hesitated. "I don't dislike her…We're very different, that's all."

They watched the sunset in silence. The beach was now empty and there were only the sounds of waves. A balmy breeze blew past them as the sun continued to descend and the evening twilight overtook the sky.

"Katherine's friends," Tessa said out of nowhere, "they like Anthony." She looked at William. "They want me to invite them over all the time so they can be around Anthony."

He looked back at her, and they both broke into laughter.

"You don't have to do anything you don't want to," he said.

She looked out to the lake again. She wondered how her mother felt about all that had happened between her and the Ardleys. Did she regret the lost time with Uncle William and Uncle Leon too? Did she feel the Ardleys let her down? Did she regret having been so out of touch with all the people from her past?

If she did, then perhaps it was a good thing that Tessa herself had come to Chicago. For all her misgivings about leaving London, maybe her being here could help everyone come together again.

William got up from the ground and offered her his hands. "Come on. I'll drive you home." She took them and let him pull her up. Together, they walked back to her bike and his car, ready to go home.

PART THREE
America First

Chapter 4

A shadow hung over the university campus when Anthony returned in the fall. The normal excitement that accompanied the start of a new school year was nowhere to be found. Since the order for conscription had gone into effect in September, all males between twenty-one and thirty-five years old had to register for selective services. The events of the world had spilled over beyond the confines of Europe and their impact was spreading. One by one, older male students departed to report for the draft and the student population dwindled.

The draft left even those who were not immediately affected sober and uneasy. As each week passed, more seats in the classrooms became empty. No one needed to ask why. Enthusiasm for extracurricular activities waned. In his own fraternity, the senior brothers had lost interest in initiating and organizing social or charity events. They had cut the rush events by half. Even those they did hold were more informal and pared down than usual.

America was still officially neutral, but for how long?

While Anthony studied in his dorm room, conversations of the students in the next room carried in through his open door.

"I'd rather join the army now and get it over with," someone said. "It's a peacetime draft. Eighteen months and I'll be done. My time served before FDR declares war."

"Declares war? He wouldn't dare," another person answered.

"You want to bet? He's terrible. I can't stand him."

"What about Hitler and the fascists?"

"Europe's problem, not ours. I don't want to go to war."

"Coward."

"I don't need to go to war for foreigners to prove I'm not a coward. If the Europeans want to fight, they can do it without me."

Anthony put down his textbook and closed his door. He tried to return to the chapter on the economic fallacies of Marxism, but he couldn't focus. Lately, all everyone talked about was the draft. It weighed on his mind as much as anyone else's. He hoped the war would be over before he would have to worry about it. He liked his life. He liked studying at the university and competing on the swim team. And despite the never-ending meetings, he actually liked the debate team too. He didn't want to join the military. He didn't even want to think about it.

How could he not think about it? No one thought Congress would pass the draft, but it did. No one thought France would fall, and it fell. Last week, what his parents had feared most finally happened. Germany attacked England. The London Blitz threw his parents into a panic because Tessa's parents were still over there. If something happened to them, his father would be very upset. And what would happen to Tessa?

But why should he have to go to war for them? Dean and Juliet could've come to America before England was attacked. His father had wired them many times about that over the summer. Each time, they had refused. He wished they had changed their minds. If they had come, they would be safe and his parents wouldn't have to worry about them.

If they had come, maybe they could take that rude and brooding daughter of theirs somewhere else with them.

He stared at the open pages of his book. No need to worry yet. He was still two years away from the minimum age for the draft. What he needed to do now was get back to his studies.

You can enlist, a tiny voice crept into his mind.

No. What nonsense. Why would he do that? The incessant talk on campus about the war and the draft were getting to him.

But if England surrendered, what would become of the world?

No. The answer was still no. He was nothing more than a college student. He couldn't solve the world's problems. Even if he enlisted, he would only be a soldier and he wouldn't be able to change the world anyway. He had his own life to think about. His father expected him to take over their family business someday. He had enough responsibilities at home.

If he enlisted and something happened to him, his mother would be devastated.

Enlisting was simply not an option. He pushed his thoughts about the war out of his mind and forced himself to read through every sentence and every word of the chapter he needed to finish.

#

The radio evening news program brought no new information about England other than Neville Chamberlain's worsening health. The bombing of London continued. When the program ended, Tessa turned off the radio and quietly left the den.

On her way back upstairs to her room, she passed by the parlor. The voices of everyone talking carried out into the hall and she stopped. Uncle Leon was here. He had come to talk to Uncle William and Aunt Sophia about Anthony again. He had been coming a lot since the new conscription law had passed.

"Let's not worry ourselves over nothing," William said. "Anthony's only nineteen. The minimum age for the draft is twenty-one. Everything may be over by then."

"I don't know, Will," Leon said as he paced around the Ardleys' living room. "I have a bad feeling about this. You need to call Senator Reinhardt and make sure there won't be any more to this conscription business. The only thing they should do about it is to repeal it. I can't believe Congress let this happen. Roosevelt is leading them by the nose. America should not be involved, period." He plopped down on the sofa, lit a cigarette, and took a deep drag. Still agitated, he blew out a cloud of smoke and stubbed it out.

Listening to them outside the parlor, Tessa felt sorry for him. Uncle Leon loved Anthony as much as he loved his own children.

"I know you care a great deal about him." Sophia moved closer to Leon and put her hand on his shoulder.

"We've already lost Anthony once," he said, referring to Anthony Browning. "The day your son was born, it was a miracle. He is so much like our old Anthony. It's like Anthony had come back to us." He looked helplessly at her. "He can't be taken away from us again."

Sophia gave his hand a light squeeze.

"So much of a burden on our young men these days," William said. "We had it easier when we were his age."

"No we didn't," Leon said. "Your memory's failing you. It was the same thing back then. Europe goes to war, we enact the draft and our boys are sent to fight their wars for them. That was how we lost Lex. We've sacrificed one family member to Europe's brawls already. It's enough."

"I wish Lex was still with us too. But to be fair, he wasn't drafted. He enlisted on his own."

"Anthony won't want to go. I'm sure of it." Leon got up and poured himself a glass of whiskey from the liquor cabinet. "What about

Alexander? What happens when he grows up? What if this never ends? Or it ends and repeats all over again like now? Do we send our boys to war every time Europe wants to fight?"

"Oh, Leon, don't say that," Sophia said. "I can't imagine Alexander would have to deal with this too."

"He might have to as long as that warmonger is in the White House. And he's been there forever. He won't leave."

William exchanged a glance with his wife. "I'll put a call in to Senator Reinhardt tomorrow. We'll see what he can do."

Tessa looked away from the parlor. Uncle William only said that to make Uncle Leon feel better. What could the Senator do? The draft had already passed. For now, it was here to stay.

Quietly, she walked upstairs to her room. She hoped Anthony would not have to go to war. Back in England, her parents' friends had sons who had gone to war. She even knew some of those boys. At least one of them did not come back.

Anthony was the Ardleys' only son. If something happened to him, Uncle William and Aunt Sophia surely would be devastated. Uncle Leon too.

Chapter 5

On an early November afternoon, Anthony had come to the gym half an hour early to prepare for swim team practice. He wanted to get in a few extra laps before the other team members arrived. He had just finished changing in the locker room when Brandon Lowe, his best friend and teammate, came running to him with the news.

"Anthony, Anthony. Have you heard?"

"Heard what?"

"Lloyd, he's been drafted!"

Lloyd Pearson. Their swim team captain. Anthony's heart sank.

Before Brandon could tell him more, another teammate opened the door. "Anthony, Coach Feldman wants to see you in his office."

"What does Coach want with you?" Brandon asked.

Anthony did not know. He put his clothes back on and left the locker room. In the office, Lloyd and their coach were both waiting for him.

"Anthony," Lloyd greeted him. He seemed surprisingly upbeat.

"Hey, Lloyd," Anthony said, his voice uncharacteristically reserved. He wasn't sure if he should say anything about the draft.

"Anthony, you probably heard already," Coach Feldman said. "Lloyd's leaving us."

"Yes, I heard." He should say something encouraging or sympathetic, but he didn't know what.

Lloyd, though, didn't appear concerned. Sitting on the coach's desk with his legs swinging, he seemed carefree as always. "Hey, don't worry about me." He chugged on a big bottle of water. "I'm ready and pumped. I'll kick some asses if I have to go to war."

His optimistic attitude only made Anthony sadder. Lloyd was a good team captain precisely because he always stayed positive. No matter how tough the competition, he could still convince everyone they were in for a win.

"We'll all miss you," Anthony said. "The team won't be the same without you."

"Maybe not, but they'll be in good hands. Right, Coach?

"Right. So, how about it, Ardley? You up for the job?"

"Me?" Anthony asked. "You're joking. I can't be captain. I'm only a sophomore. What about Richard and Hal? They deserve it."

"Richard and Hal are both twenty-one. It's better we have someone who we know will stick around through the end of the year. It's not good for us to keep changing captains," the coach said. "It's bad enough when we lose a team member. I don't want to keep losing captains."

He hesitated. Among their teammates, Lloyd Pearson was a legend. Coach Feldman thought he could fill in for Lloyd?

"What do you say?" the coach asked.

This didn't feel right. He would love to be the team's captain, but not like this. He wanted to feel he earned it. Right now, there were others who were just as deserving. They should be considered too.

"What about Stanley? He's a sophomore and his results are as good as mine."

"Mmm." The coach crossed his arms and drooped his lips, clearly not impressed. "Stan's a great swimmer, but he isn't captain material. He's too quiet. We need someone who everyone would rally around."

41

Really? The coach thought the team would rally around him? Why wouldn't they rally around someone else? "What about Brandon? He's a top competitor and more outgoing than Stanley. Our team would rally around him too."

The coached bobbed his head, not entirely convinced. "Brandon's not a bad choice. I'd rather have you. My own feeling is Brandon doesn't care about the team as much as you do. I've seen you cheer everyone on, helping them out even the time when you sprained your ankle and got sidelined. Brandon doesn't have the same team spirit."

Was that right? Brandon didn't have the same team spirit? Anthony never noticed. He thought everyone on the team was in this together.

"Besides," Coach Feldman smiled and loosened his arms, "if you're captain, we'll always have an advantage when the other teams hear who's leading our team. The son of William Ardley of the Ardley Group? That'll turn some heads for sure. They'll all know we mean business when we show up to compete."

Wonderful. Just what he needed. More people on other teams trying to take them down to prove they could beat an Ardley.

"The team's yours." Lloyd jumped off the desk and slapped him on the back. "Take us to the championship. You all can write me and let me know how the season goes." He winked. "Don't let me down."

Anthony tried to smile. He had never been less thrilled about being appointed to be the team leader of anything.

Chapter 6

Anthony spotted his Uncle Leon almost as soon as he entered the restaurant. The host brought him to their table, where a sommelier was showing Leon a bottle of wine. Leon looked positively dapper in his London drape suit and his gold and burgundy striped necktie.

While the choice of wine preoccupied his uncle's attention, Anthony thanked the host politely and sat down.

"...absolutely splendid, sir. It's a vintage from our private collection."

"Uh-huh." Leon studied the wine bottle's label. "All right, let's give it a try."

"Excellent choice, sir." The sommelier opened the bottle and handed Leon the cork. Leon sniffed it and nodded and he poured him a taste. Leon took a sip, his face as serious as if he were pondering a matter of utmost importance. Anthony watched him, amused.

"It's perfect." Leon put his glass down and signaled the sommelier to pour him a full glass. "Anthony, glad you could make it."

"I was looking forward to this." He opened the menu. A waitress came by and brought them each a glass of water.

"How's school?" Leon picked up his glass of wine.

"Pretty good," Anthony said, not realizing he was frowning.

"Pretty good? If it's pretty good, then why the dour face?"

Anthony closed the menu. "Lloyd left school today."

"Lloyd? Lloyd Pearson? Your swim team captain?"

"Yes. He's been drafted."

Scowling, Leon put down his glass.

"Coach Feldman made me captain, but I'm not thrilled about it. I hate seeing Lloyd go. Feldman made me captain instead of Richard or Hal because he didn't want to have to pick another replacement if they are drafted too."

Leon shook his head. "This is exactly the kind of thing I don't want to see. Our best and brightest plucked from one of the finest universities in the world to go train to be a soldier. What a waste."

"It's depressing, I have to say. Not just Lloyd being gone. A lot of the other upperclassmen are gone too. Eight of my fraternity brothers including our president. The house feels empty without them."

"You know this isn't simply a matter of your friends being taken out of school to join the army." Leon leaned forward in his chair. "You know what this war's really about? Profiteering. And I'll be the first to tell anyone all about the importance of profits. But this isn't worth it. It's not worth our boys dying so the East Coast bankers and industrialists can profit off their blood. We need to protect your friends from the profiteers."

The waiter came to take their orders. The interruption was a relief to Anthony. He didn't want to hear Uncle Leon go on another diatribe against the war. He didn't entirely disagree with Leon, but he had heard his arguments many times already.

"We need to make sure things don't get out of hand," Leon said after the waiter walked away.

"I know you're doing everything you can."

"I am, but what about you?"

"Me? I'm in school. What can I do?"

Leon pulled a pamphlet from his briefcase by the side of his seat and put it on the table in front of Anthony. The pamphlet's title, "Defend America First!" was printed in bold letters across the top. At the bottom in smaller print, the phrase "America First Committee."

"What is this?" Anthony picked it up.

"It's a new anti-intervention group. The AFC. Two Yale law students started it in September. One of them is Douglas Stuart, Jr., son of Quaker Oats' founder Doug Stuart. The AFC's setting up new chapters across the country. They have a lot of supporters."

"You're one too, I take it?"

"I'm funding it. So is Robert Wood."

"Robert Wood? Sears Roebuck's Chairman?"

Clearly pleased, Leon smiled. "And Bob McCormick. With Bob on board, we'll have a strong, influential voice through the Chicago Tribune."

"Impressive."

"UC doesn't have a chapter yet."

Anthony glanced up from the pamphlet.

Leon looked intently at him. "They need someone smart and articulate to start one at your school. You're on the debate team, right? That's for amateurs. You can put your debating skills to good use for something bigger."

Anthony didn't answer right away. "I don't know. You know I don't like politics."

"That's fine if times are normal." Leon's voice turned serious. "Times are not normal now. Lloyd, Hal, Richard, all your friends. Their lives are at stake. I don't have to remind you about that. If you don't take a stand, you might be next. Think about your parents. How would they feel if you're drafted?"

Unsure, Anthony flipped through the pages and took a closer look at the pamphlet. He stopped at the page titled "Missions" and scanned the

AFC's list of goals. "Uncle Leon, the Committee wants to stop American aid to Britain?"

Leon did not deny it. "The more aid we give, the more involved we'll get. We're funding the war."

"What if Germany defeats Britain? If that happens, Germany will rule all of Europe."

"And if that happens, so what?" Leon said. "How does it benefit us to keep pandering to the Brits? If Germany takes over Europe, we'll deal with the Germans. Germans, Brits, French, we can do business with any of them. We don't need to get involved with their squabbles and drama. What's the worst that can happen if we deal with the Germans instead of the Brits? The only important thing is we don't let any of them screw us."

Anthony opened another page of the pamphlet. "What about Juliet? Aren't you worried about her? I thought you and Father were still worried about her and her husband in London."

"I worry about her every minute. Ask Anna. I've been losing sleep every night since the Blitz started. If Juliet would agree to come back to the U.S., I'd send over a plane, a ship! Anything to bring her and Dean back. If they were here, I'd sleep a lot better, but I can't stand by and do nothing because they refuse to leave London."

The waiter returned. Anthony put the pamphlet aside to let the waiter place the first course on the table, but his eyes remained on the pamphlet. He wasn't closed to the idea of the America First Committee. He didn't want his country to go to war either. Certainly, he didn't want to be drafted. But wasn't stopping American aid to Britain too extreme?

Anyhow, even if he did join the AFC, he would rather assist than lead. Whenever the Ardleys got involved, people would have higher expectations. If he headed the chapter, people would give more weight to his every action and every word. They would expect him to deliver. They always did. People thought the Ardleys could never fall short. The new AFC chapter would have to gain influence and support very quickly, and it would be his responsibility to see to that happening. Why would he want that kind of expectation on himself, all for politics? He would rather do something else with his time. Maybe even something people never expected he would do.

"Uncle Leon?"

"Yes?"

"Why did Uncle Lex join the air force? Did he ever tell you?"

Leon's eyes softened at the mention of Lex. "No. He never said, but I knew why."

"Why?"

Leon looked away, deflated. The mention of Lex joining the air force took all his fervor away. "You know your father and I were never drafted. Lex wasn't either. Everyone chalked it up to luck, but the three of us always thought your grandpa pulled some strings to keep us out. Your grandpa was very influential and well-connected in his day. It wouldn't surprise me if he had."

He took a sip of his wine. Anthony waited for him to continue.

"We never knew for sure if your grandpa was the reason we escaped the draft. Lex thought so, and his conscience got to him. He couldn't watch other men get drafted while he got to sit it out because his family had connections. I think he went to war to prove a point."

"So it wasn't because he believed in a cause?"

"No," Leon denied firmly. "There's nothing valiant or glorious about why he went. Don't you get any of those ideas in your head. They're all lies to get young people like you to give up your lives for people with ulterior motives. Your Uncle Lex wanted to rebel against my parents and your grandpa. It was all a young man's bravado. It was a mistake."

Anthony didn't think so. If Lex went to war because he didn't want to abuse his privileged background, it was an admirable act.

Nonetheless, he held his tongue. He didn't want to contradict his uncle. He wondered how Lex broke it to the family back then when he made that decision to do what his family didn't expect.

Leon finished his glass of wine. "I need something stronger than this," he mumbled under his breath.

Anthony's heart ached for him. Uncle Leon never got over Lex's death.

"Take that pamphlet back with you," Leon said. "Think about it. The AFC will start a chapter at your school one way or another. I can think of no one more suitable than you for the job. A chapter at the University of Chicago led by William Ardley's son? That'll make a statement. Almost as strong a statement as Stuart Jr. leading one at Yale. I'll make sure you get all the support you need."

Anthony stared at his food. Doug Stuart, Jr., Anthony Ardley. It almost felt as if everyone had decided already what their roles in the world would be. He wished his name didn't always precede him in everything he did.

PART FOUR
The South Side

Chapter 7

On her way to school, Tessa passed the newsstand two blocks away from St. Mary's Academy. Today's front-page headline, "Night Raiders Bomb West End." She tightened her grip on the strap of her schoolbag. Hopefully, her father and his theater troupe weren't near the bomb sites. A magazine cover next to the newspapers showed the front side of a London building collapsing into dust clouds and rubble when a shell dropped. Another magazine showed crowds of people shuffling into an underground shelter.

An icy wind blew past. She pulled her coat collar tighter and hurried on. The Chicago winter had arrived, bringing with it insanely cold temperatures.

Coming to the school entrance, she checked her watch. It was seven-thirty in the morning. The London time now would be three-thirty in the afternoon. What were her parents doing now? Her mother should be at work at the hospital. Her father might have just finished performing a matinee. In their last letter, they told her the theater had changed to daytime performances because of the nightly raids.

Maybe he's not performing. Maybe a bomb hit him.

She squeezed her eyes shut and lowered her head.

No. They're fine. They're fine. Everybody is fine.

She looked at her watch again. Her parents had given her this watch before she left for America…

An unusually heavy fog clouded the Port of Southampton the morning she left England.

"I'm sorry we can't leave with you," her father said. "England is my country and I am needed here. You understand, right?"

She tried to hold back her tears. The night before, he had explained he would be going on another tour to perform for the British troops. He told her entertainment was vital to keep the soldiers' morale up. He said it was important that he did his part when others were fighting to keep England safe.

"Then I should stay. England is my country too."

"No. You're still young. You'll be safer in America." In recent months, the German U-boats had been edging closer and closer.

"Then why can't Mother come? She's not British."

"Tessa," her mother said, "that's a childish question. You know why. If things get worse, people may get hurt, and they'll need my help. Besides, I don't want to leave your father here all alone."

"But I don't want to go to America." She stared over at Uncle William, who was standing off to the side to let them say their private goodbyes.

"I promise you'll like it." Her mother put on a cheerful face. "Your Uncle William will take very good care of you. You'll like him. And you'll finally get to see the place where I grew up."

"When will I see you again?"

"We don't know, but very soon we hope." Her father reached into his pocket and brought out a jewelry box. "We have a present for you." He opened it. Inside was a lady's gold watch.

She took the watch, a Bulova with a solid rose gold case and rubies set into the bezel. It had indigo-colored hands shaped like the nib of a fountain pen.

"You asked when you'll see us again. We can't tell you the precise date, but it'll only be a matter of time." He took her by the shoulders. "I want you to remember that every time you look at this watch."

Holding the watch in her hand, she could not hold back her tears anymore.

"Don't cry." Her father gave her a hug. "Here. Put it on. Let's see how it looks."

She put the watch on, but it didn't make her feel any better.

"It's beautiful," her mother said. "Remember, darling, it'll only be a matter of time before we see each other again."

Uncle William led her away toward the ramp where the passengers embarked.

She turned around one more time before she boarded the ship. Her father had his arm around her mother and they both waved to her. She wanted to run back to them, but each step she took led her farther and farther away.

"Come along, Tessa. It's time to go." Uncle William put his hand on her back and urged her along.

On the rear deck of the ship, she watched the view of coastline shrink out of her sight. When she could see the port no more, she went to the bow to watch the ship head out to the open sea. The sea was so wide. She couldn't see what was ahead beyond the horizon. She felt so small in an ocean that went on without end...

She entered the school building with more than fifteen minutes to spare. While she was putting her coat away in her locker, a few students said "good morning" to her and she politely returned their hellos. She put the books she needed into her book bag, then closed her locker and headed to her classroom.

In the two months since she started school at St. Mary's, she had acquainted herself with only a few girls. If the teachers hadn't assigned them to work on projects with her, she wouldn't even have gotten to know them. Most of the time she avoided getting into conversations with the girls here. The first thing they always asked was what her father did. She didn't like that. Talking about herself and her parents with strangers always made her uncomfortable. People, outsiders of no consequence, always wanted to pry into her father's private life. Reporters from the Daily Mirror were the worst. And then, whenever people found out she was Dean Graham's daughter, they always looked her up and down with curious eyes. She would rather not draw attention to herself or her family.

Unfortunately, here at St. Mary's, the occupations of their fathers were of great importance to the girls. It was an unavoidable subject. The difference was, when they found out her father was merely an actor in England, they lost interest. Their indifference didn't bother her. She preferred to be alone anyway. She always felt more at ease in her own solitude. She had never been good at small talk and she didn't like to have to explain herself. Besides, most of the girls here reminded her of Katherine's friends she had met earlier in the summer. They bored her.

As she approached her classroom, Lilith and Isabelle walked out. Seeing them surprised her since they were upperclassmen and didn't belong there. When they saw her, they snickered and walked past her without acknowledging her. After she refused to help them with their scheme to get close to Anthony, they never spoke to her again. When they ran into her at school, they ignored her and pretended not to see her.

At least Katherine was right about one thing. The students at St. Mary's liked Lilith and Isabelle. They took their cues from those two and stayed away from her. Even Katherine. Katherine couldn't avoid her entirely because of their family relations, but at school, she tried hard not to be seen with her. That was all right too. If Katherine wanted to keep her distance, Tessa was happy to oblige. Pretending to be friends with people with whom she shared nothing in common was not something she ever did anyway.

In the classroom, scattered groups of students gossiped and laughed while they waited for class to begin. The moment she entered, their laughter and chatter turned to whispers. She had a feeling they were all watching her. Strange. The girls didn't usually pay attention to her.

The reason for their behavior soon revealed itself. A tabloid magazine, Movie Stars Weekly, lay on her desk. Right away, she recognized the annoying face of the actress and her phony smile plastered across the front cover. The tagline under the magazine title read, "Alina Fey on Love, Loss, and Regrets." She scanned the classroom for the culprit. Everyone pretended to look away, but she knew they were all waiting for her reaction. She picked up the magazine and threw it into the rubbish bin. A few girls giggled. She walked straight past them and returned to her seat.

The nun entered the classroom and everybody shushed. Class began with a morning prayer. Tessa prayed for only one thing. To be able to go home. When the prayer was over, she looked up to the front of the classroom. The clock on the wall above the blackboard struck eight.

Remember, she told herself. Time. It would only be a matter of time before she could leave and go home.

# # #

After school, Tessa took the Alley L downtown to the post office. She wrote home at least once a week and she always sent her mail at the

Main Post Office on the South Loop. Maybe she worried too much, but she didn't trust the branch post offices. She didn't want any risk of delay. She wanted to make sure her letters would get to London as fast as they could.

Today, a festive mood buzzed in downtown Chicago. Shoppers filled every street corner. Christmas lights and decorations sparkled and shone in every shop and store. The excitement even chased away the depressing boredom that always followed her when she left school.

"Merry Christmas!" A man dressed in a Santa Claus suit bellowed. "Merry Christmas!" He pulled on the bell hanging on a stand propping up a sign that read "The Salvation Army." The rings of the bell charmed all the passersby. She smiled at the man in the Santa costume and dropped a coin into the red kettle before moving on.

A rush of warm air soothed her face when she opened the door to the post office. The clock on the wall showed five-thirty. She got there just in time before the post office closed at six.

She got excited too soon. The place was packed with people sending holiday cards and packages. Last in line, she had no choice but to wait for her turn.

"Hi, Tessa. Sending letters to your folks again?" asked the girl behind the mail counter. Her name was Ruby. She was a high school sophomore too and she worked here after school.

"Hi, Ruby. Yes." Tessa took two letters out from her school bag. "Here they are. Would you please mail them for me?" She placed six cents on the counter.

"Of course." Ruby took the coins. "You must really miss them. I would be so sad if I had to live away from my parents. Here. I'll put the special Christmas stamps on your letters for them." She sealed the red and green stamps on the envelopes and showed Tessa. The stamps depicted two boys and a girl singing Christmas carols with the words "Christmas Greetings 1940" printed at the bottom.

"Thank you." Tessa brushed the stamps with her thumb. Besides the Ardleys and the Caldwells, Ruby was the only person who had ever tried to cheer her up about being away from her home.

"Do you work every day?" Tessa asked. "You're here every time I come."

"Four days a week after school. I like it. I can make extra money to help my family." She put Tessa's letters in the pile behind her. "See you next time."

Tessa took a few steps away, then turned back. "Ruby, would you like to visit sometime? My uncle has a phonograph. We can listen to music together."

"A phonograph? I would love to! I don't know anyone who has one." Her eyes brightened and she clapped her hands together, but then her smile vanished. "I better not. I don't know anyone around where you live. Nobody I know ever goes there."

"You know me, and you'll meet my Uncle William and Aunt Sophia. I know they'll welcome you."

"Meet your aunt and uncle? No thanks." She drew back into her chair. "I'd be too scared."

"Why? My aunt and uncle are very nice people."

"I'm sure they are." Ruby lowered her eyes. "It's me. I won't feel comfortable. Girls from a school like yours don't mix with girls like me. I'll feel awkward if your aunt and uncle ask me questions about myself. What if they ask me what my parents do?"

"Why would that be a problem? What do your parents do?"

"My father works at a steel mill. My mother is a maid at the Hotel Georgette. I can't tell your aunt and uncle that."

"Why not? My aunt and uncle won't think less of you, I assure you."

Ruby shook her head. "No. I appreciate your invitation, but I can't."

Disappointed, Tessa turned away, but then another idea came to her. "I know. Why don't I come to your home then?"

"You want to come to my home?"

"My aunt and uncle have a cook. She's not British but she makes fabulous scones and pudding. I can bring some over and we can have afternoon tea together."

"I don't know…" Ruby said, trying to hide a smile. "I live on the South Side. It's not like where you live. I doubt you'll like it."

"Why? Why won't I like it?"

"My neighborhood is shabby, and some of the people there are not very nice."

Tessa waved her hand. "I'm from London. We wrote the book on shabby neighborhoods. Haven't you ever read Charles Dickens?"

Ruby's face went blank.

"Never mind. I bet you there are places much worse where I come from. It can't be worse than the slums on the East End. I'd like to see if where you live is as bad as you say. Let me visit and I'll tell you all about bad neighborhoods in London. What do you say?"

"You'll bring scones and…pudding, did you say?" Ruby asked. "I like chocolate pudding."

"Sure. That would make a splendid Christmas pudding."

Ruby looked confused, but nonetheless broke into a smile. "Okay. How about this Saturday? I can meet you at the L station here at the Loop and bring you there."

"Marvelous."

"Oh, don't wear your St. Mary's uniform. If people see you're from a private school, you might get mugged," Ruby joked.

"Who wears school uniforms on Saturdays?"

Chapter 8

When Tessa came out of the train station at Canaryville with Ruby, the first impression that struck her was gray. The buildings, the streets, the people, everything was gritty and gray. It was a drastic change of scenery from the North Shore community where she and the Ardleys lived. Here, homes clustered together in old, low-rise buildings. Dull shop signs hung above dusty display windows showing even duller goods.

The only fresh color came from blood. Streams and trickles of blood flowed down the gutters, staining the streets. The blood leaked from the buildings where men were unloading carcasses of hogs and cattle from their trucks and wheeling them inside. She had never seen so many dead pigs and cows.

"You said you wanted to see this. This is the Irish neighborhood," Ruby said.

On a closer look, there was more beyond the gray. On the doorsteps outside the buildings, children played unsupervised. In front of a restaurant, a large, rotund man in an apron swung his arms in every direction, hurling commands at two smaller men delivering boxes of food and supplies. Women hurried down the sidewalks on their way to work. At a convenience store nearby, teenage boys lolled about, smoking and laughing. Everywhere she looked, there were signs of a vibrant community.

"Ruby, your home is nowhere near where you work. Why didn't you take a job at a post office closer to where you live?"

"My mother doesn't want me to work around here. She worries I might get mixed up with the gangs. The post office downtown is close to her hotel. She wants to keep an eye on me."

"Did you say gangs?"

"Uh-huh. They own this place. The Irish gangs run the Chicago police force and half the city's government. The gang everyone's afraid of is the Colt." She lowered her voice to a whisper. "They work with the Outfit."

Tessa had never heard of this before. How could a gang run and control the city's government? The Ardleys never mentioned anything about that and they were friends with all sorts of government officials and politicians. "What's the Outfit?" she asked.

"It's an Italian mob. Al Capone owns the Outfit and the Outfit backs the Colt."

They came to the steps of a four-story walk-up. "Here we are," Ruby said. "My home." She opened the building's front door. Before they went inside, a boy about fifteen years old came running up to them. "Ruby! Ruby!" he shouted. "You better come quick. Jack, they put out a fire again." Having caught up to them, he stopped and bent over, trying to catch his breath.

"He has! That's great," Ruby said. "Did he bring back anything good this time?"

"Come look."

Tessa didn't understand what they were talking about.

"Come on, Tessa, let's go." She grabbed Tessa by the hand. "By the way, this is Henry. We grew up together." She turned to the boy. "Henry, this is my friend, Tessa."

"Hi, Tessa. Nice to meet you," Henry said, taking off his hat and revealing a mop of red hair. His coat, worn-out and at least two sizes too big, drowned him, but everything awkward and dingy about him faded to insignificance when he broke into a smile. He had an infectious smile, bolstered by the freckles across the bridge of his nose. "Let's go." He ran back the way he came. Ruby ran after him, pulling Tessa along.

"Where are we going?" Tessa asked.

"We're going to Henry's home. His older brother Jack is a firefighter. Every time the firefighters put out a fire, they bring back loot from the places that were burned down. We're going to see what Jack brought back this time."

Tessa didn't know what was happening, but Ruby and Henry were so excited, they got her excited too. She ran along with them. For the first time since she came to Chicago, she was having fun.

#

Henry's home was only two blocks away. When they arrived, he led them into his building and up to the third floor where he lived. His apartment was a small unit with only a few pieces of basic furniture cramped inside. An old couch stood against the wall. The single window above it let in only dim shafts of sunlight. A wooden cupboard and a cabinet next to the couch held all of the family's shared belongings. The unit had no separate kitchen, only a cooking stove next to the living room door.

Tessa knew the housing conditions in this neighborhood would be far from luxurious, but she had never seen a more barren home. The walls didn't have a single piece of decoration. Only two framed photos of the family on top of a small icebox gave the place a homey touch.

On the right side of the room, a young man with short strawberry-blonde hair was unloading various items from his canvas bag and spreading them across the small dining table. He looked about eighteen, tall with a slender frame, and agile in the way he moved. When they entered, he looked up. His eyes crinkled when he smiled. Tessa liked him right away.

"To the victor go the spoils," the young man said.

"What've you got?" Henry rushed over to the table. "I want to see!"

The young man ignored him. "And who is this lovely young lass?" he took Tessa's hand. "I'm Jack. I slew the dragon, escaped from his breath of fire, and brought back troves of treasures." He kissed her fingers and made her laugh.

"She's my friend Tessa. Tessa's from England," Ruby said. "Tessa, this is Jack, Henry's older brother." She joined Henry at the table to examine the loot.

"Hello," Tessa said to Jack. "Ruby told me you're a firefighter. You take things from the places that burned down? Isn't that...stealing?"

"No, no, no." Jack laughed. "Stealing is too strong a word. More like taking my fair reward. All of us firefighters are volunteers. We risk our lives to save people. The loot is payment for our services. Besides, if it weren't for us, these things would've been burned to ashes." He pointed to the icebox. "See that over there? That would've been a goner if I hadn't saved it and brought it home."

"It's okay, Tessa." Ruby reassured her. "This is how things are. Everybody here knows that."

Jack picked out a silver bracelet from the table. "A gift for my sweet Ruby." Ruby happily put it on her wrist. Next, he picked out a toy machine gun for Henry. "This is for you, fearless warrior."

"All right!" Henry said. "Look. I'm a soldier." He held the toy gun up, pretending to shoot.

When it came to Tessa's turn, Jack leaned back and crossed his arms. "Hmmm...I didn't expect a new initiate today." He combed through the pile on the table. "Aha!" He found a red hair ribbon with small white polka dots. "This is for you. A welcome gift." Tessa smiled politely and accepted.

"And for all of us, this!" He pulled out a long, narrow box from his canvas bag.

"Monopoly!" Henry yelled.

"Oh, Jack!" Ruby said. "I've always wanted to play this."

After Jack passed out the gifts, they went through the rest of the loot, sorting it into separate piles. "The watches and jewelry we can sell for money," Ruby explained to Tessa. "We'll divide the rest between Jack and some of our neighbors depending on who can use them." She picked up a small, ornate silver music box. "This is beautiful!"

"Let me see," Tessa said. Ruby opened the top and Tessa recognized the music immediately. "It's 'Fur Elise!' Beethoven."

"Fur Elise." Jack took the music box from Ruby. "I like that." His eyes turned tender. "This is for Carmina."

Ruby giggled.

"Carmina's his girlfriend." Henry rolled his eyes at Tessa.

"Let's go give it to her now," Ruby said.

"Okay." Jack put the music box into his pocket. "Let's go." He headed out the door and they hurried after him.

Outside, they followed Jack to a car patched together with a mishmash of exterior parts. "This is your car?" Tessa asked him.

"Yes," Jack said. "I've had it for a year. I worked at an auto repair shop two summers ago. I was a mechanic. This car was so broken, the owner abandoned it. My boss didn't think it could be fixed. He wanted to scrap it but I made a bet with him."

"What kind of a bet?"

"I bet him if I could fix it, he'd give it to me. I worked on it for a long time and, ta-da! It's good as new." He started the car engine. "See? It's running pretty darn good again." He sounded so proud, she didn't have the heart to tell him the car was just chugging along. She thought it might fall apart any moment, but it did move.

"Are you still a mechanic?" she asked.

"No. I work in a factory now. The pay's better and the work's not as hard. We make parachutes for foreign militaries. Did you know they fly soldiers onto battlefields and drop them from the sky? Pretty crazy, huh? Hundreds of soldiers dropping out of the sky."

Of course she knew. She had seen photos of paratroopers in newspapers even before coming to America. She looked out the window at the sky. Suppose the Germans sent paratroopers into London. Could they do that? She became quiet.

"Benny said you should join the police force instead," Henry said to Jack. "He said they'll pay you even more."

"No, Henry. Don't listen to him. I won't join the police force, and neither will you."

"Who's Benny?" Tessa asked.

"Benny Flannigan. Our District Council President," Ruby said. "Everybody does what Benny says."

"No. Everybody does not have to do what Benny says," Jack said. "We have to respect Benny, but we won't let him tell us what to do."

"Why don't you want to join the police?" Tessa asked.

"Join the police?" Jack studied her more closely. "You must not have lived in Chicago very long." His face turned serious. "The police force is not what you think. It's packed with Colt members. The Colt is the biggest Irish gang. Once you're in, there'll be no way out." He turned the car left when the traffic light switched, passing by a Chinese restaurant. "Henry, Ruby, you both stay away from Benny and his people. Stay off their radar. The less they notice you, the better."

"You're not off his radar. Benny likes you. He said he's got an open slot on the force for you whenever you decide to come on board," Henry said.

Jack didn't say anything more. They drove another five minutes and came to a stop at a local diner. Jack jumped out of the car and waved to a young waitress cleaning tables by the diner's front window. She noticed him right away and her face brightened into a smile. She wiped her hands on a small towel and came out onto the street.

"Carmina's from Mexico," Henry said to Tessa. "She and Jack met last year when they worked at the YMCA. They were locker room attendants. Wonder what they were doing in the locker rooms." Ruby punched him in the arm and he stuck out his tongue.

The young waitress greeted Jack and he took her hand. At first glance, she appeared quite ordinary. Petite and shy, she rocked back and forth on her feet as she talked, like someone who wasn't too secure about herself. But when she tossed her head, her ordinariness gave way to her most attractive feature, her hair. Tied in a ponytail, her thick, luscious black hair swung back and forth. Against her light olive skin and red lips, the contrast of colors was stunning.

Standing by the car, Henry called out to her. "Hi, Carmina!" She smiled and waved back.

"She and Jack are not supposed to see each other," Ruby whispered.

"Why not?"

"The Colts don't like the Mexicans. They think the Mexicans are encroaching on our turf. They've already gotten into huge fights with the Mexican gangs because of that."

"What does that have to do with Jack?"

Instead of answering her, Ruby's eyes widened. Tessa turned around to see what Ruby had seen. A group of four young men were heading up the street behind her.

"You better go." Carmina put her hand on Jack's arm, nudging him away. "Carlos is coming. Don't let him see you."

Jack's face fell. Carmina nudged him again but he refused and moved closer to her. Distressed, she kept glancing down the street. When the group came to the crosswalk, she gave Jack a quick kiss on the cheek and ran back into the diner. Jack's eyes followed her, his spirits disappeared with her.

The four young men approached. At first, Tessa couldn't make out what they looked like under their fedoras. Their hugely oversized zoot suits distracted from their faces too. All she could see were four long baggy blazers with wide padded shoulders hanging over pants that billowed. When they came closer and saw Jack, the one in the black fedora exchanged glances with the rest and their expressions tensed. "What are you doing here?" he asked Jack, his voice hostile and contentious.

"Carlos!" Jack said, good-naturedly as if he was speaking to an old friend. "Haven't seen you in a while. How've you been?"

"I asked what are you doing here," the young man named Carlos said.

"Why, I'm taking the kids out for a ride. Can't you see?" He threw a look over at Henry, Ruby, and Tessa.

Carlos glared at him. "You stay away from my sister."

Feigning innocence, Jack held up his hands in the air, then sauntered back to his car with his hands in his pockets. Henry, Ruby, and Tessa scooted into the car. As they drove away, Tessa caught a glimpse of Carmina looking out the diner's window, her face as sad as Jack's.

Behind them, Carlos and his friends remained until their car turned a corner. When Carlos and the diner were out of their sight, Jack's jolly pretense dropped. He kept his eyes on the road and the four of them drove silently back to his home.

#

Visiting Ruby soon became one of Tessa's regular weekend pastimes. On most Saturdays, Henry would join them if they decided to play Monopoly. Jack would be around too if he didn't have to work extra shifts. Tessa always liked it more when Jack was there. He livened up the mood whenever he was around.

"Does he always work this hard?" she asked Henry once when Jack didn't join them.

"He wants us to live well. My pop died five years ago. My mom's a housemaid. She doesn't make much money. Jack dropped out of school and started working when he was sixteen. He thinks it's his responsibility to take care of us."

"I'm sorry about your father. How did he die?"

"In a work accident." His voice trailed off and she didn't ask him about it anymore. She could imagine his pain. She thought of her own father. There were worse situations than being separated from one's parents. At least her father was still alive.

After Henry left, Ruby showed her a dress she had made for her sewing class.

"Sewing class? They teach sewing at your school?" Tessa asked.

"Yes. Don't they at yours?"

"No. What else do they teach you?"

"English and mathematics, and home economics and typing for girls. They teach shop for the boys."

"Shop? You mean shopping?"

"No, silly." Ruby laughed. "Wood shop. And mechanics. What do they teach you in your school?"

"We have English and math too. I take classes in history, science, fine arts, and Latin."

"Latin? What's that?"

"It's an ancient Roman language. Nobody uses it anymore."

"Why would anyone learn a language nobody uses?"

"Because it's beautiful, and it helps people who know it to write better prose."

"I see." Dropping the subject, Ruby picked up her dress again. "There'll be a fashion show at my school next week. I hope my dress will win a prize." She laid the dress on her bed with a secretive smile. "I want to show you something." She took a sketch-book out of her desk drawer and handed it to Tessa.

"What is this?" Tessa asked.

"These are my design sketches. I've never shown them to anyone before." Ruby opened the sketch-book to a page with several illustrations of models in suits and hats. "I want to be a fashion designer when I graduate."

"You do?" Tessa leafed through the pages of drawings. They were amateurish, but she could tell Ruby had put a huge effort into them. Even some of the buttons and belts were drawn with elaborate and intricate details.

"What about you? What you want to do when you're through with school?"

"Me?" She hadn't thought seriously about that.

"Never mind." Ruby rolled her eyes at herself. "Silly of me to ask. You won't have to work. You're a St. Mary's girl. You'll meet a handsome guy from a nice family, of course."

"A handsome guy?" Tessa made a face. Was that all there would be for her in the future? The idea left her wanting. She looked at the dress Ruby made. Maybe it was time she had her own dreams too.

Chapter 9

Winter break began a week before Christmas and Anthony returned home for the holidays. Delighted their son was back for more than an evening, William and Sophia peppered him with questions during dinner.

"What classes will you be taking next semester?" William asked.

"I'll be taking American History. We have a new professor from Harvard teaching this course. I heard he's very good and his class is hard to get into." He helped himself to the gravy on the table. "And I'll be taking Food and Products Distribution Management."

"Food and Products Distribution Management? Why? You plan to get into the grocery business?" his father joked.

"No." He cut into his steak. "They changed the curriculum requirements to prepare for the war. I'll have to take two elective wartime prep courses next semester. I picked Military Science and Engineering, and Principles of Radio Communication."

"Are you serious?" Sophia stopped eating and put her knife and fork down on her plate. Tessa and William, too, paused to listen.

"Those are the courses they're teaching now. I thought the ones I picked might be useful if I work for Uncle Leon again next summer since they involve logistics." Anthony continued eating, not realizing the news had stunned his parents. "They want us to be ready. Every college is doing this, not just UC, and all the male students have to take an hour of Phys. Ed. everyday."

When neither his father nor his mother said anything, he finally sensed their unease and looked up. The changes he was speaking of had been implemented for months, old news for everyone in school. He hadn't thought they would worry his parents to this extent.

"My courses will be fairly basic." He tried to backtrack from the subject. "It's probably just for show. I doubt they'll teach me anything practical for use in a real war," he lied. Actually, he had no idea. Rumors had run rampant on campus after the school announced the changes and no one knew yet what all this meant. "You should see the classes Brandon chose. Those are real military classes. He signed up for Naval Strategic Tactics and Military Pyrotechnics. My classes will be child's play compared to his." Maybe they would feel better if they knew the changes didn't worry Brandon either.

His attempt to allay his parents' fears didn't work. They exchanged glances and continued eating in silence. He looked at Tessa, who was watching the entire exchange. He thought he saw a tinge of worry in her eyes, but she turned away from him, and he was left wondering if he had scared her with all the war talk.

# # #

On Christmas morning, Tessa sat alone on her bed, staring out the window remembering past Christmases. It was snowing outside. Light speckles of snowflakes drifted in the air. She had never been away from her parents on Christmas. Last season, her father's company had run a production of A Christmas Carol with him in the starring role as

Scrooge. Her mother said that it was the perfect role for him because he always grumbled about how much he hated the holidays.

But it was not true that he hated holidays. He didn't like going to Christmas parties. Like her, he loathed being around crowds where he had to fake an interest in people. He said he felt phony pretending to admire every theater patron in attendance. Her mother would laugh and tell him his acting skills should save him in that case.

At home was a different story. They always had happy Christmases as a family. Her father would buy her and her mother a lot of presents. Her mother, certainly not the world's greatest cook, would attempt to make a holiday feast.

She wondered what they had planned for today. It felt so lonely without them this time of the year.

A knock interrupted her thoughts. She glanced at the door. "Come in."

The door opened. "Merry Christmas, Tessa," Anthony said without entering the room.

"Merry Christmas." Still sitting on the bed, she mustered as much enthusiasm as she could.

"Uncle Leon and everyone have arrived." He stood in the doorway. "You should come down." He grinned as if he had something good to reveal. "Mother and Father got you a Christmas present they want you to see." He sounded anxious for her to get excited too.

"Okay." She twitched her lips to suppress a smile of amusement. The genuine sincerity on his face was always funny to watch. For someone so smart, he was very simple and easy to figure out. Whether he was sad, or happy, or grouchy, he always let his emotions show.

She got off the bed and put on her shoes. The Ardleys were hosting a Christmas luncheon for their friends and relatives. Privately, she wished she could skip the meal. There would be so many people downstairs. Some of them she had never met. She would feel out of place among them. Besides, to have to sit among strangers for hours when she could barely keep herself from crying was the last thing she wanted to do. She wished she could spend the day alone and keep to herself, but Aunt Sophia had been planning this luncheon for weeks. She didn't want to be difficult and upset her and Uncle William. With so many guests, they had enough to handle today without having to worry about her.

She went to her dresser and brushed her hair. The whole time, Anthony stood in the doorway watching her. She wondered why he was still there. "You don't have to wait for me."

"It's all right," he said, his voice gentler than usual. "I'll wait. You don't have to come down alone."

She didn't know how to respond. They usually stayed out of each other's way. It was so awkward that he was being nice. She quickly finished brushing her hair and straightened her skirt. "I'm ready."

He waited for her to walk ahead of him. As they walked down the stairs and the guests' voices in the main parlor grew louder, she was glad he stayed with her after all and she wouldn't have to enter a room full of people by herself. She didn't want to be the center of attention.

When she entered, everyone stopped talking and laughing and looked at her. Seeing the large gathering of people, she wanted to turn around and run back upstairs. Instead, she took a deep breath and forced herself to smile. "Merry Christmas," she said.

"Merry Christmas, Tessa," William said.

"You waited too long to come down." Sophia came over. "Look what just came for you." She handed her a telegram.

With timid hands, Tessa took the telegram. When she saw the names of the senders, her heart stopped.

"It's from your parents," Sophia said. "Go on. Read it."

Without another moment's hesitation, she opened it and devoured every word.

73

Dear Tessa,

Merry Christmas. We wish you a wonderful holiday with William and his family. We are thinking of you all the time, and we miss you very much. We cannot wait to hear all about your first Christmas in America. We hope we will be back together with you very soon. — Love, Mother and Father

Her eyes smarted with tears as she read. She pretended to rub her eyes and wiped them off before her tears fell and everyone could see her cry.

"We have something we want to show you," William said. Only then did she see something in the middle of the parlor that hadn't been there last night. A white cloth covered it but she could guess the object by its shape. Still, it was hard to believe. Could it really be?

William took the cloth off to unveil a brand new baby grand piano. "Juliet told me you're an excellent piano player. Sophia and I thought you might like this." He opened the keyboard cover. "Want to take a look?"

In a daze, she walked to the piano. She never expected this. Her heart felt so full of emotions, she could hardly breathe. Ever so lightly, she ran her fingers across the keyboard. She almost didn't dare to touch it for fear that if she did, it would dematerialize and she would wake up to find this was but a dream. "This is so generous. Thank you, Uncle William. Aunt Sophia. Thank you."

"Would you play something for us?" Sophia asked.

"I'll be delighted." She looked around at everyone in the room. They didn't look so oppressive to her anymore. "I can't play as well as my father. He taught me how to play when I was little." She sat down in front of the piano and tried out a few keys. Finding her rhythm, she began to play. The uplifting melodies of "Ode to Joy" filled the air, mesmerizing all those who were listening. When she finished, the guests gave her a resounding round of applause and she bowed her head.

"Tessa, you're amazing," said Alexander. "Can you play 'Winter Wonderland'?"

"Of course!" Her fingers danced on the keys, bringing the notes of the music to life. Alexander started to sing and everyone followed. The song ended with everyone in joyful spirits and in awe of her masterful performance.

"Ladies and gentlemen, may I invite you to the dining room?" Sophia said to the guests. "Tessa can play more songs for us later."

As the group retreated from the parlor, Tessa couldn't resist and took to the piano once more. This time, she chose a Bach piece with a private message. As she played, she looked at Anthony. She hoped he knew this music and that he would understand.

Her stare caught his attention. He leaned against the wall and listened while the others left the room. She hoped he could hear the message that she also wished he would not have to go to war. It was the only way she knew to let him know how she felt. When they were the only ones remaining, she turned her attention back to the keyboard. She realized then what she really wanted for Christmas this year, not just for Anthony but for everyone else in the world.

"Dona Nobis Pacem." Grant us peace.

PART FIVE
The Hand of God

Chapter 10

"Anthony! Anthony!"

"Go! Go, go, go, go, go!"

"Come on, Anthony, faster, faster, go!"

In the pool, all the shouts and shrieks of Anthony's teammates blended into background noises along with the ripples and splashes of the water. He couldn't hear them. Nothing they said or did would help. It was all up to him.

Their relay team started off with Brandon in the lead, but somehow, their second and third swimmers lost the edge. By the time he dived in, they were fifteen seconds behind the leader. The leader in the next lane had pulled a daunting distance ahead.

Anthony swung his arms and kicked with all his strength. This competition would determine whether they would qualify to advance to the finals. Everything now depended on him. He could not let everyone down.

With sheer force of will, he pushed ahead. When he caught up with the leading swimmer, the swimmer increased speed, giving him no choice but to push even harder. His arms and legs burned but he refused to let the swimmer regain the lead. The end was in sight, only inches away. He reached out his arm. His fingertip touched the wall of the pool, ahead of his opponent by a mere second.

After the competition, Anthony entered the locker room with the rest of the swim team cheering him and slapping him on the back. The relay was close, but they had done their job. They would advance. Moreover, Hal and Richard had posted personal best times in their individual events. Their team members advanced in every category.

Their victory was a huge relief to him. Being the team's standard-bearer after Lloyd Pearson was no easy task. Thankfully, everyone had rallied behind him. "Great job, everyone," he told the rowdy bunch when the swim meet was over. "Don't forget practice at seven a.m. tomorrow."

"Time for beef!" Hal shouted as he walked out of the shower. "Hey Anthony, you should be the one rounding everyone up."

"Right." Anthony picked up his gym bag from the bench. He was still adjusting to his role and didn't even think of being the one to lead the team's tradition of going to Marconi's for Chicago beef after they qualified for the finals. "Who's up for Marconi's?" he shouted to the rest of the team.

A chorus of "me" answered him. He hurried up and put on his clothes, ready to take everyone out for a celebratory meal. Before they left, he scoured the lockers. "Where's Brandon?"

His teammates looked around. A few shrugged and shook their heads.

"He left a few minutes ago," Stanley said.

"He left?" Anthony looked at the door. What could be so important for Brandon to skip their beef sandwich victory dinner?

When Anthony returned to his dorm room later that night, Brandon was already getting ready for bed.

"Where'd you go?" Anthony asked his friend.

"I had an appointment to get to," Brandon said.

"It was that important? You missed all the fun at Marconi's."

"Yeah. Sorry about that. It was a great win today, wasn't it?"

"Sure was," Anthony said, excited. "Stanley's time for the butterfly was amazing. He must've practiced over the holidays. I wonder…"

"I got to get some sleep." Brandon climbed into bed and turned off his lights.

Anthony held back, surprised that Brandon didn't want to talk about their competition. In fact, he didn't seem all that excited. "What appointment did you have tonight?" He was curious.

"I'll tell you about it later. It's late. We have to wake up early for practice tomorrow." Brandon turned toward the wall. "Good night."

Anthony didn't say anything more. He wondered all night why Brandon seemed so odd today.

# # #

Of the classes offered during the spring semester, American History garnered the longest waiting list. The reason for that was Garrett Collins. A visiting professor from Harvard in his early thirties, he related to the students better than most of the other faculty members. The line between them often blurred both inside or outside of the classroom.

"Joining us for another basketball game tonight, Prof?" asked a male student passing by to take a seat.

"Not tonight. Got a History Department meeting," the young professor said while he organized his notes behind the lecturer's podium.

"Professor, can we schedule a time to meet with you? We need help with our term papers," asked a female student with her friend standing behind her.

"Sure. My office hours are three to six, Mondays and Thursdays. Sign-up sheet's posted outside my office."

The girls returned happily to their seats.

When class began, he stood at the podium and pushed his lecture notes aside. "Let's put our reading aside for today. We have a more urgent topic to discuss than the Louisiana Purchase, important subject as that may be."

Paper-shuffling sounds and mumbles filled the room as everyone closed their books. Collins walked away from the podium.

"There's nothing better than to live our lessons when significant moments of history fall upon us." He picked up the newspaper on the table in the front of the lecture hall. "The House of Representatives today passed the Lend-Lease Bill." He held up the newspaper to show them the headline. "You all have been thinking about the war, I'm sure. So. The war. Let's talk about it." He sat down on the edge of the table facing them. "I want to hear what you all think."

The students smirked at each other, the way they did when they thought their own opinions were superior to others.

"You know we are mobilizing, right? It doesn't matter the government and the press keep telling you we're not. We are preparing for war. You're all smart enough to know that."

His declaration invited only confused whispers.

"Universities across the country are preparing their students to go to war." He watched for their reactions. "Students such as yourselves. The school administration is sadly not as Fred with you as they should be, but you don't need everything spelled out for you. You see what's happening. Your curriculum has changed. Military officials are visiting the campus. Why are they here?"

No one volunteered to speak. Some of them threw each other nervous glances.

"Because faculty committees are actively collaborating with the U.S. Army. They've been doing so for months."

The mood in the classroom changed from playfully smug to sober. Everyone had heard the rumors. Their school had subjected the students' interests to the army's priorities. They had all whispered about it. They had all guessed it even if no one in the school administration would confirm it. Collins' open admission cemented the rumors into reality.

"Your university leaders believe intervention is inevitable. What do you think? Is American intervention inevitable?"

No one raised their hand. The subject of the war made them uncomfortable and no one knew the right thing to say.

"Well, you better have an opinion. When we declare war, your generation will be the ones most affected." He looked at the naive and confused faces before him. His eyes settled on one whose easy self-assurance had caught his attention since the first day of class. The young man had the presence of a leader, but at only nineteen, he had no awareness yet of his natural ability to draw people to follow him.

"Mr. Ardley."

"Yes," Anthony answered. In the seat next to him, Brandon raised an eyebrow with the corner of his lip turned up. He could almost hear Brandon say, "Poor you."

"Do you think intervention is inevitable?"

Everyone's eyes turned to Anthony. Too modest to take pleasure at being the center of attention, he drew slightly back into his seat. "I hope not."

"Why is that?"

"Because..." he glanced down for a moment, then gazed up directly at Collins. "I wish I could give you a more intelligent answer, Professor, but the truth is, my family lost my uncle to the last war. I don't want them to go through that again."

"Hmm." Collins held his hand to his chin. He hadn't expected this response.

"I know it sounds selfish…"

"No," Collins interrupted him. "It's a valid answer." He picked up the newspaper to show them the headline again. "In the coming months, you'll hear many arguments for and against American involvement. Political arguments. Economic arguments. Ethical arguments." He put down the newspaper. "But remember this. If America goes to war, your generation, all of you who sit here in this classroom today, will be the ones to bear the bulk of the burden and consequences. The question is, are you ready?"

The class remained quiet. Some averted their eyes and others pretended to take notes. No one wanted to deal with the question.

"I'm not ready," Collins said, not letting go of the issue on account of their unease.

"You side with the isolationists?" Brandon spoke up.

"No," he said. "I'm actually appalled at how callous they are about what's happening in the other parts of the world. I'm not against intervention. I'm against war."

"What's the difference?" Brandon asked.

"The difference is as Mr. Ardley said."

Anthony shifted in his seat, self-conscious at the uninvited attention.

"War is an ugly business," Collins continued. "It takes a human toll. It breaks families apart. It displaces people. Destroys them, physically and mentally. War is never the answer."

While the class thought about what Collins said, Brandon held up his notebook to Anthony, showing him the word "Coward" written in large letters and an arrow pointed in Collins' direction.

Anthony frowned. That was an unfair assessment. Collins was right. War was brutal and it usually didn't change anything. "Professor," he said, "what if we're called to fight?"

Collins smiled. "That's the ultimate question, isn't it? What will be your choice if the call comes?"

Anthony didn't know. He looked at Brandon. Brandon was no longer listening. He had his head down and was scribbling something into his notebook. Anthony never found out what he was writing, but the look of contempt on Brandon's face remained for the rest of the class.

#

Two weeks later, Brandon announced he would quit the swim team to devote more time to writing op-ed columns for The Daily Maroon, the University's student newspaper.

"Is this necessary?" Anthony asked. "You've been doing both since our freshman year and you handled everything fine." Taking over the role of captain from Lloyd Pearson was hard enough. The last thing he needed was to lose another strong swimmer like Brandon.

"My heart's not in it anymore." Brandon tossed his book onto the desk and flopped down on his bed. "When I think of all the things happening in the world, swimming doesn't feel all that important."

Anthony sank into his chair. He didn't know how Brandon could say that. They had competed together since junior high school. Swimming was an integral part of who they were. They planned their lives around it. Besides, he and Brandon were best friends. They had grown up together and were now roommates at school. The swim team wouldn't be the same without him.

More than that, why didn't he know anything about what Brandon had been thinking? Why hadn't Brandon said anything about this until now?

"We Americans are turning a blind eye while Hitler is taking over Europe," Brandon said. "Everyone says they don't want to get involved, that they want peace. You know something? There is no peace. How can we have peace when democracies are being destroyed?"

Anthony crossed his arms and listened. Uncle Leon would have a fit if he heard this.

"The people arguing against intervention have dominated the debate for far too long. Everyone hears only their side because our chancellor supports them. It's time we all hear something else." Brandon sat up on his bed, his eyes fired up the same way they always did during a swim meet. "I'm going to make sure everyone hears the other side, loud and clear."

Anthony looked away. Good thing he hadn't mentioned anything about America First. He had no idea Brandon felt this way. "I don't see why you have to quit the swim team. You're a good writer. Writing articles for the Maroon can't take that much time. Why quit now? We need you on the team."

Brandon flicked the pen in his hand the way he always did when he was losing his patience. "It's not just the newspaper." He took a flyer out of his book bag and gave it to Anthony. "Some of us are starting a new advocacy group to support American involvement. We're going to turn opinions around."

Anthony took the flyer. It called for America to defend Britain. Beneath the call, a giant foot in a black boot marked with a swastika was about to crush the Statue of Liberty.

"Our first meeting is tomorrow night. You should come."

Right. As if he could. If Uncle Leon found out, all hell would break loose. "Brandon, do your parents know what you're doing?" He needed to ask. The Lowes had been his neighbors for years. Their parents were good friends. Mr. and Mrs. Lowe practically watched him grow up with their son. With conscription now in effect, they would be worried for sure if they knew what Brandon was planning to do.

Brandon shrugged and didn't answer.

"Are you going to tell them?"

"Look. This isn't about my parents." Brandon avoided his question. "The important thing is, we have to convince people to do what's right."

The passion in Brandon's voice and his dismissive attitude about his parents worried and surprised Anthony.

"Come to our meeting tomorrow."

Go to a pro-intervention meeting? Him? Was Brandon out of his mind?

"We can use all the support we can get."

"I can't do that. You know what Uncle Leon thinks about this."

"It doesn't matter what he thinks. He's him and you're you." Brandon pressed on. "One meeting. Come." He looked Anthony in the eye. "Don't you trust me?"

Anthony hesitated. Trust had nothing to do with anything. It was a noble thing to care about what was happening in the world, but he cared more about the people close to him. He didn't want anyone he knew or loved to be drawn into the war, least of all Brandon. Why couldn't they leave things be and let everything take its own course?

He wanted to refuse. He didn't want to push for more American involvement, but he didn't know how to decline without upsetting his friend.

"You know," Brandon said, "sooner or later you're going to have to decide which side you're on."

# # #

The first meeting of the new pro-intervention group attracted only ten people. Brandon, along with Nate Sanders and Gretchen Moore, led the meeting. Anthony knew Gretchen, but not well. Like him, she was a sophomore, and she had been in his archaeology class last year. He had seen Nate, a junior, around campus, but they had never met.

Part of him regretted letting Brandon talk him into coming tonight. He hadn't given Uncle Leon an answer yet about starting a chapter of the AFC, but here he was, at a meeting for a new group advocating the exact opposite. If anyone else but Brandon had asked, he most certainly would have refused. He came for one reason only, to find out what his friend was up to. Brandon had never been politically active about anything. What brought this on? Why the sudden interest?

Except it wasn't a sudden interest. Watching Brandon interact with Nate and Gretchen, it was clear the three of them were more than mere acquaintances supporting the same cause. They had the rapport of that of old friends. Brandon knew what Nate and Gretchen wanted to say before they finished speaking. Sometimes, they would laugh at jokes only they could understand.

Brandon used to behave this way only with him.

Searching his memory, Anthony tried to remember if Brandon had acted differently or shown any changes last semester. Nothing came to mind. Brandon never even mentioned Nate, Gretchen, or anything about their pro-intervention work. Was Brandon hiding this from him? Or was he himself the one to blame? Had he been so engrossed in himself that he overlooked what Brandon had been doing?

"Thank you all for coming." Nate Sanders took to the front of the classroom. At five-foot-six, slightly chubby and with beady eyes, he didn't look the part of a leader of a political movement. Brandon would've made a more convincing leader. Anthony wondered why Nate was the one in charge.

Nate cleared his throat. "We formed this group as the University of Chicago branch of the National Committee to Defend America." Behind him, Brandon wrote "CDA" in large letters on the blackboard.

"For now, our objective is to call for more military aid to Britain." Nate puffed out his chest and stood straighter as he spoke, perhaps trying to compensate for his lack of height. "We do not rule out support for direct military intervention. If Britain falls, American security will no longer be guaranteed. We must prepare ourselves. Starting now." Strangely enough, when he talked, everyone paid attention and listened. It wasn't the substance of what he said, but how he said it. He spoke with a provocative sense of urgency, sounding almost a little shrill. With just those few sentences, he spurred a round of applause.

His style of speaking—Anthony had heard it before, but where? He crossed his arms and drew back into his seat, trying to figure Nate out. Something about Nate bothered him, but he couldn't say what.

"One by one, countries in Europe have fallen. At this rate, Britain will not hold. It will fall! If we don't do something, America will be next. None of us will be safe. It is now up to us to take up the mantle of freedom and democracy." Nate paused and made eye contact with each person in front of him as though he was speaking personally to each of them. Sly move, Anthony thought. Senator Reinhardt always did that too whenever he was introduced to new campaign donors.

That was it. Senator Reinhardt. Nate spoke like Senator Reinhardt. Only Nate was worse in the way he was fanning fear.

"We must take a stand against German fascism and dictatorship. Neutrality is not an option." The urgency in Nate's voice heightened. A few students shouted out their agreement.

Anthony looked around. Unbelievable. Nate was winning them over, even the few who he suspected had come tonight solely out of curiosity. Did they really believe Nate's false sympathy and fear-mongering? Were people this gullible?

"We must assert ourselves in the war and lead the world to do what's right." Nate continued to stoke the small crowd. "We are the last line of defense. America is meant for greatness. We will not let the weak and the cowards speak for us anymore."

Everyone in the room applauded. Anthony remained the only one unmoved. To him, Nate sounded like a buffoon, but the others had inexplicably fallen under his spell. He glanced at Brandon. Brandon's face glowed with inspiration as if he had found a new religion, and Nate Sanders was the high priest. He had never seen Brandon like this before. What happened to him?

They needed to talk. He didn't like Nate Sanders. Whatever else the CDA might be about, he didn't want Brandon involved with Nate. He needed to get him out of this. When the meeting ended, he tried to get Brandon to leave.

Brandon brushed him off. "I'll catch up with you when I get back. I have some things to wrap up with Nate and Gretchen." He continued talking to Nate. Regardless of what Anthony wanted, it would have to wait.

While Brandon practically ignored him, Nate made a point of smiling at him. It was a friendly smile, too friendly from someone he hardly knew. Anthony excused himself and headed for the door. The whole situation made him uncomfortable.

"Anthony. Wait." Gretchen Moore chased after him on his way out. "Thank you for joining us. Your coming means a lot to us."

Out of courtesy, he nodded. He didn't know why she singled him out.

"I can't tell you how glad we are to see you with us." She gave him a demure smile. "Maybe you aren't aware, but you influence people." Her eyes were serious and sincere. "The guys, they follow you. The girls, they like you. Your being a part of us will help convince others to join us."

Her blunt compliment embarrassed him. "Nate's doing a fine job convincing others without me."

"Maybe so. It would still help a lot if we have the Ardley family's support."

His family's support. Of course. He could never do anything without someone calculating what the Ardley family could bring to the table. Too bad she thought that too. He wasn't about to commit his family to supporting anything. He came to the meeting because of Brandon, not for anything else. He gave her a polite but noncommittal smile.

She looked back at Nate and Brandon. "I know it sounds easy for me to say, but if I were a male student, I would enlist. As it is, this is all I can do." She sounded almost disappointed. "I promised Brandon and Nate if they're drafted, I will continue the CDA's work here. You do see the importance of what we do, don't you?"

He couldn't honestly say he did, especially with Nate leading their cause. She spoke so earnestly, though, he didn't want to contradict her outright. "You and Brandon are dedicated to a cause bigger than all of us. I admire that."

His answer was enough to satisfy her. "Thank you again for coming. Please come again next time." She smiled and walked away.

Yes. He might have no choice but to come again if he couldn't convince Brandon to drop this. Immediately.

# # #

"Anthony. What do you think of this?" Brandon asked from his desk in their dorm room. He had been working on another article for The Daily Maroon all night.

On his bed with his textbook on his lap and leaning back against the wall, Anthony glanced at his clock. Eleven p.m.

Oblivious to the time, Brandon read from his draft without looking up. "America is and remains a beacon for freedom and democracy for the world. We cannot isolate ourselves as the world descends into chaos. We have a moral duty to stand up for our fundamental values and principles…"

"Too pompous. Since when did we become a beacon for the world?"

"Nate said we should open people's eyes to America's potential. We have the resources and ability to lead the world."

Lead the world? He wasn't even convinced America should go to war, let alone lead the world. Besides, what Professor Collins had said in class was still fresh in his mind. War destroyed people. It had left lasting consequences on his own family already. Did Brandon have any true idea what it all entailed? "Brandon, if you tell people to fight for your values and principles, then you have to be ready to go to war and defend your values."

"I'm ready," Brandon said without hesitation. "We have to do what's right and take a stand for our beliefs."

Anthony closed his book. Their conversation was going nowhere. Lately, he and Brandon were out of sync on everything. "Do you understand what fighting a war means? It's not a game. It's real. People get hurt. People die. It changes people's lives." He thought of his Uncle Leon. "Sometimes people never get over it."

"Of course things will change." Brandon turned around from his desk. "But we can't think about insignificant things like changes to our own lives now. We have a chance to do something much bigger and be a part of a new movement. We can bring changes to the whole world."

Anthony wasn't convinced. Brandon didn't have an inkling of what it was like to lose a family member to war.

His quiet dissent went unnoticed as Brandon went on. "It's like what Nate's been saying." That glow of inspiration shone on his face again. "We have to think bigger than ourselves."

Even the mention of Nate's name irritated Anthony. "You put a lot of stock lately in what Nate says."

"Because everything he says is true. I wish more people would listen to him."

Not wanting to argue, Anthony turned out the light on his nightstand. "I'm going to sleep. Goodnight." He pulled his cover over himself.

A moment later, he opened his eyes and stole a glance at Brandon, who had returned to his draft. Brandon used to be an independent thinker. He didn't like the growing influence Nate Sanders had over him. Not at all.

Chapter 11

"I'm sorry, Uncle Leon. The AFC's a good cause, but I have other priorities right now." In Leon's office, Anthony finally let it out. He had stalled his uncle for weeks and had finally run out of excuses.

Leon's disappointment was as great as he expected.

"What other priorities? Your classwork? Swimming? The AFC won't get in your way of those. I'll see to that. I'll give you whatever support you need."

"It's not that. It's Brandon."

"What about him?"

"He's not himself lately."

Leon stared at him, puzzled.

"He and some students started a UC branch of the Committee to Defend America."

"Committee to Defend America...What?!"

Anthony shrank in the chair. He had been dreading this moment.

"You're telling me Brandon supports intervention? He's working against me? Has he lost his mind?"

"He's been brainwashed..."

"I'll say!" Leon lit a cigarette and took a deep drag.

"There's this guy, Nate Sanders. He's a junior. He's the ringleader. He has a hold over Brandon. It's the way he speaks. He's very persuasive." He fiddled his fingers on his lap, trying to think of how not to aggravate his uncle any further. "Brandon listens to everything he says. I don't like the influence Nate has over him. I want to try to get Brandon out. If I get involved with the AFC now, Brandon might not talk to me."

"What can you do to get Brandon out?"

"I go to their CDA meetings."

"You what?" Leon looked like he was ready to explode.

"To keep an eye on Brandon. That's all. I swear."

Leon swiveled his chair sideways and took another drag of his cigarette.

"I want to know what Brandon's doing. I'm worried he might enlist on impulse. If that happens, I want to be there to talk him out of it."

"Everybody knows I'm an AFC supporter, and my own nephew goes to CDA meetings. How does that look?"

"I'm not there to support the CDA." He tried to appease his uncle. "I won't participate in their rallies. I won't speak on their behalf. I won't do anything to embarrass you. I just want to be there for him. If I had paid more attention last semester, maybe Brandon wouldn't have gotten roped into the CDA to begin with."

Leon didn't answer. He stared at the old photo of Lex on his desk.

"He's my best friend. I feel responsible. If Brandon enlists, what would Mr. and Mrs. Lowe do? He's their only son."

Turning his chair to face Anthony again, Leon asked, "That's your decision then?"

Anthony lowered his head. He did feel he was letting his uncle down.

Leon dropped his shoulders and rubbed his forehead between his brows. In that instant, he looked older than Anthony had ever seen him.

95

His eyelids sagged and his hair seemed unusually dull. "I can't fault you for being a good friend. Watch out for him then. Don't let him make the same mistake Lex made." His lips turned up in a sad smile. "At least I know you're not thinking of enlisting."

"Thanks, Uncle Leon." He could breathe easy again, although he didn't tell Leon he was also relieved to not have to be a part of the AFC. In truth, he didn't care for either the AFC or the CDA.

"You still want to work for me this summer?" Leon asked.

"I'm thinking about it. I want to see what I can learn elsewhere before I start to work for Father."

"You can learn a lot from your father. He's a brilliant businessman and an honorable civic leader. The Ardley Group is yours to take when he steps down and you're ready."

"Sometimes I wonder if it should be that way."

Leon looked at him, perplexed.

"There's got to be a better reason for me to take over his business than simply me being his son. What if I'm not the right person? What if there's someone else more capable or deserving?"

Leon studied him with an amused smile. "Don't be ridiculous. A father passing his work on to his son is the natural order of things."

Still, Anthony wished there was another reason besides his birth. "I'd like to try working somewhere else first and see how I'd do. I might learn something I can bring into Father's companies."

"All right. Just let me know. My door's always open."

# # #

Arriving in American History class a week later, the students found Professor Leif McLaren, the head of the History Department, standing before them in the lecture hall instead of Garrett Collins.

"I regret to inform you Professor Collins will no longer be with us," McLaren announced to the class. "He's been summoned to service for the United States Army this morning and so cannot finish out this term. I will take his place as your instructor for the remainder of this semester."

The students let out a collective moan.

"Don't all get too excited now," McLaren said in his forever-flat voice.

Next to him, Brandon whispered, "Good riddance."

Anthony didn't say anything. He liked Collins. Collins cared about the students, challenged them and made them think and learn. His departure was their loss.

"Serves him right. Now he has no choice but to fight for what's right." Brandon said. His tone of contempt upset Anthony. He wished Brandon wouldn't detest Collins so much because of ideological differences. Collins was one of the best professors they had ever had.

As soon as class finished, he rushed to the faculty offices in the History Department, hoping to catch Collins before he took off for the next train back to Harvard. In his office, Collins was taking down a painting from the wall.

"Professor Collins."

"Anthony." Collins seemed pleased he had come.

"Professor, we just heard…Here, let me help you." The large painting started to tip over and he stepped up to give Collins a hand.

"Thanks."

"We'll all miss you." He helped Collins set the painting on the floor.

Collins stared at the draft letter on his desk. "I'm rejecting the summons."

"What do you mean?"

"I'm refusing service as a conscientious objector."

"They'll let you do that?"

"I'll petition. My prospects are good. My antiwar views are well-known from my publications."

"People will think you're a coward. They'll think you're trying to escape the draft."

"I'm not escaping anything. I won't participate in any war. It's against my principles."

"You'll be sent to a conscientious objectors' camp."

"It's better than going to prison, and I won't have to go to war against my conscience."

"It's almost like a prison. You won't be free."

"No, but if this war gets any worse, none of us will be free. There's no freedom in the military. There's no freedom in prison. There's no freedom in the conscientious objectors' camps. The only choice you'll have is which prison you'd rather be in."

How ironic, Anthony thought, considering that Brandon had been talking non-stop about America being a beacon for freedom.

"It's not so bad. They'll put me to work on national conservation projects and services. I'll be doing something positive. It'll be my way of contributing to our society." Collins put the notebooks and stationery pads on his desk into a box. Lastly, he picked up the draft letter. He held it for a moment, then dropped it in with the rest of this things. "My conscience is clear."

"Professor, is it true the government performs medical experiments on people at the conscientious objectors' camps?"

Collins closed his box. "I don't know. I've heard the rumors too. I suppose I'll find out." He scanned his office one more time to make sure he hadn't forgotten anything. "I'll miss this place."

The empty office was a depressing sight.

"Would you do one thing for me?" Collins asked.

"Anything, Professor."

"You have a gift. People listen to you. Remind them often of what I said. War is an ugly business. It brings changes in ways people can't begin to imagine, usually not for the good. There are always consequences. War never solves anything."

Those were Collins' parting words.

# # #

In less than three months' time, the CDA chapter on campus had grown to more than three hundred members. The combination of Nate Sanders' fiery speeches and Brandon's newspaper articles had swayed people's minds like a one-two punch. At rallies, Nate's oratory skills provoked raw emotions. Through *The Daily Maroon*, Brandon made his case for intervention with sound, logical reasons. Their momentum surged.

The CDA's rise was all the more remarkable considering the dominance of the anti-intervention faction on campus and the rest of Chicago. The UC CDA Chapter rivaled the new UC AFC chapter, even though the AFC chapter had the support and backing of some of Chicago's most powerful men.

With the CDA's rise, Nate became the face of those in support of intervention. When journals or publications needed alternative opinions to the isolationist groups, they sought him out before anyone else. As his influence grew, he attracted more and more people to their cause. Classroom meetings no longer sufficed. They now held rallies indoor and outdoor all over campus wherever there were crowds so they could spread their word. Nate Sanders was everywhere. People began to listen. They came to rallies to hear him speak and he relished the limelight.

On his way to class, Anthony passed by Nate proselytizing again in front of the university chancellor's building.

"We can help England win this war!" Nate roused the crowd from the podium. "We can set the stage for global democracy. Those who argue for non-intervention would turn a blind eye to the atrocities happening in Europe. They go about their business as usual. They don't care that people are dying and suffering. They don't care if Hitler takes over half the world." He paused to let the crowd stew in their indignation. "But we care. We must defeat the isolationists and bring our glorious nation to its full potential." A wave of cheers and applause followed.

Anthony walked on. Wasn't defeating Hitler and Germany their real goal? If the CDA thought their mission was to defeat the isolationists, then they had lost their way.

If it weren't for Brandon, he would quit the CDA. He kept hoping this was a phase. He held out hope that when it passed, things would return to the way they used to be.

Deep down, he knew it wasn't so simple. Supporting intervention was all Brandon cared about anymore. Going to CDA meetings was the only way he could remain relevant in Brandon's life.

But he came close to abandoning even that.

At tonight's meeting, a student reporter writing a feature article about the pro-intervention movement for *The Daily Maroon* had joined them and she had brought along a student photographer. Everyone had arrived, but the meeting couldn't start because Nate was fussing about who should appear in the photo.

"I'll stand in the front here because I'm leading the meeting." Nate pointed to the front of the classroom. The poor photographer dragged his equipment back and forth, trying to capture the angle Nate wanted. "If you can take the picture from this spot, then you can show the others in these seats…" He indicated four seats in the first two rows in front of him. "Jeremy," he called out to Jeremy Heller, a freshman who everyone knew as the younger brother of the Chicago Cubs left fielder Brett

Heller. "Yes. You'll be good. Why don't you sit right here?" He pointed to one of the two seats in the first row. "Ethan, I'm sorry. Would you mind changing seats with Jeremy?" Ethan, a shy freshman, obliged and Jeremy moved to his seat.

Far in the back of the classroom, Anthony glanced impatiently at his watch.

"Beth, Carol," Nate said to two of the most attractive female students in the group. "Why don't you two sit behind Tom?" Beth and Carol moved to the seats he pointed out.

"Okay..." He scanned the room. "Anthony!"

Anthony winced.

"Would you please take a seat next to Jeremy?"

"No. I prefer not." Anthony remained in his seat. "Actually, you, Brandon, and Gretchen should line up together for a photo and get this over with. They deserve to be in the picture. It's getting late. We all have homework to do."

His refusal threw Nate off. "Of course. Brandon and Gretchen are invaluable to us. They are absolutely essential to what we do. We all know that, right?" Nate looked at the rest of the students, seeking their affirmation. Some mumbled yes. Everyone seemed to agree. "However, this photo is a rare opportunity to send a message. Brandon and Gretchen are already represented by me. For publicity's sake, it'll be good to show different types of students supporting our cause."

"You mean to show people who will make you look good."

Everyone stared at them. Nate held up his index finger, signaling a request to the student reporter and photographer to give him a minute, then turned to Anthony. "No," he said in a conciliatory tone. "Not to make me look good. To make the CDA look good."

Anthony sat unmoved. How could anyone believe that? Part of him wanted to expose Nate, but he had no desire to prolong his own part in this nonsense. He stood up and swung his school bag onto his shoulder.

"I'm done here for tonight. You all carry on." He walked out of the classroom, leaving Nate to deal with the photographer who had snapped multiple shots of their falling-out.

"Anthony. Anthony! Wait up!" Brandon chased after him in the hallway.

Anthony stopped.

"I'm sorry about all that. Nate got carried away. He only wants to do what's best for the group."

"How was that best for the group? You did so much work and he wouldn't even publicly acknowledge you for it."

"The newspaper photo? I don't care about that." Brandon held out his hand.

"He wants to hog the spotlight for himself. He doesn't want you or Gretchen to get the credit."

"That's not true." Brandon shook his head. "Nate's right. It would bring more publicity to our cause if people know you and Jeremy are a part of us."

He couldn't contain his irritation any longer. Why couldn't Brandon see what was happening? This was not the Brandon he knew. "You know, this cult of Nate Sanders, it has to stop."

"Cult of Nate Sanders?" Brandon chuckled. "What are you talking about?"

"You listen to him too much. He's a demagogue. You're better off without him."

"No. You're wrong about him. I know Nate. Everything he does is to gain us support. Look how big the CDA has grown since we started. You remember, don't you? Our first meeting? Ten people besides us came. Look where we are now. It's all because of Nate."

It was hopeless. He didn't want to listen anymore. It hurt him to see Brandon lose his senses under Nate's influence. "I'll see you back in the room." He turned around and walked away.

Brandon watched him leave, then turned in the other direction back to the classroom.

#

"I'm sorry about Nate earlier," Brandon apologized again when he returned to their room. "He got carried away."

"It's okay." Anthony pretended to study without looking up from his book. "It wasn't your fault."

"You won't stop coming to our meetings, will you?"

He wanted to say yes, but couldn't bring himself to turn Brandon down. "No. Of course I'm still coming." He turned around from his desk. "We won again yesterday." He tried to change the subject.

"What?" Brandon looked at him, confused.

"The swim team. We advanced to the finals for the relay."

"Oh. Yeah." Brandon sat down and pulled out his books. "Congratulations. That's really great." He hardly sounded like he cared.

His utter disinterest hurt, but Anthony forced himself to let it go. It would do no good to dwell on this if Brandon no longer cared. "What time do you want to head to the lake on Sunday?"

"The lake?"

"The polar plunge. It's this Sunday, remember?"

"Is it this Sunday? I forgot all about it." He looked at the calendar on the wall. "I can't."

"You can't?" Anthony couldn't believe it. They had been doing the polar plunge together since they were sixteen. They made a pact since then to do it every year. How could he not go? How could he forget?

"I'm sorry. Nate and I have plans on Sunday to draft the speech we'll be giving at the national CDA meeting in two weeks."

Trying not to show he was upset, Anthony said quietly while he avoided looking at Brandon, "You have two weeks. Can't it wait? The polar plunge is only one afternoon."

"I am sorry. I really am, but I already told Nate I'd work on the speech with him. It's important. We want to do everything right before the national committee. There's a lot of work still to be done."

Disappointed and angry, Anthony returned to his studies and flipped to the next page of his book.

"Hey, you're okay with this, right?" Brandon asked. "I mean, some of the other guys on the swim team will be going too, won't they? You won't have to go alone."

"Sure. It's okay." What more was there to say? Whether he would go to the polar plunge alone or with other people was not the issue. He kept his head down and his back toward Brandon, pretending to be busy his homework.

# # #

Easter holiday was a welcome break. Although he hated to admit it, Anthony had looked forward to getting away from the ever-present tension that now hung between him and Brandon. Maybe a time-out from each other would do them good.

Returning from the gym late one afternoon, he came into the parlor, where his father was reading the newspaper and his mother was listening to the radio detective series *The Adventures of Ellery Queen*. The program had just reached the part where the guest armchair detectives, this time four people all with the name John Smith, gave their theories on whodunnit. The fireplace crackled and the warmth of the room thawed his skin.

"They're all wrong," his mother said and proffered her own theory which character had committed the murder to his father.

"Why don't you join us?" his father asked.

"I will. After I shower."

William returned to the newspaper and Sophia continued listening to the show. He left them and went upstairs.

Could life stay peaceful like this, always?

He knew right then he wouldn't want to leave his family to fight a war in Europe. Let those who had bigger dreams and higher ambitions run the world. He loved life the way it was. He wouldn't want to change anything.

He went to his room and took a quick shower, then headed downstairs to the library to pick a book to read. Not expecting to find anyone inside, he shoved the door open. The sun had gone down and the lights were off. In the dim interior of the library, the lone silhouette by the window took him by surprise.

Startled, Tessa turned around.

Recomposing herself, she picked up the envelopes on the window-sill. "Excuse me." In a hurry to leave, she jostled him as she passed through the door. Her eyes looked wet like she had been crying. In the faint light, he couldn't tell for sure.

He switched on the lights. A newspaper clipping lay on the floor. Tessa must have dropped it when she rushed out the door. He picked it up. "Blitz Bombing Goes On All Night," the headline read, followed by the subhead, "Hospital ringed by explosions."

Was this the hospital where her mother worked? He wondered if he should return the news clip to her.

He pulled an old book of Greek mythology off the bookshelf and returned to the parlor. At the bottom of the stairs, he looked up to the second floor toward her bedroom. No. Better to keep the news clip.

Returning it to her would only remind her of the sad news. He slid it under the cover of his book and joined his parents.

"Would you like some cake?" his mother asked him when he entered. Two empty desert plates and cups sat on the coffee table.

"No thanks."

The radio show was still going. Sophia listened with a huge smile on her face. William took a puff of his pipe, occasionally nodding to himself when he read something he liked in the newspaper.

It was so comforting to be home on an ordinary day, to see his parents alive and well. He sat down with them and opened his book.

The news clip about the London hospital bombing stared back at him. What did Tessa think when she saw how peacefully they lived every day while her own parents were under siege in London?

On the display case behind his father, the old photo of Uncle Lex in his air force uniform showed him proudly climbing into his airplane.

At CDA meetings, Nate Sanders espoused the principles of preservation of democracies and the righteousness of supporting Britain. He warned of a doomsday of apocalyptic proportions if America refused to take a stand. So far, nothing Nate had said had convinced him. He didn't care for these lofty ideals and grandstanding. Uncle Leon was right. Lex died, but the wars didn't end. Nothing Lex fought for had lasted.

But what about those who didn't have a choice?

He picked up the news clip. Did Tessa cry because her mother might have been at the hospital? If he were in her place, he would want to be in England too where his parents were, not far away in a distant country.

Next to the radio, Sophia fiddled with the tuner to search for a different radio station. The detective adventure program she was listening to earlier had ended.

He looked at the news headline again. Brandon didn't understand. He was just an ordinary college student. They both were. They had no power to change the world or alter the course of history by themselves no matter how passionate they felt. He didn't want to go to war for some lofty, far-fetched ideal. Not when his family had already suffered one great loss from which they had never truly recovered. He wanted his mother happy and free of worries like she was now. His family, that was what mattered to him the most.

But if the war ever threatened his family, if anything ever placed his parents at risk, he would do everything he could to defend them.

Chapter 12

"Brandon! Anthony!" Gretchen Moore came running after them as they came out of Phys. Ed. class. "Nate's disappeared. He's gone."

"What do you mean, gone?" Brandon asked.

"He took all his things and left school. No one has seen him for days."

"Are you sure?" Anthony asked. "Did he go home? Maybe he had something to do outside of school?"

"No." She shook her head. "It's more than that."

"What is it?" Brandon asked.

"He got a summons from the County Draft Board five days ago. I was with him when he got it. We picked up our mail together at the mailroom. When he saw the summons, he panicked. He said he can't go. He said his work here getting the message out was too important. He wanted me to help him figure out how to get exempted. I was so surprised to hear him say that, but I thought he was in shock. I thought he needed time for the news to sink in." She looked at Brandon. "He asked me not to tell you. He said he wanted to tell you himself."

Speechless, Brandon's face dropped.

"That was before the weekend," Gretchen said. "I didn't see him again after that. He and I were supposed to meet today to prep for the

CDA rally this evening but he never showed up. I went to his dorm. No one has seen him. The last time anyone saw him was five days ago, the same day he got the summons. His dorm advisor checked his room. He's not there. All of his things are gone."

"Could he have left to report for duty?" Brandon asked.

Anthony was about to make a snide remark, but held back when he saw how distressed Gretchen was.

"I don't know." Gretchen considered the possibility. "His dorm advisor called the County Draft Board. He's due to report for his qualifications exam tomorrow." Hope returned to her eyes. "He wouldn't leave for duty without saying goodbye, would he?"

"He might. Maybe he didn't want us to worry about him," Brandon said.

Anthony turned his head in case he appeared too unsympathetic. The blind faith Brandon had in Nate annoyed him.

"Let's not jump to conclusions," Brandon said, more to himself than to anyone else. "He's not missing. He'll report for his exam tomorrow. He will. There has to be a good reason why he left without telling us. He didn't want to upset us. That has to be it."

"What about our CDA rally tonight?" she asked. "What should we do?"

"Cancel it. We'll figure something out. Let's go to his dorm. I'll check his room. Maybe he left us a note or message."

Maybe pigs will fly, Anthony wanted to say when Brandon left with Gretchen. He felt sorry for them. By tomorrow this time, they would have to face the truth. Not a chance in a million would Nate show up for his qualifications exam. The guy had skipped town to evade the draft. He was sure of it.

He would have to be there for Brandon when the truth came out. This would be a hard blow to him.

On the bright side, maybe things would return to normal again. Maybe Brandon would finally see that all Nate orchestrated was nothing but a sham and drop the CDA. Maybe he would even return to the swim team.

# # #

As Anthony expected, Nate Sanders never showed up at the County Draft Board. Two days later, the military police came to his dorm with his arrest warrant, but no one knew where to find him. Nate Sanders had gone AWOL.

Outside Nate's dormitory, Brandon and Gretchen watched the events unfold. When they entered the student center afterward and sat down at his table, Anthony lost any interest he had in telling them what he had always thought about Nate. From the shock and disappointment on their faces, it was clear how hard Nate's disappearance had struck them.

"What are we going to do?" Gretchen asked. "How will we explain this to everyone?"

Brandon had no answer.

Anthony kept his feelings to himself. He didn't want to upset them any further.

Chapter 13

For all the distress it was causing his friend, the disappearance of Nate Sanders and what should be done about it were the farthest things from Anthony's mind. Good riddance as far as he was concerned. One less thing to contend with as the busy semester came to an end. He had term papers to write and exams to study for. He also had to decide whether to work for Uncle Leon this summer. On top of everything else, Professor Vinci wanted to see him.

Vinci taught his Applied Physics class. A renowned physicist and a giant in his field, his name was known throughout the campus. Everyone revered him, even the university chancellor. Vinci looked the part of a cerebral scientist too. His silver-gray hair was always in need of a trim, and his suit was always wrinkled as if he had slept in it. His appearance didn't concern him in the slightest. He always gave off the impression that he had bigger, more important matters on his mind, and he had no time for the mundane details of life.

Mundane details like teaching. At higher learning institutions, there were always brilliant figures who took pride in cultivating young minds. They were academics who believed in spreading their knowledge. Those were the kind of instructors Anthony liked.

Vinci was not one of them. For students, he was as remote as could be. Everyone knew Vinci's purpose at the university was research. Even in class, they could sense teaching was a necessary burden for him, a nuisance he must endure in exchange for the benefits of access to facilities and resources for his own great work. He did accept requests for tutorial help from his students. His job duties required it. Beyond that, private access to him was rare. His engagement with students went no further than his office hours, which he kept at no more than the university required minimum of three hours per week.

Not that his availability was ever an issue. Students wouldn't go to him for help if they could avoid it. A meeting with Vinci would mean a full session of humiliating talk-down. He treated everyone who asked questions as if they were stupid.

When he specifically asked Anthony to come by his office, Anthony didn't know if that meant good news or bad luck. He couldn't imagine why the professor wanted to see him. He thought he did well enough in class. Hopefully, Vinci wasn't calling him in to disparage him.

"Anthony! Come in, please." Vinci gave him a warm welcome.

"Professor," he said with the normal deference he would give to any authority figure in school. The professor's friendly attitude confounded him. Keeping his distance, he took a seat in the guest chair.

Vinci's office reflected his person, somewhat messy and unorganized. Sketches and papers piled up on his desk. Books on physics, chemistry, and engineering lay in disorder on the shelves. Oddly, he had no personal effects in his office. Not a single photo of family, loved ones, or pets. No personal mementos or anything of sentimental value. Not even displays of awards or special acknowledgments or distinctions, although everyone knew he owned a collection of them. In this office, only work mattered.

Except for one single sculpture amidst the stack of notes on his desk. Right away, Anthony recognized it as a replica of Auguste Rodin's *Hand of God.* The sculpture was of a half-open palm holding two figures, presumably Adam and Eve, both curled in a struggling fetal position. The sculpture stood out prominently in sharp contrast to the bare practicality of the rest of the room.

"Your performance in my class has been impressive," Vinci said from behind his desk.

"Thank you."

"Have you ever considered a career in science or engineering?"

The thought never crossed Anthony's mind. "Not really."

"You should. You have a lot of potential."

Unprepared for the compliment, Anthony didn't know what to say. He responded with a deferential smile.

"Would you consider working for me this summer? And perhaps beyond that?"

Anthony did not expect this at all. "You mean a summer internship? What would I be doing? Scientific research?"

"It'll be a little more than that." Vinci sat back in his chair as if he was withholding a sought-after surprise. "I'd like to tell you more about it. Before I do, you'll have to sign a confidentiality agreement. My work involves national intelligence. It is classified." He took a document out of his drawer and placed it in front of Anthony. "Read it. Take your time. Ask me any questions you may have. Nothing in it should alarm you. It only requires you to keep confidential everything we discuss today."

Anthony reviewed the document. The contract prohibited the signee from disclosing any information about something called the Manhattan Project. One of the clauses read, "unauthorized disclosure will result in imprisonment and the violator will be deemed to have committed an act of treason."

"Professor. This clause here, it sounds a bit frightening." He pointed to the part about treason and imprisonment while trying to make light of his concerns.

"Oh, that." Vinci dismissed it with a wave of his hand. "It's nothing, I assure you. As long as you keep secret what we talk about today, you'll have nothing to worry about."

Anthony weighed the situation. The Manhattan Project? Already, he could feel his curiosity getting the better of him. And a chance to work with someone as important as Vinci? Who in his right mind would turn that down?

Treason and imprisonment? Why would he ever disclose information his professor showed him? And Vinci was a person of high esteem. Surely he could trust Vinci, whatever he was doing.

He picked up a pen and signed the document.

"Good." Vinci smiled as though he knew all along Anthony would accept his terms. "Now come with me. I want to show you something." He got up and led Anthony out of the office.

They walked until they reached Stagg Field, the university's old football field that the school had abandoned over a year and a half ago. The university administration had terminated the program after deciding that football distracted the students from their academics. On the way, Vinci asked him questions about his classes and his exam preparations. Anthony answered each question with due respect, but he could tell Vinci was not in fact listening. The professor had his mind on something else. His eyes looked wild like a mad scientist. As they got closer to the old football field, the shine in his eyes became fanatical.

Vinci took him to the west side of the football field and led him down a stairway to the underground. In the basement, they followed a short walkway to the abandoned squash courts.

"You see these?" Vinci asked, referring to the blocks of minerals stacked in the squash courts. "You're looking at the future of America."

Anthony walked closer. The stacks looked like large piles of bricks lined up high within the walls of the courts. He could not tell what they were.

"This uranium-laced graphite will alter the course of modern warfare and ultimately, human history."

He still didn't understand.

"This is a top-secret government experiment. What we're doing here is testing for the first self-sustaining controlled release of nuclear energy. If we succeed, we will create a weapon, a bomb so powerful we will be able to destroy entire countries, continents, and populations. It will be a threat so frightening, all our enemies will have no choice but to surrender to us."

Anthony widened his eyes and took a better look. Fear was not something he felt often, but what Vinci said alarmed him. He looked at Vinci. Vinci still had the fanatical shine in his eyes, except now it was accompanied by an equally fanatical smile.

"Think of all the possibilities." Vinci put his hand against the wall of one of the squash courts. "If we succeed, America can stop the war immediately without ever sending our own troops to Europe. We can deter aggression of any kind even before it starts."

A chill ran up Anthony's spine. The basement suddenly felt frigid and he shuddered. "Professor," he said, keeping his voice soft and cautious. An irrational fear overcame him and he worried a loud voice might set off the graphite. "Are there any plans to use this weapon if the experiment succeeds?"

"Umm…" Vinci muttered, seemingly uninterested in the question. "One would hope never, of course. I certainly would not advise it."

Turning to observe the graphite, Anthony pretended not to notice the professor's insincere tone of voice. He had a gut feeling that if the experiment succeeded, Vinci would want to see his creation in action, in use to its full effect, for validation of his own genius.

"I'll leave that decision to wiser men than I," Vinci said. The wild look in his eyes now tamed and he sounded more restrained. "The United States government initiated this experiment and the president endorsed it. I trust that our government officials will take all things into consideration and do what's best for our country and the world."

In other words, you don't care, the thought jumped to Anthony's mind.

That thought was immediately superseded by another one. "Professor, this experiment here, in this place. Is it safe? What will happen if you make a mistake and cause an accident?"

"In that case, half of Chicago will blow up and the city will be obliterated to the ground." Vinci laughed, but from the way he sounded, he was only half joking.

"Don't worry." Vinci patted the wall surrounding the pile. "My team and I have taken every precaution." His face then turned solemn. "I do not make mistakes. We will succeed." In the dark, isolated basement, his voice sounded haunting. Anthony swallowed hard and pulled on the strap of his school bag on his shoulder.

"What do you say?" the professor asked. "I'm offering you a chance to join my team. You must know this is a rare, special opportunity. It's not one I easily offer to anyone." He moved closer to Anthony. "You have a chance to be part of something that will change this world. When this project succeeds, your name will be alongside those of a very highly select group of men to be written into history for this great creation."

It would be the chance of a lifetime indeed, but all Anthony wanted was to leave. The basement felt oppressive. He wanted space. "Professor, I'm honored, but I'm not qualified. I'm a college sophomore. I don't know nearly enough about science and physics to be of use to you."

"Nonsense," Vinci said. "I know talent when I see it. The knowledge, you will learn from me soon enough. You're smart. I know that from your classwork. What I want on my team are people who can handle pressure, people who have what it takes to be a part of a project of this magnitude. You, Anthony, I believe in you."

Anthony took a step back.

"If you work for me, you'll not only be a part of something extraordinary." Vinci lowered his voice. "You'll be relieved from all possibility of being drafted, for you will be deemed a part of the most essential personnel for the war industry."

Stunned, Anthony looked up. The professor's last remark rang in his mind.

Vinci nodded. It was a nod of conspirators sharing a secret.

"But what you'll have will be so much more than that. You'll be one of the few individuals to have a hand in influencing the world's ultimate destiny."

The Hand of God, Anthony thought. Like the Rodin sculpture on Vinci's desk.

An opportunity of a lifetime. A chance to join a selective group of men and go down in history. No possibility of being drafted…

Overwhelmed, he stared at the piles.

A bomb that can destroy whole populations…

Professor Collins. Collins came to his mind like a buoy in the sea.

"Do me a favor," Collins had said. *"Remind them often of what I said. War. It brings changes in ways people can't begin to imagine, and not always for the good. There are always consequences. War never solves anything."*

He touched the wall shielding the graphite.

"Think about it," Vinci said. "I await your acceptance of my offer."

Chapter 14

Back in his dorm room, Anthony reflected on everything he had learned about the Manhattan Project. He wished he could talk to someone about it. His father, maybe. If only he hadn't signed that confidentiality agreement. Then again, if he hadn't signed it, Vinci would never have told him about the project.

He wished he had never learned about it. The idea that his professor and his own government were building a weapon that could destroy entire continents and populations shocked him beyond belief. He wanted to think through the implications of what such a weapon could do, but he couldn't because Brandon wouldn't stop urging him to take over Nate's role in the CDA.

"You're the best person to do this," Brandon said. "You know how to talk to people and motivate them. That's why you were named captain of the swim team, and class president back in high school. They're going to make you president of the debate team too. I know it. People listen to you. They follow you."

"Brandon, you founded the CDA. I only attend meetings. I don't even participate in any activities. You should be the face of the group. Or Gretchen. Why don't you take over?"

"Because I'm no good at talking in front of people. I can write. If I can put things down on paper, I can be eloquent. But let's face it. I'm not good at public speaking like you or Nate. I don't have your kind of natural charisma."

"Natural charisma? Stop that. I'll gag."

"I'm serious." Brandon showed him a CDA flyer. Someone had drawn a cross over it and written the word "hypocrites" on top. "This was taped to our door when I came back. What Nate did, going AWOL like that, it's a disaster. The AFC's laughing at us. You can bring people back on board again."

Anthony pushed the flyer away. He couldn't assume a leadership role in the CDA. For one thing, it would enrage Uncle Leon, especially after he had declined to help with the AFC. More importantly, he didn't believe in the CDA. Professor Collins was right. War never solved anything. Uncle Lex fighting and dying didn't change anything. And after what he had learned from Vinci today, he would much rather America steer clear of the war. If there was any chance America would launch such a weapon, he wanted no part of it. He would explain that to Brandon if he could.

Come to think of it, he didn't even want to be part of the CDA anymore. His continued presence at CDA meetings hadn't helped to bridge the growing gap between him and Brandon in any way. Their views and interests diverged now more than ever. With Nate gone, he had no reason to stay with the CDA to try to keep Brandon from Nate's influence.

"I can't," he said. "I'm sorry but I don't want to do it. In fact, I want to withdraw from the CDA."

"Withdraw? Now?" Brandon sounded devastated. "You don't care that Germany might win and the fascists will take over Europe, maybe even here? You don't care if the security of our country is at risk?"

"Of course I care."

"Then what is it? We have a chance to change things and make things better. Why are you refusing?"

Anthony clasped his hands together. He could still see the replica of Rodin's sculpture on Vinci's desk in his mind. "I can't talk about it. I don't want to be a part of this now. That's all I can say."

Brandon's face darkened. "Well then." A cold silence cut between them. "There's nothing more to say. I'm very disappointed in you." He got up and left the room.

Alone, Anthony tried to think. When did everything become so complicated?

Brandon had never walked out on him before. Never.

#

Two days passed. Brandon never said another word to him. He left the room early in the morning and returned late at night. Every time Anthony tried to initiate a conversation, Brandon ignored him.

Brandon wasn't his only problem. There was also Professor Vinci. He had decided to decline the summer job offer. Whatever the outcome of this war might be and whatever would happen in the future, he didn't want to be a part of something so destructive.

"I'm disappointed to hear that," Vinci said when he gave him his answer. "I expected great things from you. I guess I was wrong." The tone of belittlement in the professor's voice was hard to miss.

He waited for the professor to say more, but Vinci kept his head down and his attention on the papers on his desk. He wasn't sure if Vinci wanted him to stay or go. After a minute of awkward silence, he decided he should leave. "Thank you for offering me the opportunity."

The professor mumbled something without looking up.

When he reached the door, Vinci glanced up. "Don't forget you signed the agreement, Mr. Ardley. Any breach of confidentiality will be a cause for imprisonment."

He tightened his grip on the doorknob. He wished he had never found out that Vinci, a scientist admired by the world, was nothing more than a cold, heartless man. "I understand. Good day, Professor."

Anthony left Vinci's office and walked across campus back to his dorm. On the way, he passed by the university chancellor's office building. Another CDA rally, this time led by Brandon and Gretchen. Brandon stood behind a podium and spoke to the crowd with Gretchen behind him.

Did Brandon finally decide to step into Nate's role himself? He changed direction and went toward the rally.

"As you all know, Nate Sanders has deceived us, myself and Gretchen included." Brandon spoke into the microphone. Unlike their past rallies, the crowd today was silent and tense. Anger festered beneath the outward calm.

"But our cause is bigger than one man," Brandon continued. "Our efforts cannot go to waste because of the actions of one Nate Sanders. We have to continue our work. We must make our voices heard."

"Why should we believe you?" someone wearing an AFC pin shouted from the crowd. "You all talk a good fight but when your life's on the line, you run like a scared chicken."

The crowd grumbled in agreement. Brandon hunched his shoulders and gripped the edges of the top of the podium. Anthony walked closer. He wondered if he should get behind Brandon.

Brandon looked up and stared into the crowd, his eyes determined. "You can believe us because..." He took a deep breath. "You can believe us because I will go in his place. As of yesterday, I have voluntarily enlisted with the United States Navy. I'll be reporting for duty in one week."

The crowd buzzed as everybody began talking all at once. Anthony stood frozen, too stunned to react.

"To prove to you we are truly committed, I will take the first step to make our goals a reality. We believe wholeheartedly in our cause. I hope you will join me and continue the work we have started." Gretchen stepped up next to him. "In my absence, Gretchen Moore will be the new CDA leader. I will send word to her whenever I can to let you all know what I am doing. She will keep me informed of the CDA's efforts."

Anthony watched the entire scene in disbelief.

"Even away, I will do everything I can to help," Brandon said, his voice now firm and assured. "We will not stop until we defeat Hitler. We will stamp out fascism and keep the world safe." When he walked away from the podium, the crowd broke into applause.

"Brandon! Brandon!" Anthony ran toward his friend.

Brandon and Gretchen stopped. They looked at him with cool and guarded eyes.

"What are you doing?" Anthony asked. "You don't have to do this. You don't have to enlist for Nate. What about your parents? What will they think?"

Brandon responded with a smile of contempt. "My parents? Yeah, you just go on and think about your own self-interest with your small mind, Anthony."

The words stung, but at the moment his concern for Brandon overrode his feelings. "Please, Brandon. Can't you reconsider?"

The firm look on Brandon's face softened. A glimpse of the old Brandon returned. "It's too late. The navy already accepted my application. There's no turning back." For a few brief seconds, it felt like they were back to their old selves again. "Goodbye, Anthony."

With that, Brandon walked away. Gretchen took one look at Anthony, then she too followed Brandon. The crowd had dispersed. The yard in front of the chancellor's building became deserted.

Alone, Anthony remained, trying to come to terms with the truth that he had lost his friend.

That same night, Brandon left school. His personal belongings were gone and his half of the dorm room was now empty. Anthony sat by himself at his desk and tried to study, but all he could think about were the good times he and Brandon had spent together. Summer camps, birthday parties, swim team, high school graduation, college. How did so many years of friendship fall apart just like that?

But life went on. Summer had arrived again.

When the semester was finally over, he was more than relieved to pack up his things and go home. This had been a lousy school year. He disappointed Uncle Leon. He disappointed his best friend. He disappointed Professor Vinci. Professor Collins asked him to remind people about the dangers of war and he had done nothing about it. Everyone wanted him to take a side regarding the war and all he wanted was to not deal with it.

He never thought he would be so happy to start work with Uncle Leon and leave all this behind.

PART SIX

A Chicago Summer

Chapter 15

Summer again.

Tessa shed her school uniform the minute she came home and shoved it into the closet. The last day of school was over. She couldn't be happier putting the St. Mary's emblem and colors out of her sight for the next two months.

A full year had passed since she had left England. The London bombing had finally stopped in March when Germany turned its attention eastward to Russia. For the time being, her parents were safe. She had hoped they would let her return home, but the U-boat attacks had gotten fierce and frequent and they didn't want her to travel by sea. For the same reason, they couldn't come visit her in America either.

What would she do here all summer long?

Aunt Anna wanted her and Katherine to join the Junior League. That would be awkward. She and Katherine hardly talked to each other at school. Why would they want to see each other during the summer? Besides, the Junior League was filled with St. Mary's girls. All they did was host soirées to gossip and socialize under the guise of charity functions. She must find an excuse to get out of this.

What she really wanted was to spend the summer with Ruby and Henry, but they both had to work. Henry started a new part-time job as a busboy at Murphy's Tavern, the Irish pub where Jack bartended three nights a week. Ruby quit working at the post office to be a waitress at the Bistro Montmartre, the restaurant at the hotel where her mother worked. The worst part was, Ruby had to work the lunch shift on weekends. Their Saturdays together were now on hold.

Before leaving to meet them at a soda fountain, she changed into her favorite summer outfit, a light summer dress with a tiny daffodil print. She had waited for the right moment to pull it out. The end of school called for a celebration.

The zipper came up half way and then stuck. No matter what she did, the two sides of the back of her dress wouldn't come together. The dress didn't fit. She had grown out of it.

She looked at herself in the mirror. Even if she could pull up the zipper, the waist would be too high and the top would be too tight. Disappointed, she wriggled out of it and folded it away back into her drawer.

Time didn't stop for anyone.

At the soda fountain, Ruby and Henry told her all about their new summer gigs.

"You both work so much. I feel useless," she said to them.

"No way. I'm jealous you don't have to work. I'd trade places with you," Henry said.

"We should still find something to do together now that we don't have school. What do you all do for fun in the summer?"

"Go to a baseball game."

"We can go to Riverview Park," Ruby said.

"Riverview Park. The amusement park?" Tessa asked. "I'd like that. A baseball game sounds good too. I've never been to one."

"You know what we should do?" Henry said with a secretive smile.

"What?" Ruby asked.

"We should ask Jack to take us swing dancing. He's been going swing dancing with his friends every week at the youth center. I heard them talking about going to real dance halls."

"I don't know," Ruby said. "I'm not good at dancing and neither are you. You just want to go to meet girls."

"What's wrong with that?"

"I want to go," Tessa said. "I can dance."

"You know how to swing dance?" Henry asked.

"No, but I can learn. I can do the tango and the foxtrot. My father taught me. He's a fabulous dancer."

"Swing dancing's not the same."

"How hard can it be?" she said. "I can try it, then I can tell my father all about it."

"We can't," Ruby said. "How would we pay for everything? I don't have any money. I give most of what I make to my parents."

"Yeah, me too." Henry slouched over the table. "I give my paychecks to my mom. I won't feel right keeping money from her to spend on carnivals and baseball games."

Tessa never knew Ruby and Henry gave their earnings to their parents. Their families weren't wealthy like the Ardleys, but she had thought they were working for their own spending money.

Two teenage boys came in and sat down at the counter next to them. She watched the waitress take their drink orders. What the waitress had to do didn't look so hard.

"I have an idea," she said to Ruby and Henry. "What if I get a summer job? I don't have to give money to my family. If I work, I can pay for us to go play. We can go to Riverview Park and baseball games. Even dance halls." She turned to Ruby. "Maybe I'll even make enough for us to buy dresses to wear to go dancing."

"You can't pay for us," Ruby said. "That wouldn't be fair."

"Of course I can. I want to. If we don't do it this way, we won't be able to do anything this summer." It then struck her that if she worked, she would be able to tell Aunt Anna she had no time for the Junior League. "I must work. I have to do this. I've never worked before. I want to try it. Ruby, do you think I can be a waitress at your restaurant too? Then we can work together!"

"They're still hiring. They always hire extra staff for the summer season, but…are you sure about this?"

"Absolutely. Let's go to the Montmartre now and ask them to hire me." She pulled on Ruby's arm. "Now I will have a perfect excuse to get out of the house, and I can get away from all the ladies' socials Aunt Anna wants to take me to because she thinks I have nothing better to do."

"You're out of your mind," Henry said, chewing on his straw. "I don't know anyone who wants to work. And you go to St. Mary's. Who from St. Mary's would want to wait tables?"

She shrugged. "I meant what I said. I want to make enough money for us to go play."

"Thank you then." Ruby couldn't hide her joy any longer. "But this is only for this summer, and only so we can do fun things together. You cannot pay for us any other times." She gave Tessa a hug. "Oh Tessa, what an unbelievable thing you're offering to do for us."

"Of course. We're friends, right?" She winked at them. "We're in this together."

# # #

"You're going to be a waitress?" Sophia nearly dropped her fork. "What kind of restaurant is it?"

"It's a very nice bistro at the Hotel Georgette downtown." Tessa helped herself to another serving of roast potatoes. "I'll be working the lunch shift, Monday to Thursday, and Saturday."

"I know the Hotel Georgette. It's not too far from my office," William said.

"Do you have enough spending money?" Sophia asked, worried. "Is your allowance too low?"

"No," Tessa said without looking up from her food. "I'm fine on money. I want to work, that's all. Ruby's working there for the summer and I want to work with her."

"Ruby? Your friend from the post office?"

"Yes. Her mother's a maid at the Georgette." Tessa finished eating and wiped her lips with the dinner napkin. "I'm done. May I please be excused?"

Sophia eyed William, signaling him to say something authoritative. William, however, merely said, "Of course."

Tessa put down her napkin and left the dining room.

"Why didn't you say something?" Sophia asked William after Tessa was gone.

"I didn't know what to say." He looked at his son. "Anthony never had a summer job until he went to college. I couldn't think of any reason why she shouldn't work."

"Why are you looking at me?" Anthony asked. "What could I have done back then? I guess I could've taught kids how to swim." Truthfully, he had too many other priorities than a summer job when he was in high school. When he was fifteen, his father took him and Brandon to the Grand Canyon. The following summer, he went with his mother to Palm Springs to visit his grandparents. After graduation, he spent all of July and August in Florida. His family owned a resort hotel in Miami. Brandon came with him and they went to the beach every day. He became quite good at tennis too after that.

131

"I never expected she would want to work. What if Juliet and Dean don't approve?" Sophia asked. "We're responsible for her. How will we make it up to them if something happens to her?"

"Nothing's going to happen," William said. "We'll wire Juliet and tell her. If she and Dean object, we'll have a good excuse to ask Tessa to quit." He looked at Tessa's empty dinner plate. "You realize she wasn't asking our permission. If we stop her, she might resent us."

Sophia put down her water glass. "You're right," she said. "Sometimes I don't know what to do. I want her to be safe, but I don't want her to feel stifled either. The last thing I want is for her to think we don't trust her."

"Don't worry," William said. "It's just a summer job. It could be a good experience for her."

"I hope you're right. Well, Anna will be disappointed."

Watching his parents, Anthony felt for them. They had taken on a huge responsibility bringing someone else's child into their home. If only Tessa would be more considerate sometimes, everything would be easier. His parents never had to worry about him. Maybe he should have a talk with her about that. Maybe she was too young to understand that people worried about her.

Moreover, her own parents had sent her here to keep her safe. It would be terrible if something bad happened to her here.

# # #

The warm light of the den spilled from the crack of the door out into the hallway. Inside, the soft strains of Louis Armstrong's "I'm Confessin' that I Love You" played on the phonograph, beckoning those who heard the soul of the music. Anthony pushed the door open, careful not to disturb the sound.

Lying on her stomach, Tessa hummed along to the song. She flipped through the record albums spread out on the floor one by one until Anthony, standing by the door but saying nothing, got on her nerves.

"What?" she turned her head and asked.

Unsure how to broach the subject, he said the first thought on his mind. "You should've asked my parents first before you took a summer job."

"Why?"

"It's irresponsible what you did."

"How is it irresponsible? I took a job. I'll be working. What's more responsible than working?"

"You didn't ask for their permission. They're worried."

"Worried about what? I'm not doing anything bad."

"It would've been more considerate if you had asked them first."

"You didn't ask for their permission when you took your summer job with Uncle Leon."

"That's different!"

"Why? Why's that different?"

He didn't know how to answer her twisted logic. He didn't understand how she could not see, or why she was being argumentative. He was only watching out for her. Everything with this girl was always so difficult.

"Forget it." He gave up and walked away.

The music continued while she watched him leave, baffled. She didn't see why she needed anyone's permission to do something as innocuous as taking a summer job. What he said made no sense to her at all.

She tried to return to her music, but he had ruined her mood. Only recently, she began to think they could get along. He had been all-around nicer since last Christmas. What brought this on again? Did he know how overbearing he could be when he was around her, or Alexander, and even Katherine? At least Alexander was a child, and Katherine seemed to like having him decide what was best. But why did he think he could tell her what was right or wrong?

She picked up the cushion on the floor and threw it at the door.

Chapter 16

The jitterbug!

Tessa could hardly believe how much fun it was.

Every Thursday and Saturday, Jack and his friends Fred and Janie would go to swing dance night at the youth center around the corner from where he lived. After much cajoling, Jack finally agreed to take her, Henry, and Ruby along.

"You go like this," Janie tried to teach them. "Step back with your right foot off your heel and make a quick step in one beat of music. When you're comfortable with that, you can do triple steps instead of one."

Tessa got it after just a few tries, but Ruby and Henry both struggled.

"You're a natural, Tessa!" Ruby said.

Of course she was. She wasn't Dean Graham's daughter for nothing.

"Come with me." Jack took her hand and led her to the middle of the dance floor while Ruby and Henry were still learning on the side of the room. He twirled her around and around. She loved the way her skirt swirled. It felt so liberating. So titillating and wild! When the music stopped, she fell into his arms, unable to stop laughing.

Jack was incredible. His feet moved so quickly, yet his every movement was smooth and controlled. She mimicked his steps, determined to keep up with him and the music.

How she loved the music! The tempos, the sounds, the beats. It filled the place with energy and heat. If the music didn't stop, she could keep on dancing forever.

When the night was over and she must stop, she couldn't wait to go back again. And again.

It wasn't long before others took notice of her, the girl whose swing moves could dazzle the crowd. Every time she came, dozens of boys would line up to dance with her. If they could follow her pace, she would take turns dancing with each of them.

But she loved dancing with Jack the most. In fact, she wanted to dance with only him. He could do the jitterbug better than anyone. When he flipped her into the air, she never had to worry about crashing or tripping. He always caught her. He would never let her fall.

That was not all. The first time he put his arm around her, her heart jumped. He held her the way a boy would hold a girl, not a friend or a sister. When he pulled her back to him following a release, his breath fell on her neck and she wished he would hold her even closer. She loved it when his body glided against hers.

The other boys did the same moves, but they couldn't compare. Those boys were clumsy when they danced. The ones with weak arms could barely lift her and the others were too rough. They got out of breath like they were exercising, like Anthony when he came back from a jog.

Dancing with her father wasn't the same either. He taught her like a trainer coaching his protégé.

By mid-summer, they all wanted something more exciting than the youth center. The Melody Mill became their new haunt. An old windmill converted into a dance hall, it looked like a dollhouse from the outside. Inside, it had a giant ballroom, a soda fountain, a roller rink, and a cocktail lounge. It was the ultimate recreational hot spot. Every Friday, girls got in free.

One night, Carmina came along too.

Jack's eyes shone the minute he saw her on the street corner when they picked her up. While driving, he didn't talk much to her, but he would look at her at times and she would smile back. They were in their own world, the passengers in the backseats were nearly forgotten.

"Carmina, I can teach you the new steps I learned," Henry said.

"She doesn't need you," Ruby said. "She has Jack."

Carmina turned around. Her large, round eyes reminded Tessa of an actress her father worked with once. A lot of men loved her. In the magazines, they said her eyes captivated souls.

"I'd love for you to teach me, Henry," Carmina said.

"Carmina, what color lipstick are you wearing?" Ruby asked. "It's beautiful."

"Thank you. It's called Eternal Flame." She dipped her chin and smiled. So striking was the red color against her black eyes and hair, Tessa couldn't turn her eyes away.

Noticing Tessa staring at her, Carmina took her lipstick out of her purse to show her.

Embarrassed, Tessa pretended to examine it, then handed it to Ruby and stared out the car window. Her own reflection looked so pale.

As Jack spent most of the night with Carmina, Tessa had no choice but to dance with other people. She didn't lack dance partners. Once the boys saw how good she was, they all wanted to dance with her. But the excitement wasn't there. Even the music sounded flat.

On the dance floor, she looked over at Jack and Carmina. Everyone was jiving to the fast tunes of Benny Goodman's "Sing Sing Sing," but in a corner, they slow-danced. They had eyes only for each other. What the rest of the world was doing didn't matter. She sighed and stopped dancing. When the song finished, she left with Henry and Ruby for the soda fountain.

"Why doesn't Carmina come dancing with us more often?" she asked Henry.

"She doesn't like coming to our youth center. You know, her people and our people don't get along. Besides, she can only come out to see Jack when Carlos isn't paying attention. He'll give her hell if he finds out she's still dating Jack."

"That's terrible. How often do they see each other, then?"

"I think they try to meet up whenever they can in places away from where we live and where she lives. How often? I don't know. He doesn't tell me these things."

She sipped on her soda. A large poster behind the bar caught her attention. The Melody Mill would be holding a jitterbug competition the last Saturday of August. The grand prize was two tickets to dinner and dancing at the Edgewater Hotel on a night when Duke Ellington would perform.

"What do you think? Are we good enough to win?" Jack asked. She hadn't noticed him coming up behind her while she stared at the poster. His arm hung loosely over Carmina's shoulders. Carmina nodded, encouraging her.

"You're interested?" Tessa asked, surprised he made the suggestion.

"Sure. Duke Ellington at the Edgewater. You bet!"

"He only wants a free meal at a fine hotel," Henry said. Jack playfully slapped the back of his head.

Ignoring Henry's joke, she watched him give Carmina a little hug. "Wouldn't you two rather compete together?"

"I'm not nearly as good a dancer as you," Carmina said. "Jack's been telling me how great you are, and I saw it tonight myself. If he competes with me, we'll lose. Anyway, you know our situation. I can't practice with him as often as needed to win."

"That's right. My time with you is too precious to spend on dance practices." He pulled her close to him and kissed the top of her head. She laughed and didn't shy away.

"You and Jack should go for it." She squeezed Tessa's arm.

"Are you in, Tessa?" Jack asked.

She thought about it. "Sure." How could she say no to him?

"Fantastic!" He gave her a warm smile.

Fearing she might give away her feelings, she cast down her eyes and looked away.

"All right, people. Time to go," he said to Henry and Ruby as he and Carmina turned to leave. His arm never left her. Tessa got off her seat and followed behind.

How good it must be to be in love like that.

Oh well, she told herself. At least she got to dance with him.

Chapter 17

The lunch rush at the Bistro Montmartre would begin in less than fifteen minutes. Tessa quickly gathered her apron, notepad, and pen. She needed to be ready before her first customers arrived.

When she took this job, she had done it on a whim to earn money for her, Ruby, and Henry to go play. But now, the job had become an experience in and of itself. With a staff full of neurotic characters, the restaurant never had a dull moment. The prep time before the lunch rush reminded her of her father's troupe getting ready to open a show. Actually, one of the waitresses, Elsie, was an aspiring actress.

"Tessa, hurry up." Ruby came looking for her. "Louis is serving today's lunch special." Louis was their head chef. Only thirty years old, the local restaurant reviewers had written several glowing articles about the Montmartre after he took the helm at their kitchen.

"Quiche Lorraine." Louis gave a slice to each of the wait staff. "How does it taste?"

"Wonderful!" Elsie grabbed the first piece and ate a mouthful. "I haven't had lunch yet."

"Watch it there." Walter, the restaurant manager, strutted in. "No theater will hire a fat actress."

"Walter, this is why your wife left you. You never have anything good to say to people." She pouted and left the kitchen with her quiche. Walter ignored her and came closer to the counter to get his slice.

"Ugh," Ruby whispered and made a face. "I'm outta here." She took her plate and left. Ruby didn't like being near Walter. He wore heavy cologne and she hated it.

"Tessa," Louis said, "do you like it?" Generous to a fault, he always offered full servings of his creations to the restaurant staff under the guise of "taste testing."

Tessa took a bite. "Delicious." Louis gave her a thumbs-up and returned to the stove.

A whiff of bergamot swept past her, wiping away the savory aroma of the freshly baked quiches.

"Hi, Walter. How are you?" Tessa asked.

"Terrible. I'm having the worst day of my life. I found out my ex-wife is running around with some idiot working at a bank. That wench. She's a gold digger. She sucks everyone dry."

"But you're divorced." Tessa handed him his plate. "Why do you care?"

He ignored her question. "She sucked me dry. You know how much I have to pay in alimony each month? That woman sees money and off she goes like a bee lured by honey. She's terrible. I curse the day I ever met her." He was talking very loudly now and gesticulating wildly with his hands while holding his plate. His quiche fell to the ground. Tessa tightened her lips to stop herself from laughing.

"What's a man to do? That sonofabitch from the bank's just using her. I warned her but she wouldn't listen."

She cleaned his quiche off the floor. "I have to start my shift," she said and darted out of the kitchen. She had worked here for only a month, but she must have heard him talk about his divorce woes a thousand times already.

Out in the restaurant's dining room, she found Uncle William seated in her section reading the menu.

"Uncle William!" She hurried over to him. He had never come here for lunch before.

"Hello, Tessa. I thought I'd pay a visit to my favorite waitress in town." He closed the menu. "What's cooking?"

"Quiche Lorraine. It's today's lunch special. It's very good."

"All right. I'll have that and a French Onion soup."

"Coming right up." Excited, she jotted the items down on her notepad. "You'll love the quiche. I had some earlier. It's very delicious. I'll sneak you a free dessert too. Our pastry chef makes a wonderful chocolate mousse…Wait a minute, did you come here to check up on me?"

"Me? Never!" He opened his hands with an exaggerated look of denial. "I came because I'm hungry. Why? You don't think I trust you?"

She eyed him with suspicion, then rushed off to place his order. Of course he had come to check up on her, but she was thrilled he came anyway.

By the end of her four-hour shift, the restaurant had emptied and Tessa sat down with Ruby to count their tips. Uncle William had given her the biggest tip of all. A full dollar!

While they sipped on iced tea and rested their sore feet, Walter came out of his office and handed each of the staff an envelope.

"Payday!" She clapped her hands lightly.

"Henry's going to be so happy," Ruby said.

Tessa opened her envelope. Sixteen dollars. Adding the money she had made from gratuities, she had more than enough for three baseball tickets.

All those hours she had worked on her feet were well worth it.

#

Tessa had no idea a baseball game was such a big event. More and more fans filled the train at each station. The passengers' excitement simmered, brewing and ready to be unleashed as they approached the final stop.

Last summer, Uncle William had wanted to take her to a game, but she turned him down as she knew nothing about it. In any case, she was homesick and resented everything that had to do with Chicago or America. Even now, she could barely muster an ounce of interest in the sport itself. The reason she came was to treat her friends.

They got off the train and followed the crowd. Hordes of people swarmed the ballpark entrance under the large green marquee displaying the words "Wrigley Field Home of the Cubs." Inside, lines of people waited to buy hot dogs and peanuts. Amidst the exuberant atmosphere, she soon found herself enjoying the event as much as everyone else. With the gorgeous sun shining on the ivy that lined the outfield wall, she felt like she was at a summer picnic.

The way Henry explained it, they had to root for the Cubs, their "home team." Today, the Cubs were playing against the Braves. That much she knew even before coming to the game, although heaven only knew who the Braves were and where they came from.

To say Henry was excited was an understatement. He wouldn't stop telling her the "stats" about every player on the roster.

"See that guy over there? That's Billy Herman. He hit over 300 four years in a row." He switched his attention abruptly away and pointed to the left fielder. "Look at him. That guy's playing too deep."

Everything he told her went in one ear and out the other. She hadn't a clue what he was talking about. The only time she could see something was happening was when a player hit the ball with the bat and started running.

She liked the music. Occasionally, the organist would begin playing and the loudspeaker would broadcast fun and cheerful tunes. During the seventh inning, he even played a whole song. Everyone knew the lyrics. Everyone except her, of course.

"We're the first baseball park in the whole country to have live organ music," Henry told her, his eyes full of pride.

"I'll get us Crackerjacks and Cokes." Ruby got up from her seat. After she left, Henry suddenly stopped talking.

"What's wrong?" Tessa asked him.

He stared out to home plate with a faraway look in his eyes. "I was just thinking, this is only the second time I've been to a baseball game. The last time I went to one was five years ago."

"Why haven't you gone to one again in so long? You certainly love it."

"My father took Jack and me to my first game on my tenth birthday. He promised we'd go to more, but he died a few months after that." He took a baseball trading card out of his pocket. "I bought a pack of gum that day. This card came with it." The card showed a photo of a player named Dizzy Dean. "See the guy at bat now? That's him. He played for the Cardinals back then. I was going to trade this card for one of Larry French. Then my father died and I decided to keep it. How funny. Dean pitches for the Cubs now."

The crowd erupted in cheers. Dizzy Dean had hit the ball and made it to first base.

"When Jack got his first job, he said he'd take me to a game again. I know he wanted to, but he made very little money when he first started working. He makes more now, but he works two jobs and he has so little time."

"You all have it pretty rough, don't you?"

"It's not too bad. Jack has it the toughest. He puts a lot of pressure on himself to make sure Mom and I are comfortable. He takes too many extra shifts at the factory. Mom tells him he doesn't have to work so hard. She said we could do without the extra cash. He says it's okay because he's young, but a lot of times when he comes home, he's very tired."

"I had no idea," she said. When Jack was with them, he always looked so easy-going, like he didn't have a care in the world. "I never knew he was this serious."

"He doesn't want us to worry about him. He wants us to think everything he does is for fun and games. Like fixing up that junky car. He played it off like he wanted to figure out how the machines and engines worked, but what he really wanted was to have a car to drive us all around. He worked on it for months. He scraped together every penny to buy spare parts. We would never be able to afford a car if he didn't do that. And the fireman thing? He risks his life. He could get hurt or killed if he's not careful, but he does it to bring looted gifts back for us."

And he's only eighteen. No one she knew at this age had taken on so many responsibilities.

"After all he's done for Mom and me, it's enough. I don't need him to take me to a baseball game."

Ruby joined them again and Henry's attention quickly turned to the snacks she brought back. Tessa sipped her Coke and thought of Jack. What Henry said remained on her mind for a long time.

#

For Tessa, the one negative thing about the jitterbug was that it had turned her into a frequent shopper. Normally, shopping bored her, but looking for dresses to wear for dancing was a matter of high priority. More than that, it was such a treat for Ruby.

The first time they went to Marshall Fields together, Ruby was ecstatic. "I'd never dared to come in here before," she said as they wandered around the racks of clothing on display. "Everything's so expensive." She checked the price tag on every piece she looked at. When they passed by a mannequin in a pretty white blouse with a Peter Pan collar and a powder-blue skirt, her eyes would not leave that outfit.

"Want to try it on?" Tessa asked.

Ruby touched the fabric of the blouse and shook her head.

"Come on. We're here to splurge." Tessa picked out the same blouse and skirt as displayed on the mannequin from the stacks laid out on sale and handed them to her. "At least try it on and see how you look in it."

Ruby tucked her neck and giggled. "Okay." She looked lovingly at the outfit. "What about you? Do you see anything you like?"

Tessa took a scarlet red dress off a nearby rack. She knew she wanted this the minute she saw it. Its sweetheart neckline was a bit too low, but it was the only dress that matched the color of the polka-dot hair ribbon Jack gave her. "Let's try these on." She took Ruby's arm and led her to the fitting room.

Before the mirror, Ruby stood hypnotized.

"You look so pretty," Tessa said to her.

"I've never worn something this beautiful." She picked up the skirt. "Look at the fabric. It's so soft, and the seams are so even."

"We'll get this outfit for you then." Tessa pulled the red dress up her own shoulders and zipped the back. "The boys will drool all over you when they see you in it."

"They will not, but thanks anyway for saying that. And thanks for everything."

"No need to thank me. It's why I'm working this summer, remember?" She twirled around. The skirt of the red dress flared open high above her waist.

"Tessa!" Ruby said. "This skirt won't cover you when you swing or do your aerial moves."

Tessa raised an eyebrow with a flirtatious smile.

"You knew!" Ruby gasped and put her hand to her mouth. They both laughed.

She twirled again and watched herself in the mirror. The skirt flying high was exactly what she intended. Why not? She had seen how boys looked at her when she danced. Sometimes, she even let her skirt swing higher just to see their reactions.

If only Jack would look. When they danced together, she couldn't help but check to see if he noticed how high her skirt flew. But he was always so immersed in dancing and they moved so fast, she could never tell for sure.

Did he not know she wore nice dresses just for dancing with him? She didn't even like shopping. She only dressed up so people could see he had the prettiest dance partner.

Would he notice if she wore this dress?

Chapter 18

Originally, Tessa had wanted to treat Henry and Ruby to a trip to the Riverview Park, but Jack decided he would come too and insisted on buying everyone's tickets.

And he brought Carmina along.

Henry didn't care who came. He hopped in line as soon as they came upon the flying scooter. It gave them tons of fun for sure, but the big attraction was the Bobs, the eighty-seven-foot tall roller coaster famous for its steeply banked turns, abrupt drops, and wicked angles. Tessa had never screamed so loud as when the Bobs' cart dropped from its highest rail.

After the Bobs, they went for the Shoot the Chutes. When the coaster dropped from altitude and landed, water splashed all over their bodies, soaking them wet.

Recovering from the thriller rides, they followed the trail to the Aladdin Castle. Live bands played throughout the park, spreading music in the air everywhere. Aladdin's giant face greeted them at the castle entrance like a magician promising to show them a world of wonders, and he didn't disappoint. The castle was packed with surprises. They scooted past the collapsing stairways, figured their way out of a maze, and arrived at the hall of the twisted mirrors. Their distorted reflections looked so hysterical, Tessa laughed with Ruby until her stomach hurt. She was easily having the time of her life until they came to what was next, the Tunnel of Love.

"Sorry guys. We're going into this one without you," Jack said, then looked at Ruby and Tessa. "Unless either of you wants to go in with Henry."

"No!" she and Ruby both screamed at the same time. Laughing, Jack pulled Carmina away to the line and left them all behind.

"I don't want to go there with you either. I'm getting me some popcorn." Henry made a face and went to the concession stand while they waited for him by the spinning teacups.

"Ruby." Tessa leaned over the rails and watched Jack and Carmina hold hands as they waited for their turn at the Tunnel of Love. "Have you ever been in love?"

Ruby chuckled. "I had my first boyfriend when I was thirteen. It was puppy love. We never did anything, not even kissed. We only sat with each other during lunch period."

"Where is he now?"

"I don't know. After junior high, we went off to different high schools and we lost touch. He used to live near me but I think his family moved."

The teacups' rotation cycle began. The accompanying music blared and the cups spun around and around. In her mind, Tessa could see Jack and herself spinning to the beats.

"What about now?" she asked. "Is there anyone you like now?"

"There is this boy in school. His name's Evan. He's one year ahead of us but last year, we were both on the homecoming committee." Ruby stopped and put her fingers over her lips.

"Tell me!"

"There's nothing to tell. He already has a girlfriend."

The teacups slowed and the riders' screams softened into laughs and moans.

"Oh." Tessa felt bad she asked. The music stopped and the cups came to a halt. "It's maddening when the guy you like already has a girlfriend, isn't it?"

"Yes. It's terrible."

The next batch of riders jumped into the teacups' seats.

"What about you?" Ruby asked. "Is there anyone you have your eyes on?"

"No." Tessa's heart flipped. "No, there isn't. There isn't anyone," she said as she looked over at Jack. In a little boat, he and Carmina disappeared into the Tunnel of Love into the dark.

After the Tunnel of Love, Jack and Carmina wanted to slow down. "Let's go to the Ferris wheel," he said.

"The Ferris wheel?" Henry groaned.

"The carousel then."

"Boring!" Henry rolled his eyes. "Come on," he said to Ruby and Tessa, "they just want to find places to make out. Let's go look for rides that won't put us to sleep."

Jack threw his hands in the air and Tessa gave him an apologetic look. She wanted to stop Henry, but he and Ruby had already walked away and she could do nothing but to follow them.

Having separated from Jack and Carmina, the three of them wandered around. They rode the Boomerang and watched a freak show starring a muscular man with tattoos over his entire body. They then came to the bumper cars and Henry wanted to go for a ride, but the cars only seated two people.

"You two go ahead," Ruby said. "I don't like bumper cars. It's so uncomfortable being hit and bumped over and over."

With no waiting line, Henry and Tessa ran to the entrance gate.

"I'm going to drive," he said.

"No. I want to drive."

Conceding to her, he said, "All right. We'll go twice and take turns. I'll even let you go first 'cause you're a girl."

At his patronizing tone, Tessa pursed her lips and threw popcorn at him.

In the bumper car, Tessa drove around and around in laps and circles. She was doing her best to avoid the other riders when suddenly, another car rammed into them from behind. Unconcerned at first, she steered left out of its way, but the car crashed into them again, this time even harder. Both she and Henry looked back. In the other bumper car were two boys about their own age. The scrawny one with curly hair stuck his tongue out at them. The bigger, stockier one with the buzz cut bared his teeth at them with mean, threatening eyes.

"Oh no," Henry said.

"What?" She steered their car to the side. "Who are they? Do you know them?"

"It's Don and Lester." He shrank into his seat.

"Don and Lester?"

"The fat one's Don and the skinny one's Lester." His voice turned to a whimper and his ears turned red. "They always pick on me at school."

She glanced at the boys in the other car. They shouted something at Henry, although they were too far away and she couldn't make out what they said. Henry looked to the side away from them, his earlier excitement vanished.

Without thinking, she turned their car around, stomped on the pedal, and slammed into the side of the car Don and Lester were riding in. Shocked, Henry's mouth dropped open. Don and Lester too were stunned and sat frozen in their seats.

She didn't stop there. Reversing backward, she pumped the pedal again with all her might and jammed hard into them.

Don was the first to recover. He pulled his car back and drove it head-on toward them. Rather than backing down or driving away, Tessa looked him in the eye and drove the car forward on a collision course.

"No!" Henry shouted and grabbed his seat. Don would not stop, and neither would she. The fronts of the two cars collided in a huge bang. Simultaneously, Henry and Lester both screamed.

Reeling from the crash, Don squinted his eyes at her, looking confused. He went at her again, but that only incited her more. They chased and smashed into each other over and over, each ramming against the other as hard as possible to try to claim dominance. Neither would give up. Next to her, Henry started to pray.

When the ride was over, Don and Lester jumped out of their seats and raced for the exit. Tessa rubbed her knee. She had bruised herself during one of the crashes.

"I can't believe you did that," Henry said. "You gave me a heart attack."

"I'm sorry."

"No. Don't be." He smiled. "You were nuts, but you were an ace nuts."

They got out of their car, unaware they were being watched. At the exit, Don walked up from behind them and knocked Henry over. Henry tripped. Luckily, Tessa caught him in time and stopped him from falling.

"Watch where you're going," Henry said before he saw who had bumped into him. When he saw Don, he shushed.

"What's the matter, fat-head? You dare to tell me to watch it?" Don moved closer and hovered over him. Behind Don, Lester snickered. Ruby ran up to Henry and Tessa and stood by them.

"Ruby! You're here too," Lester said. "Why the gloomy face? Aren't you happy to see us? Well, good to see you too."

"Leave us alone," she said.

"Who do we have here?" Don asked, looking at Tessa. "Who are you, doll? What are you doing with this ninny? I like how you rode your car. Want to ride with me next time?" He tried to touch her face. She slapped his hand away.

Incensed, he scowled. "Nobody does that to me." He pushed Henry out of the way to grab her shoulders. She glared at him, ready to defend herself when someone else shouted, "Leave them alone, Don."

It was Jack, returning to them with Carmina. "Knock it off. All of you."

Don took a hesitant step backward.

"You two should leave now," Jack told Don and Lester.

The two bullies exchanged a glance. Don muttered something under his breath and walked away. Lester followed. Before he left, he wrinkled his nose at Carmina. She turned her head away, clearly uncomfortable.

Still angry, Henry, Ruby, and Tessa stood together stone-faced.

"Who else is hungry?" Jack asked. "I'm getting one of those famous foot-long hot dogs. Anyone else want one?"

The three of them suddenly realized they were starving.

"Well, let's go then." He took Carmina's hand and started walking. Subdued, they walked slowly behind them.

"Thank God Jack showed up," Ruby said to Tessa.

"I don't understand," Tessa said. "They pick on Henry but they're afraid of Jack?"

"Don and Lester are cowards. They only dare to pick on Henry when he's alone. Jack's different. He's older and he knows a lot of folks who can get them into serious trouble. Besides," she lowered her voice, "Benny likes Jack. They wouldn't dare mess with anyone Benny likes. But then..." She gazed proudly at Jack.

"But then what?"

"Everybody likes Jack." They had now come upon the hot dog stand. Ruby pulled her arm to hurry her along. Tessa acquiesced, but her mind was on something else.

Everybody likes Jack.

But Jack only liked Carmina.

Chapter 19

The jitterbug competition was coming up in less than a week. At the youth center, Tessa practiced with Jack for the last time. Their performance drew a group of onlookers clapping along as they danced.

Considering his busy work schedule, Jack sure was setting aside a lot of time to practice with her. The competition meant a lot to him, it seemed. Not wanting to disappoint him, she practiced as hard as she could. By now, she had mastered their routines and learned to match her steps to his fast-paced footwork.

Swinging to the music, he picked her up in one swift move, threw her onto his back, and let her roll right off him. Their fans cheered. Without missing a beat, she grabbed his wrist, landed perfectly and hopped into the next set of kicks. She could still see his winning smile through their rapid speed and blurred vision. His face glowed with excitement, all from their dancing.

When they finished, the group gave them a resounding round of applause.

"That was fantastic, Tessa," one of the girls who had watched them said.

"Great job, Jack. Good luck this weekend," said one of his friends from the dispersing crowd.

Still catching his breath, he waved and thanked them. "We're going to win this thing, right?" he asked Tessa.

"I hope so. Do you think I'm good enough? I only learned this dance a few months ago."

"Don't worry. You're a natural. If we mess up, we can always improvise." And then he told her, "Carmina's coming."

"She is?" She didn't know Carmina would be there. This was the first time he had mentioned it.

He nodded. "I want her to see me win. Promise me we'll try to win?"

She lowered her eyes, then mustered up the best smile she could. "I promise."

"We'll win." He tapped her lightly on the forehead.

# # #

On the night of the competition, a large gathering of spectators filed into the ballroom, all buzzing with anticipation. Long before the contestants started to dance, the band had already begun to rouse the crowd. So much energy had filled the air, Tessa thought the roof might burst.

For tonight, she wore a new dress she had bought especially for this occasion, a short-sleeved white dress with black polka dots and a round neckline. It fit snugly around her waist and accentuated the shape of her body. The skirt ran longer than what she usually wore and fell below her knees. It swung when she danced and flared out like a peacock spreading its feathers when she twirled. It was perfect for showing off their moves.

Originally, she had planned to wear her special scarlet red dress, but she changed her mind after Jack told her Carmina was coming.

Everyone started cheering and clapping as soon as the competition got under way. The contestants surrounded the dance floor, each pair awaiting their turn. She sized up each team during the elimination rounds. None of them did anything she and Jack could not match or outdo. In fact, Jack was way more attractive and nimble than all the other guys competing. They easily advanced to the final round.

When their turn came in the first heat, they started off with a series of rapid steps. He followed with several sets of pulls and releases, drawing her close, then releasing her while she waved her hand in the air and twisted her hips to the beats. He then grabbed her waist, lifted her into the air on his side, and rolled her off his back to let her slide off his other side. The crowd whistled.

In the next heat, they started off with a series of hops. Next, he lifted her and swung her body horizontally sideways one hundred and eighty degrees around his body several times. Everyone watching went wild. He continued to swing her into the air in between steps, exciting the crowd. With each heat, they raised the bar another notch, adding more spectacular and racier moves to stir the audience and the judges.

They saved her favorite routine for the final heat. He started by pulling her body up against him and they stepped into a long series of back kicks. Their movements were fast, clean, and crisp. Impressed, the crowd gave them a long round of applause. Then, from behind her, he picked her up from her waist and threw her over his head. As soon as she glided down his back, he pulled her through from the bottom and she slid between his legs back to the front. He twirled her around while she spun to a blur with her skirt flying in the air. The move electrified the room.

To close the dance, she tugged his tie and pulled him toward her. He leaned forward, pretending to be led by her while he flailed his arms and kicked his feet back up high. Laughter broke out among the audience. Finally, he swung her body around him one more time. When she landed, he slid into a split on the floor in front of her. The comical but sensational final move sent the audience into frenzied cheers.

There was no contest. They were the decisive winners. He grabbed her hand and held it up in the air to clinch their victory.

As soon as they came off the dance floor, he rushed over to Carmina, embraced her and gave her a deep kiss on the lips. Tessa held her first place ribbon. A bittersweet smile hung on her face.

"You two were wonderful," Carmina said.

"I said I would dance for you tonight. It was a special dedicated performance." He pinned his first place ribbon onto her dress. "Happy birthday," he said softly to her.

"Jack!" She touched the ribbon gently with her hand. "This is the best birthday present."

"And special thanks to Tessa for being the most sensational dance partner." He smiled at Tessa.

"Today's your birthday, Carmina?" she asked. Jack never told her his dancing today was a birthday gift to his girlfriend.

Carmina confirmed it with a shy smile.

"Tessa! Jack!" Henry said. "Do you know what this means? This means you're both going to see Duke Ellington live at the Edgewater."

"That'll be pretty amazing," Jack said. "Too bad we can't all go." He turned to his girlfriend. "Do you want to go with Tessa instead? You can have my ticket."

"No." She refused. "You worked hard for this. You deserve to go. You can't miss an experience to dance at the Edgewater. Anyway, I don't dance well. Don't waste the chance on me. You can't leave Tessa in a bind without a dance partner." She smiled at Tessa, and Tessa smiled back.

"Tessa will have no problem finding dance partners." Jack dismissed her worries. "She dances so well, all she'll have to do is walk onto the dance floor and people will line up out the door to dance with her. You're the one who'll be sitting alone all night." He leaned in and whispered in her ear. "Maybe I'll have to sneak in to keep you company."

"For the love of God." Henry rolled his eyes. "Don't you two ever get sick of this?"

"I heard the Edgewater's outdoor dance floor is very romantic," Ruby chimed in. "People say it's dancing under the stars."

Tessa had heard that too. She wanted to dance there with Jack more than anything. But what was she thinking? He and Carmina were so in love. Any talk about romantic outdoor dancing felt pointless.

"It's not romantic at all," Jack said, interrupting her thoughts. "There'll be more than a thousand people there. I just hope it won't rain that night or we'll get soaked. Right, Tessa?"

Tessa forced herself to smile, then turned her face away so he wouldn't see her disappointment.

# # #

There was only one right thing to do.

She had never been to Murphy's Tavern before. It was five in the afternoon and the place was almost empty, too early yet for the dinner crowd.

Jack was there. He was talking to a couple while he cleaned the glasses. Off toward the back, Henry was bussing a table.

She took a deep breath, then walked up to the bar and sat down.

"Tessa? What brought you here?" Jack asked, surprised to see her.

"I came to see where you and Henry work. Is it all right for me to be here?"

"Of course. Can I get you something?"

She gathered her nerves and asked, "Would you get me something from the bar?"

"From the bar?" He had never seen her drink before. "Okay. What would you like?" he asked, a bit hesitant.

"Would you make something special for me? Something you've never made for anyone else?"

"All right." He eyed her with a curious smile, but nonetheless obliged. He scanned the alcohol on the shelf behind him and picked out several bottles. With expert hands, he mixed the liquor together and returned with a beautiful cocktail garnished with berries. "Try this." He put the glass in front of her.

"What is it?"

"It's the sum of what I think of you. Apple cider with cranberries, cinnamon, bourbon, and lemon juice. Sweet and spicy, with just a tiny hint of sour." This was the first time he had ever told her what he thought of her. She could almost feel her face turning red. "How about we call it the Sugar Tuck?" he asked.

Sugar Tuck. Of course. So he did notice when her skirt swirled. She smiled to herself and took a sip. The alcohol burned her throat and stung her stomach, but it didn't matter. He created this just for her.

He watched her on the other side of the bar.

"You don't approve of me drinking?" she asked. "I only wanted to try it because you mix drinks."

He poured himself a glass of whiskey with ice. "I don't disapprove. I started drinking when I was fifteen." He clinked his glass against hers. "I'm an Irishman. Who am I to tell anyone not to drink?"

She rested her chin on her hand and laughed. The alcohol gave her a light head rush. The sweetness of the drink grew on her.

"If you're going to drink, then better that you do it here where I can keep an eye on you." He gave her a glass of water. "Is this why you came? To learn how to drink?"

"No." She took a card out of her purse and gave it to him. "This is my ticket for the night at the Edgewater. Why don't you go with Carmina instead?"

He looked at the certificate in her hand. "That wouldn't be right. You won it. Don't you want to see Duke Ellington?"

"It's nothing, really," she lied and put the certificate on the bar. "If I want to go, I can always ask Uncle William and Aunt Sophia to go with me. Take Carmina. It'll be my present to both of you for her birthday."

"Are you sure?"

She pushed the certificate toward him. He took the gift. His eyes brightened and he broke into a huge smile. "This means a lot to us."

"I know." She held her glass to her lips and pretended to take a sip to mask the hurt she felt inside. Of course Uncle William and Aunt Sophia would take her to see Duke Ellington if she asked, except the band and the musician were not what she wanted.

But Carmina was the one he wanted to go with.

"On one condition," she said.

"Anything. What is it?"

She finished her drink. "I want another one."

He leaned back, impressed. "Of course. As long as you can handle it." He took her empty glass and turned it upside down. "Look at that. Not a drop left. I do like a woman who can handle her liquor." He grabbed the bottles from the shelves and made her another one.

"Tessa, what are you doing here?" Henry came up next to her.

"Having a drink." She began sipping her second glass of Sugar Tuck.

She didn't stay long. When she walked out of Murphy's Tavern, a cool breeze blew by and swept away her tipsy feelings. The smoldering summer heat had tapered off. The air felt lighter now. Next week would

161

be her last week of work at the Montmartre. School would be starting again.

It had been an incredible summer in many ways. She didn't expect to enjoy herself so much in America. But somehow, a tinge of loneliness tapped against her heart.

PART SEVEN
Star-Crossed Lovers

Chapter 20

As it turned out, sacrificing her chance for a night dancing with Jack at the Edgewater Hotel had its own reward. If she hadn't given up her prize, she might have never set foot in Murphy's Tavern.

When summer ended, Henry stopped working there and took a weekend job at the YMCA, but he still went there to play darts and billiards with Murphy's waiters and regulars. And if Henry was going, how could Tessa resist? Not to mention, Jack bartended there three nights a week. Too bad Ruby couldn't join them most of the time. She had returned to her after-school job at the post office.

Murphy's attracted a young crowd. Residents of the Irish neighborhood and students from nearby colleges and universities alike found their haven here. Mr. Murphy, the tavern's owner in his fifties, mingled with the guests all the time. "See you in church," he would say to them every night by the door when they left.

Once, Tessa asked him, "Which church?"

"This is the Church!" He laughed.

Everyone loved Mr. Murphy, but Nadine Kelly was the one who ran the place. Nadine bartended full time and managed the tavern. A beautiful, fiery redhead in her mid-twenties, she took no nonsense from anyone. She didn't have to. Her godfather, Benny Flannigan, saw to that. If anyone caused trouble on the premises, she would boot them out before anyone else, and they were lucky if that was all she did. At Murphy's, everyone knew not to cross Nadine.

"You don't look happy," she said when Tessa came in early Friday evening after school.

"My teacher's making me write an extra essay this weekend."

"Why?"

"We're reading *The Scarlet Letter* in English class. I said in class that if Hester Prynne's husband was such a mean-spirited bloke and was always away, then maybe she wasn't physically fulfilled."

"You did not!" Nadine bent over laughing.

"I said what was on my mind."

"So what now?"

"Now I have to write an essay on why Hester Prynne would have been wrong to have these thoughts."

"I have a suggestion." Nadine leaned across the bar. "Why don't you write this? 'Hester should not have these thoughts because it led her to a wimpy priest who satisfied her even less.'"

Tessa's mouth dropped open and they both broke into laughter.

"What's so funny?" An attractive man in his late thirties entered. His French accent made him a standout among the tavern's other patrons. Nadine did not look up right away, but her lips curled up slowly into a seductive smile. The Frenchman came up to her and hugged her from behind. Unabashed, she turned around and kissed him.

"Good afternoon, Tessa." He winked at her.

"Hello, Laurent." Laurent was Nadine's lover, the one for whom she left her husband two years ago.

"Why don't you marry him?" Tessa asked after Laurent left.

"Because I'm already married," Nadine grunted. "It was the biggest mistake of my life. The bastard won't accept a divorce, out of spite, and the Catholic Church won't let me divorce."

Tessa didn't know Nadine was still married. The nuns at St. Mary's would have a fit if they heard this. A married woman with an open lover? Must be a loose woman. Immoral. A scandal!

"I don't care." Nadine tossed her hair, nonchalant. "I'm in love. Laurent loves me. That's all I care about." She gave Tessa a glass of orange blossom. "I'm not corrupting your innocent mind, am I?"

Tessa smiled and sipped the drink. She loved being in Nadine's company. Nadine was so audacious. So romantic! She reminded her of the way things were back at the West End, where women knew how to live and how to love. There was no one like her at St. Mary's. There, the girls all reminded her of damsels trapped in a castle. They never wanted to know any fire or thunder. They were like flowers in a glasshouse, never knowing any storms or wind. She would rather be like Nadine, who did what she wanted and lived as she pleased.

Who dared to live for love.

There would be love like that out there for her too, would there?

Chapter 21

The physical training of male students for military readiness continued when the next fall semester began. Now they must take Phys. Ed. class five days a week. Every high school and college in the country had adopted this requirement, and UC was no exception. The school administration still made no explicit announcement as to why this was happening, but everyone knew.

Anthony didn't mind the additional athletic training. He was in such good shape, Phys. Ed. was easy for him. It was extra conditioning for swimming.

Not so for his classmate Warren Hendricks. Warren loathed exercise. Always had. He never liked sports growing up. And now, Phys. Ed. class was his daily torture.

Their instructor wanted them to run eight laps around the track. He had only reached the fourth lap, but his legs were already dragging. When the others started their fifth lap, he fell further and further behind. The instructor watched him with disgust.

"Mr. Hendricks. Get moving! We don't have all day."

He tried, but he was so far behind everyone and he could hardly breathe. By the time everybody else had finished, he still had two more laps to go. The entire class stood and watched him finish last by himself.

He took his final steps past his classmates' sneering smiles. His face burned with embarrassment.

The instructor led them away from the track. Warren followed, unaware of two of his classmates walking behind him and mocking the way he dragged himself when he ran his last lap.

Anthony threw them a quick glance and watched Warren walk on.

Next came the push-ups. Warren struggled to push himself off the ground. Big drops of sweat dripped from his face down to his chin. After the eighth count, his arms gave out. He couldn't finish the twenty counts everybody else was doing.

"Mr. Hendricks!" The instructor lost his patience. "Never mind counting on you to save the world. You'd be dead if your own life depended on it. What have you been doing all summer?"

"Sorry, sir." Warren bowed his head. He could hardly look up to face him.

When class was over, he was the last to walk into the locker room. Tired and miserable, he kept his head down, hoping to remain inconspicuous. No such luck. A few students laughed as he passed by and one whacked him with a towel. He grimaced and shifted his body to the side to avoid being hit.

"Hey! Creampuff!"

"Twerp."

"You're in the wrong room. The girls' locker room's across the hall."

Anthony watched them quietly as he got dressed by his locker. When everyone had left and only the two of them remained, he picked up his gym bag and went over to Warren. Warren sat slouched on the bench and paid no attention to him.

"You can build up your body," Anthony said. "It takes time and you have to work at it, but it's possible."

"Easy for you to say."

"That attitude won't help."

Warren bent down even lower, his shoulders and back tensed. "I know I'm pathetic. You don't have to remind me."

"You're not pathetic. You need to train more, that's all." Anthony walked closer to him. "I'll help you. We can train an extra hour every morning and on weekends too."

Warren looked up, his doubtful eyes buoyed by a trace of hope.

"At least give it a try."

Warren opened his mouth, but couldn't let any word out.

"I'll meet you here tomorrow morning. Early before classes start. Seven a.m. sharp." Anthony left the locker room, not waiting for him to have a chance to say no.

# # #

Outside, Anthony took a deep breath of the crisp autumn air. It was a nice change from the boiling summer heat. He loved this time of the year. Everything was orange, good and comforting, from the gorgeous change of colors of the leaves, to Halloween and Thanksgiving, and pumpkin bread and apple pies.

A disquieting mood nonetheless remained and hovered over their campus. It was even more disturbing than last year. The student population continued to dwindle. Brandon was gone. The swim team competed only half as often as previous years. Some of the schools they competed against had suspended their men's athletic programs altogether due to lack of participation when too many students had left for the draft.

He wished something good, something less depressing, would happen for a change.

His next class wouldn't begin for another hour. He headed to the student center for a cup of coffee and to get a head start on his reading assignments. While waiting in line, he noticed the student sitting at the table in the center of the room. The sunlight through the windows gleamed on her golden blonde hair, which fell neatly on her shoulders on top of her cashmere sweater. The sweater, matched with her white blouse underneath and her tailored wool skirt, made her a perfect picture of beauty and form. She would have gotten everyone's attention even if she had sat in a corner rather than the most obvious spot here.

He watched her turn the pages of her book. Mary Winters. She was a sophomore, just a year behind him. When she first entered UC last year, his fraternity brothers couldn't stop talking about her. A number of them had met her and a few had tried to date her. He might have tried to meet her himself if he hadn't been so wrapped up with all the changes with the swim team and all the drama with Brandon, Nate, the CDC, and the AFC.

The server at the food counter poured him his cup of coffee.

"Can I have a cup of lemon tea too?" He kept his eyes on her while the server prepared the beverages.

With his book bag over his shoulder, he took the coffee and the tea over to her table.

"Hi." He put the tea down in front of her. "I'm Anthony Ardley. Mind if I sit down?"

Mary slowly glanced up, her brown eyes keen and sharp. Her lips turned up into a half smile. She showed no surprise at all, as if she always knew the moment would come when he would approach her. "Hello."

Chapter 22

Tessa knew something odd must have happened when Carmina came to Murphy's to look for Jack at work. Jack and Carmina had always been careful to keep their relationship secret. Carmina would not come looking for him at work if it wasn't serious.

She came on a Friday evening. It was still early, not even eight o'clock yet. The tavern was only half full. Except for a table of crass young men gabbing and guffawing loudly like they owned the place, most of the guests at this time had come for dinner rather than for drinks. The crowd didn't usually fill the place until later in the night. At the bar, Tessa and Henry were about to beat Jack at a game of dice when Carmina pulled him away.

"There's going to be a big fight tomorrow night between Carlos and the Colts," they overheard her say to Jack. "The Colts want Carlos' people out of Moore Street. They said that's their territory, but Carlos and his boys won't budge."

Jack's face darkened.

"I tried to stop him but he won't listen." Carmina grabbed Jack's forearm, her voice desperate. "This won't be like their usual squabbles. This time, it's serious. I'm scared for Carlos. What if he gets hurt? You have to help me. We have to try and stop them. If you can do anything or talk to anyone…"

Henry and Tessa looked at each other. They both knew Jack didn't like to get involved with the gangs' affairs. Jack looked more than conflicted.

"I'll talk to Benny Flannigan tomorrow," he told her.

"Thank you." She left the tavern looking grateful but still concerned.

"Why'd you tell her that?" Henry said to him after she left. "Talking to Benny won't help. What if he takes sides? That'll make things worse. Don't get mixed up in this."

"I can't stand by and do nothing," Jack said. "She's worried about her brother." He whipped a wet towel onto the bar and walked away.

Henry frowned. "Yeah. And I'm worried about him," he said to Tessa.

Tessa put her hand on his back and watched Jack speak to the group of loutish young men at a table. Jack's expression grew more and more tense as they talked.

Tessa didn't give any more thought to Carmina's visit to Murphy's or the gang fight Carmina had talked about. The gangs' clashes and rivalries didn't concern her. Her homework kept her busy enough, and Jack always told her, Ruby, and Henry to stay out of the gangs' businesses. The whole ruckus was far removed from her life until she visited the post office days later to mail another letter back to London.

"Jack's hurt," Ruby told her. "Carlos' friends beat him up really bad."

"Why? What happened? Is he all right?"

173

"He went to ask Benny for help. He told Benny the big fight was coming up and asked him to stop the Colts. I'm not really sure what happened after that, but instead of telling the Colts to stay away, Benny sent the police. The fight broke out anyway and Carlos got stabbed. Then the police showed up. They let most of the Colt members go but arrested Carlos and his gang. Beat them and messed them up pretty badly too during the arrest."

"But how did Jack get hurt? Was he there?"

Ruby shook her head. "Jack wasn't there, but Carlos' people heard it was Jack who told Benny about the fight. They thought Jack did it to send the police to back up the Colts. When they got out on bail, they found Jack and beat him senseless."

"That can't be! All Jack wanted was to stop the fight. How could they think Jack would send the police against them?"

"It's just the way things are." Ruby took the letter Tessa gave her, then sighed and tossed it into the bin behind her.

Tessa thought of the day when Carmina came to Murphy's. She had no idea then what a difficult situation Jack had in hand. "I'll go see him." She rushed out of the post office as fast as she could to the train station.

# # #

She came to the now familiar street where Jack lived and headed into his building, up the stairs to the small third-floor apartment. The door was ajar. The voices of people talking inside stopped her. She could see a partial view of Jack lying on the couch and Carmina standing in front of him.

"...Please don't do this," Jack pleaded, his voice weak and muffled. "You can't marry Luis. You don't even like him."

174

Luis? Tessa didn't mean to eavesdrop, but she didn't expect to see Carmina here and couldn't decide whether she should knock or leave.

"It'll never work between us, Jack. Not after what happened last week. No one will forgive me if I stay with you. And if I do, where will I go? Come here? Everyone here despises me."

"…Maybe we can elope. Let's run away from this place…"

Carmina let out a sad, helpless laugh. "That's a dream. You know you can't do that. You can't leave your mother and Henry. They need you."

"…There has to be a way…"

"There is no way. This is what Carlos wants. I have to show my family and everyone I'm loyal to them."

"Carmina, please…"

"Goodbye, Jack." She pulled the door open. The sight of Tessa standing there surprised her. Equally surprised to see Carmina face-to-face so suddenly, Tessa took a step back and stood aside. Carmina quickly turned away and ran down the stairs. Tessa glanced into the apartment, then ran downstairs after her.

"Carmina! Carmina! Wait!"

Carmina stopped halfway down the block and looked back, her face riddled with pain.

"You can't leave Jack! You can't leave him like this. He loves you, and you love him," Tessa cried out. A spark of injustice rose within her. "Who's Luis? How can you leave Jack for somebody you don't love?"

"It's the only way Jack will forget about me. I don't want him to have any more hope."

"After all he's done for you?" She was angry now. More than angry. She was outraged. "How can you leave him now? He wouldn't even have gotten hurt if you hadn't asked him to intervene. He's hurt because of it and you don't even care."

"I care!" Carmina said. "If we stay together, more people will get hurt. If I stay with him, I might put his life in danger. Don't you understand?" She hardened her eyes, then turned to go away, leaving Tessa standing at a loss on the street.

As Carmina disappeared down the road, Tessa ran back to Jack's apartment. The door was still open. She pushed it lightly and went inside. On the couch, Jack lay limp in his worn, wrinkled clothes. His hair was disheveled as she had never seen before, but it was his face that shocked her the most. A large black and blue bruise covered one side of his cheek. His left eye was red and swollen and his disfigured lips puffed out. No wonder he sounded faint and muffled when he talked.

"Jack!" She ran over to kneel beside him. His shirt, unbuttoned, revealed bandages wrapped around his ribs. "My God!" Tears swelled in her eyes as she ran her hand across his forehead, stroking and smoothing out his hair.

"Tessa…" he mumbled. He tried to smile but couldn't. "Sorry you have to see me like this."

She shook her head.

"Did you see her when you came up?" A tear fell from his eye. "She left me."

She continued stroking his hair and forehead. She only wished she could make his pain go away.

"I used to think, if I can just save up enough money, then I can get everyone out of this god-forsaken place. Mom, Henry, her. We could all move away to some place nicer and quieter. Don't need anything big or fancy, just some place comfortable and away from all this crap."

She picked up his hand and held it between her own.

"I thought, if I can just get a better job, then I can take her with me too." He laughed. A bitter, ironic laugh. "I had this stupid thought that she and I could live in our own little place, and I could take her out to a nice dinner and a movie on weekends. We could leave all this petty gang garbage behind."

There was nothing she could say. She could only squeeze his hand and hope it would make him feel better.

"What are they fighting about all the time anyway? Why do we have to be this group or that group? Why did she and I always have to hide? Why is it such a big deal to everyone if I want to live an ordinary, normal life with her?"

She had no answers to all his questions. She didn't know he had all these thoughts. All the nights on the dance floor, he always looked as if he didn't have a care in the world. He lived it up like the rest of them. Who would have known all his aspirations, and all that he wanted to do for the people he loved? Within his ability, he already did everything he could.

All this time, she never knew. How could she have been so thoughtless to have never noticed or questioned?

"Thanks for coming to see me," he said to her. His voice waned to a whisper. "I need some time alone. Is that all right?"

"Will you be okay?" She didn't want to leave him by himself like this.

"I'll be fine. Don't worry." He closed his eyes.

Reluctantly, she let go of his hand. She touched him on his forehead once more, then closed the door quietly behind her and left.

Outside, everything felt cold. Not just temperature cold, but the entire place. She could see now the dilapidated buildings for what they were, impersonal, merciless jail cells. Unlike the Ardleys' mansion hidden far behind the driveway and rose garden in the front, the homes here offered no protection to those who lived in it.

All this time, she thought St. Mary's and the Ardleys' home were the prisons from which she wanted to break free. Only now did she realize how this place was its own trap to those who dwelled in it. Worse, actually. For Jack, it was not only a trap, but also a wild jungle in which he must fend for himself, and everything here ensnarled him and pulled him back until he was entangled in all its quagmire.

If she could, she would help him escape. He, Ruby, and Henry welcomed her here with open arms when she sought refuge, and yet, she had no way of doing the same for them. She felt so powerless.

Chapter 23

Three weeks passed before Jack fully recovered. When Tessa saw him again, he announced to everyone he had decided to join the army.

Stunned into silence, they sat in a booth at Murphy's. Tessa thought of Uncle William, Aunt Sophia, and Uncle Leon at home. Whenever the subject of the army came up, keeping Anthony out of it was all they ever talked about. It only occurred to her now that no one in Jack's home or neighborhood ever worried whether Jack would be drafted.

Jack said he wanted to get away for a while.

She couldn't believe it. The Ardleys' worst fear was Jack's way out.

"The army will pay me," he said to Henry. "I'll send money home."

Henry stared at the table. His soda was only half finished and all the ice had melted.

Jack barely touched his sandwich. "I don't know what everyone's fighting about here, but if I'm being sucked into fighting one way or another anyway, I might as well go fight for something worthwhile. At least I'll be fighting a real war. Against real bad guys. We are the good guys, right?" He glanced at Tessa, as if she would know. "I hope so. I don't keep up with the news."

Henry's face scrunched up like he wanted to cry. Jack pushed him playfully on the shoulder. "Cheer up! I'll come back a war hero."

Tessa looked away. She felt like crying herself.

"It's probably for the best," Ruby said later on after they left the tavern.

"Why?"

"Benny and his boys are pushing Jack to join their side. They're going after Carlos' people for beating him up, whether Jack wanted revenge or not."

#

The last night before Jack left for basic training, Fred and Janie, his friends who always came dancing with them, wanted to throw him a going away party. Henry, Ruby, and Tessa were all for it. They wanted to take him to dinner and swing dancing one more time. At first, Jack refused, saying he wasn't in a party mood, but he gave in because they all insisted.

And because Tessa told him in private she would ask Carmina to come see him one last time.

She went to the diner where Carmina worked. As much as it made her heart ache to do this, she knew it would mean a lot to Jack if Carmina would see him off. Surely, Carmina would do at least that.

But she wouldn't.

"There's no point. It'll only prolong the misery and drag things on. Better to not give him any false hope." Carmina continued wiping the table without looking at her.

She couldn't understand how Carmina could refuse. It would be such a small thing for her to do after all he had been through. "Can't you stop by anyway? You don't have to stay long. He'll be gone and you won't see him again for a long time."

"I don't plan to see him again, ever." she picked up the dirty dishes and headed to the back. Tessa followed her. She couldn't hide her resentment. Did Carmina not care how much she had hurt Jack?

Carmina put down the dishes. "It hurts me too, you know."

It was hopeless. Poor Jack. He had a spineless girlfriend.

"We'll be taking him to the Chez Parée Saturday night," Tessa told her before she left. "Please think about it. It would mean the world to him if you come."

She did not have the heart to tell Jack Carmina said no. She told him Carmina would think about it. Maybe Carmina would change her mind.

Even if Carmina didn't care Jack was going away, she cared.

She clipped on the red polka-dot ribbon Jack had given her. Looking into the mirror, she adjusted it several times so her hair would flow down the side of her face and highlight her profile exactly the way she wanted. The ribbon matched her scarlet red dress perfectly.

When she came downstairs, Aunt Sophia's eyes popped open and fixed on the low neckline of her dress. Quickly, she headed for the door before her aunt might comment on what she wore. "Goodbye. I'll be back by eleven."

To make it the best night ever for Jack, they took him to Chicago's hottest nightclub, the ever-sensational Chez Parée.

Jack looked to be in good spirits when they arrived. When they told the club's host that Jack had enlisted and this was his send-off party, the host took them to a table near the stage next to the dance floor. In fact, the club had reserved all the most coveted tables for men in military uniforms and their guests.

"Look! You're special now," Fred joked when the host pulled out the seat facing the stage for Jack. For once, Jack let go of his usual humble self and took the seat like he was entitled.

The spectacular setting of the Chez Parée awed Tessa the minute they walked in. Its art deco style lobby, with its red carpet and large paintings of nude women hanging on the walls, instantly set it apart from the Melody Mill. Stylishly dressed guests congregated on the long, elegant white leather seats in the lounge. In the ballroom, tables covered in white linen and set with fine china and silverware surrounded the dance floor. A gold curtain hung in front of the performance stage. When the curtain opened, the brilliantly shining stage lights took her breath away.

The band began. Instantly, their fantastic big band music energized the room. Out came the Chez Parée Adorables, a troupe of dancers in glittering outfits with large, dramatically designed feathers attached to the back. They waltzed around the audience, performing their dances and dazzling acrobatic moves to fire up the crowd. She had never seen anything like this even in the West End.

After the Adorables, it was the guests' turn. They flooded the dance floor, swinging to the band's fast, rolling tunes. Fred and Janie dragged Jack out of his seat. Tessa followed them with Henry and Ruby. For a while, Jack seemed to have left his troubles behind. He pulled Tessa in and out, circled around her, and lifted her up and rolled her off his back like he always did. He almost convinced them he was okay again.

But he was off. His movements were a beat behind and his feet were less adept than usual. Between steps, he gazed at the doors, distracted. They danced farther and farther away from the others while he led her around the ballroom as though he was looking for someone. The joy on his face disappeared as the minutes passed.

Suddenly, he stopped. He pulled Tessa in and said into her ear under the loud music, "I'm sorry. I can't do this anymore." He let go of her hand and went back to their table.

She went after him. At the table, he sat down, picked up his whiskey and drank the entire glass. She stood next to him, her heart broke for him.

"She's not coming, is she?" he said to no one in particular.

Tessa didn't answer. How could she tell him Carmina wasn't coming?

"I guess it's better this way." He stared at the door, dispirited.

She sat down next to him and gently touched his face. "Jack, remember this ribbon?" She turned her head to show him the ribbon clipped to the right side of her head. "You gave it to me the first time we met."

He smiled.

"You know that when a girl wears her hair ribbon on the back of her head, it means she's not interested in any boy. When she wears it on the top of her head, it means she's out to get a boy." She half closed her eyelids and held up her chin like a flirtatious actress in a movie and it made him laugh.

"When she wears it on the right side of her head, it means she's deeply in love." She looked him in the eyes, not playing or joking anymore. "Tonight, Jack Morrissey, I'll be the girl who's deeply in love with you."

Jack started laughing again. "Tessa, you don't have to try to cheer me up..." She leaned forward and kissed him softly on his lips. Surprised, he tensed up. But as her soft breath fell on him, he closed his eyes, relaxed and accepted her kiss.

When she pulled back, he looked at her. Those green eyes that she had wished would look at her, although until now she dared not admit it.

"Tessa. You little vixen. Where did you learn to look at a guy this way?" He reached out and lifted a lock of her hair. "You're beautiful, do you know that?"

She gazed at him, waiting for him to tell her more.

"If we had met at a different time, in a different place…" He looked down. "If my heart wasn't already taken, I might seriously fall in love with you." He looked up again, stroking her hair. "If our worlds weren't so different. If you were in my world, or if I was in yours…" He didn't finish what he meant to say.

"You and Carmina are in different worlds." She leaned closer into him. "That didn't stop you."

"That's not the same." He pulled back away from her. "She and I, our people are different, but she and I are the same. Our world is the same."

She didn't understand.

"You're in a different world, Tessa. Whatever you think you see in me, whatever you're infatuated with, it's an illusion. In a few years, you'll find me very…uninteresting."

"That's not true."

"You have bigger and better things waiting for you. You really don't have to be here with us."

"You think I'm a snob!"

"That's not what I mean. It's not what I mean at all." He withdrew his hand. "In a couple of years, maybe even less time than that, you'll change your mind."

"No, I won't. I won't change!" She didn't know how to convince him. "I'm not that type of person."

They looked at each other. Rather than contradict her, he gave her hand a light squeeze. "Of course you won't change. You're very special. And, wow! The most beautiful girl in Chez Parée tonight just confessed to me and kissed me. I can't possibly get a better send-off than that!" As he said this, his eyes shone. For a fleeting moment, she thought she caught a glimpse of the fun-loving, carefree Jack she had always known.

By this time, Fred, Janie, Ruby, and Henry had returned. "What are you two doing here?" Henry asked. "We were looking all over for you. You're not dancing anymore?"

"No," Jack said. "I'm done for the night." He stood up. "Thanks for such a great evening. At such a great place too. Must have cost you all a fortune."

"Don't mention it," Fred said.

"We'll miss you, Jack." Ruby gave him a hug.

"I'll miss you all too."

"When you come back, we'll dance together again," Tessa said to him, her voice still hopeful.

"Of course," he said without hesitation.

She didn't believe him. Something in his voice was missing. She had a bad feeling things would never be the same again.

# # #

At first, they were all depressed. When Jack departed, he took all the energy and excitement with him. They were now on their own. Jack was no longer here to look out for them. No more Jack to drive them and take them to dance halls or any other place.

He gave Henry the car, but it didn't feel right for anyone else to drive it.

Henry especially had a hard time. When Jack was here, he always took care of his family. He made sure Henry got good part-time jobs, stayed out of trouble and stayed in school. He saw to it their mother didn't have much to worry about with money. Henry couldn't do half of what Jack did. He couldn't handle it.

"I'm letting him down," Henry told Tessa and Ruby. "He was only fifteen when Dad died. I thought fifteen was so old back then, and he always knew what to do. I'm sixteen! Jack stopped going to school when he was sixteen. I don't know how to do anything. Maybe I should quit school and work too. Learn a trade or something."

"He wants you to stay in school," Tessa said. "You promised him." It must have been so tough for Jack growing up. Henry was falling to pieces.

"Let's write him together," Ruby said. "He'll be happy to hear from us. We can send postcards too. The post office sells them."

"What if we go trick or treating on Halloween and send him all our candy?"

"We're too old to trick or treat, you idiot."

Tessa had no heart to join their banter. She wondered how long it would be before they would see Jack again.

By December 7, it was clear to her it would be a very long time before he would return.

The Japanese attacked Pearl Harbor.

America was now at war too.

Jack wired his family shortly after that. He was being deployed overseas.

Chapter 24

Nervous agitation filled the room as Anthony and his fraternity brothers gathered around the radio to listen to what the President had to say.

"Yesterday, December 7, 1941, a date which will live in infamy, the United States of America was suddenly and deliberately attacked by naval and air forces of the Empire of Japan..."

Until yesterday, they were all ambivalent about enlisting. Risks and dangers aside, why would they want to be grunts in the army? They were scholars among the brightest minds of their generation. Their possibilities and potential were endless.

The attack on Pearl Harbor changed everything. It shattered their trust in the safety of their own world. Reality set in as they realized the war was not bound by distance to a faraway land. Overnight, foreign attackers could come and destroy their own ports, their own cities, and their own people.

Five American battleships sunk.

Two hundred aircrafts shot down.

Two thousand four hundred people dead.

Goosebumps chilled Anthony's arms as he thought of the number of people killed. People who were going about their day one moment and violently killed the next without warning. So many lives lost.

Brandon was right. He had been right all along.

The president's stern voice continued from the radio. "The American people in their righteous might will win through to absolute victory."

Before yesterday, those words might have sounded empty. Today, they were what he needed to hear. He needed reassurance that they would prevail. He wanted to bring back what was lost and restore everything back to the way it should be.

You know, sooner or later you're going to have to decide which side you're on, Brandon had said to him.

Maybe that time had come.

Everyone felt the same way. In the following weeks, the patriotic sentiment on campus rose to a fever pitch. Droves of students left to join the armed forces. No one blinked an eye when Congress amended the conscription law to lower the age of induction to eighteen.

He had no doubt anymore. He would have to enlist. They all had to. If they didn't defend their own country, who would?

There was only one thing he must settle before he joined. Uncle Leon's phone call came as though he had read his mind.

"Don't make any hasty decisions," Leon urged him. "Come home this weekend. We'll all talk about it."

He didn't want to say no to Leon on the phone. He owed it to him and his parents to tell them in person.

"Promise me you won't do anything until you've talked to us," Leon begged in a state of panic.

Not wanting to upset his uncle any further, Anthony agreed. "Okay. I promise." It was the only thing holding him back. He would have to break the news to them when he went home.

Meanwhile, he watched a number of his classmates leave for service. Even Warren Hendricks had decided to go. In fact, he volunteered the very next week after Pearl Harbor.

"Thank you, Anthony, for everything." Warren came to him before he left. "I never would have qualified to do this if you hadn't helped me train all these months."

In three months' time, Warren had already improved to the point where he could keep up with the rest of the class during Phys. Ed. That was not all. He found new confidence and transformed before everyone's eyes. No longer the self-pitying young man who only wanted to deflect attention, he pushed himself to the limit and beyond no matter what their instructor threw at them.

"I only gave you a push. You did all the work yourself."

"Do you plan to enlist?"

"I'm breaking the news to my parents this weekend." Uncle Leon would not be happy to hear what he had to say, but he could not stand by and let the Japanese get away with this. The enemies would have to answer for what they had done. They would see what America was made of yet.

As expected, Uncle Leon was dead-set against any suggestion of him enlisting. "You can go to Chile. Our trading partner owns a company there. He'll set you up with a good job. You can stay there till the war's over."

"And be an outlaw? That's absolutely out of the question." Anthony couldn't believe Uncle Leon would even suggest this. "Many of my friends have already left. Brandon's gone. I'm not running the other way when all my friends are risking their lives."

"It doesn't matter what others do."

"Of course it does. There's no other acceptable or honorable option. I want to go. They attacked us on our land. Don't you care about that?"

Leon sat down lamely on the couch. "This is a nightmare. It's Lex all over again. And Anthony too." He was referring to Anthony

Browning. "Our family doesn't need more young people dying before their time. Won't you at least think about us?" He looked at Anthony with pleading eyes.

Anthony couldn't argue with that. Uncle Leon looked so sad and helpless.

"I spoke to Senator Reinhardt earlier today," William said. "We won't stop you if you've made up your mind to enlist, but would you wait? The Senator said they have too many people enlisting right now because of Pearl Harbor. So many, in fact, they can't take the volume of people signing up all at once. There isn't enough room. All the basic training camps are filled to capacity. Why don't you wait and see? If you're drafted, then you go." He spoke like his usual, reasoned self, but the appealing tone in his voice betrayed how much he wanted his son to stay.

The way William put it, it was hard for Anthony to refuse, even though he knew his father was only stalling. "And if I'm not drafted, then what?"

"Then it's your choice what you want to do." Resigned, William shifted his eyes to the photos of him, Leon, Lex and Anthony Browning on the display cabinet.

His father's reaction gave Anthony second thoughts. If he went to war and didn't come back, would his father be looking at old photos of him this way too? An older man regretting the loss of too many loved ones for the rest of his days? The last thing he wanted was to cause his parents pain.

And his mother? This whole time they were talking, he couldn't even look at her. She hadn't said a thing.

"All right. I'll wait," he said, almost angry with himself for backing down. "But only until the wave of people enlisting calms down."

"Of course." William let out a sigh of relief.

The end of the evening left Anthony feeling more conflicted than ever. Part of him wished he didn't let his father and uncle talk him into waiting. His resolve to stand up for his own country was real, but it was so difficult to disregard what they wanted. Seeing their worried faces made him hesitate. He was his father's sole heir and only son. His father had great hopes and plans for him. He didn't have the heart to leave his father with an empty world of broken dreams.

#

After Uncle Leon left and his father withdrew into the study, Anthony finally had a chance to talk alone with his mother. What she had to say, though, surprised him.

"I'm very proud of you."

"You are?" He sat down next to her on the couch.

"I'm deathly afraid of what might happen to you," his mother admitted. "Ever since Pearl Harbor, I can't sleep thinking about you." She put her hand on his arm. "You've grown into a fine young man. I feel so blessed to have you in my life. I can't bear to think of life without you."

Her words weighed on him even more than Uncle Leon's and his father's.

"But I'm so proud to know my son is not a coward. When Leon first told us he could arrange to send you to Chile, your father and I thought it could be a good way out too. We couldn't help it. But we had doubts. Your father thought it should be your decision."

"And you? What did you think?"

"I think like all mothers do. I want to protect you and keep you out of harm's way. His offer was very tempting." She looked helpless and resigned. "I can't, though." She looked around the room at all the valuable paintings on the walls and their expensive furniture. "Look at us. We're so privileged. I thought of all the mothers out there who don't have a choice, and I felt so selfish." She was close to tears.

"You're not selfish, Mother." He took her hand.

"Your father's right. It should be your choice. If you want to enlist, I'll understand."

His mother was being so brave. It pained him to see her like this.

"If you want to do what Leon suggested, of course I won't try to stop you."

"I can't do that." He wished he knew what to say to comfort her, but that was not an option he would consider.

"I know. I'm proud you turned him down."

Her support was a great relief. "If everyone ran away like he suggested, who'd be left to protect Alexander and Katherine? I'd like to think I would do that, to protect them if I can."

She held onto his hand. "He never got over Lex's death. It's hard for him, and he loves you very much. You made up for all the losses he suffered when Anthony Browning died."

"I know."

"Maybe the army will never summon you. Maybe the war will end before you have to make any decision. I wish this war would end tomorrow. No, I wish it ended yesterday. But if they do summon you, we must have faith God will watch over you."

He put his arm around her and hugged her. He felt a great weight lifted off him. At least his mother was on his side, and she understood.

# # #

When Tessa heard Anthony returning to his room, she climbed off her bed and went to see him.

A heavy silence had taken over their house ever since the conscription law was amended. Every night, Uncle William retreated early into his study. Aunt Sophia had lost her appetite. Her cheeks looked hollow and had lost their usual radiance. Uncle Leon came over three times last week. They talked for long hours. She didn't know what they decided, but all their talk only made them more nervous and gloomier. Then Anthony came home.

She felt bad being here. When London was bombed, her parents had sent her here to keep her safe. Now America was bombed, but Uncle William and Aunt Sophia could do nothing to keep Anthony safe. The situation was so unfair. She wondered if it upset them to see her. Did seeing her remind them that someone else's child could escape the war but their own child might not?

She tried to keep herself unobtrusive and stayed out of their way. Since Anthony had come home, she felt she should tell him she was sorry he might have to go to war. She never meant to take his place here. If she could, she would even trade places with him. After all, this began as Europe's war.

His door was open. At first, she thought he was studying. But in fact, he looked like he was just staring at a book on his desk. She knocked, feeling a bit awkward.

He looked up. All of a sudden, she lost all the words she wanted to say. To begin with, nothing irked her more than talking to people about feelings. She was lousy at it even with people she knew well. Years of watching Alina Fey airing her grievances everywhere had made her averse to anything involving talks about feelings. She couldn't bring herself to openly tell him what she thought.

"Hi," he said.

"Hello." She stood at the door. She didn't know how to begin. "Are you going to war?"

He seemed surprised she asked. "No. Not for now."

"Oh." That was a relief. She wanted to tell him she was glad to hear that, but the words would not come out. Everything she wanted to say was stuck in her throat.

"You can come in," he said.

She entered, wondering what she should do. She had lived here for more than a year, but she had never come into his room. Most of the time, he was away at school and his room was not used.

He kept his room very organized. His swimming trophies were lined up on a shelf against the wall according to the years when they were won. The clothes he had worn earlier in the day were neatly folded on his bed. She didn't know why, but she had a strange urge to mess things up a little in here. What would happen if he came home one day and found his trophies in the wrong order?

"How've you been?" he asked.

Great. Now, instead of her inquiring about him to let him know she felt sorry for what was happening, he was making sure she was okay. "I'm fine. Thank you for asking." She wandered over to his bookshelf. *Advanced Economics. College Physics. The Iliad. Ancient Archeology of the Mesopotamia.* Why did the books look so complicated? Did he ever read for pleasure?

She turned around. He was looking at her, puzzled.

"Well. Good night." She hurried out of the room.

Talking to Anthony wasn't such a good idea after all.

PART EIGHT
The Rose Pendant

Chapter 25

"Here, give this a try." Nadine put two glasses of red wine on the bar, one for Tessa and one for herself. "It's a Cabernet. This one is rare now since we can't get imports from France anymore. I took it from Laurent's cellar. Good thing he's got them stocked up." Laurent ran a wholesale wine import business, which had suffered setbacks since the war began. "It's time you graduated from those frou-frou drinks Jack used to give you."

"Frou-frou drinks?"

"Those juice cocktails." Nadine moved the glass of Sugar Tuck Tessa was drinking aside. "Try wine instead. Wine's an art."

Tessa tasted a sip. She did like the thick, woody intensity of it more than the juice cocktails.

While Tessa enjoyed her first experience of fine wine, Nadine stared out from behind the bar, mindlessly twirling her hair.

"What's the matter?" Tessa asked. "You look down."

Nadine put down her glass. "This place has changed. Things aren't what they used to be anymore."

"What do you mean?"

"I used to know almost everyone who came here. Now, so many regulars are gone. All we get are servicemen passing through town." She tilted her head toward the tables of soldiers. It was true. Men in military uniforms were everywhere these days.

As they spoke, three soldiers entered. They all looked no older than twenty. Nadine put on her most welcoming face. "Hello, boys. What can I get for you?" She swung her long red hair sideways and threw them a coquettish smile. As if under a spell, the young men came over to her at once. She invited them to sit down and poured them their beers.

As it looked like Nadine would be occupied for a while, Tessa finished her wine and left the bar, ready to go home. When she passed by a table of soldiers, one called out to her. "Hey, sweetheart, want to join us?"

She ignored him. Before she left, she looked at Nadine again. The three soldiers sitting before her were now telling Nadine exaggerated tales trying to impress her. Nadine gave Tessa a quick glance and rolled her eyes. Tessa waved goodbye and headed out of the tavern.

On her way home, servicemen packed the streets and the trains. Nadine was right. This place had changed. Half the population, it seemed, wore the olive drab. She wondered what Jack was doing now.

Thank goodness for Nadine. She filled the void Jack had left behind. Nadine reminded her of her father. They often invited unwanted attention because of their jobs. Sometimes, they even pretended to be flattered to keep their patrons happy. But they both understood real love. The way Nadine looked into Laurent's eyes—Tessa had seen that look before. Her father looked at her mother that same way.

An inspiration struck her. She wanted to create a new painting, one of Nadine and Laurent. She had taken up painting in school as part of her fine arts class. Everything went along fine until she started painting nudes. The nuns would not allow that. Luckily, Uncle William and Aunt Sophia let her use that little spare room on the third floor. She had turned it into her own private studio.

Yes. Definitely she would paint Nadine and Laurent. The painting would be a very nice present for them.

Chapter 26

Late April.

Another school year was coming to an end. Although he didn't frequent local bars, Anthony decided to make an exception tonight. It was the weekend before final exams, and the swim team wanted a fun night out.

More importantly, this might be the last chance for him to do something together with them as a group. For all he knew, they could be drafted any time. When school began again next fall, who could guess how many of them would return?

They had only just sat down at Murphy's Tavern when he caught sight of Tessa at the bar. Was that really her? What was she doing here?

The bartender in a provocatively tight dress handed her a glass of wine, and she drank it!

This wasn't the first time she had been here. Clearly, the bartender knew her from the way they chatted with each other. How could this be? This was not the aloof, introverted girl he was used to seeing at home.

She took her wine and walked away. As she did, a soldier she passed by propositioned her.

What a jackass! She's only a kid. He watched them, wide-eyed. She gave the soldier the cold shoulder and went to join a group of rough-looking boys.

Who were those boys? The redheaded one looked about her age. The other two were slightly older, maybe eighteen or nineteen. She was the only girl among them. The guy on her right in the blue shirt disturbed him the most. He kept sidling in closer and closer to her, although she didn't seem bothered by it. He kept talking to her. Occasionally, she would say something back to him, or nodded, or shook her head.

Why was she shaking her head? What did he want from her?

What was wrong with all these guys? Did they not see how young she was? He had to stop this. "I'm sorry," he said to his teammates. "I can't stay after all. You all have a good time." Without any explanation, he left their table and walked over to her.

He touched her on the shoulder and she turned around. Her eyes widened when she saw him. "Anthony. What are you doing here?"

"I should be asking you that question," he said. "You're coming with me. I'm taking you home. You shouldn't be here."

She drew her shoulder back to get his hand off her. "You can't tell me what to do."

"I can't? All right. I'll call my father and tell him to come and get you."

She started to say something, but stopped. The threat to call his father made her hesitate.

"Keep your hands off her." The redheaded boy stood up from the table. The boy had the audacity to challenge him! He took a step closer to her.

201

Tessa got up from her seat. "Fine. I'll leave with you," she said to him. "But you're being a royal pain in the neck."

"Tessa, wait. Where are you going? Who is he?" the redheaded boy asked.

"It's all right, Henry," she said. "I have to leave. I'll see you next time."

Not wanting Henry to bother Tessa any further, Anthony glared at him. Henry glared right back.

"Stop it. Come with me." Tessa grabbed Anthony's arm. "Let's go." She pulled him toward the door. Before they exited, the sultry bartender came up to them.

"Tessa, is everything okay? Is this person giving you trouble?"

He could not believe his ears. With all the rough boys and soldiers making inappropriate advances toward her, this woman thought he was the one giving her trouble?

"No," Tessa said. "Everything's fine, Nadine. I know him."

"Are you sure?" Nadine asked, still giving Anthony suspicious looks.

"I'm sure. I'll see you later." She tugged his arm again and pulled him out of the bar.

Once outside, Tessa stood on the street and refused to go any further.

"What in the world are you doing here?" he demanded to know.

"Same thing you're doing. Enjoying a good drink and passing time with my friends."

"Friends? Those are your friends? Hardly. You're too young to be here, and the guy in the blue shirt was making improper advances toward you."

"What guy in the blue shirt? What are you talking about?" she asked. "Neal? Do you mean Neal? He wasn't making advances toward me, he was asking me questions about working backstage. He's starting a new job as a stagehand at the Blackstone Theater. I was trying to help him. What is wrong with you?"

A stagehand? Was that all? He was sure that guy had ulterior motives. Could he have been mistaken? Still, everything felt wrong to him. "You were drinking," he said.

"So were you."

"You're a girl."

"I can't drink because I'm a girl? Don't patronize me."

"You're too young to be drinking. You're fifteen."

"Sixteen. I'll be sixteen next week."

"That's a very mature argument there."

Furious, she turned her back to him.

"Look. You shouldn't be here. It's not safe. The bar isn't the kind of place where a nice young girl should go. Strange men come here." He tried to reason with her.

She turned around. "Then why are you here? Are you one of those strange men too? Did you come here to make improper advances to girls?"

Her question rendered him speechless.

"I am so tired of you telling me what I should or should not do. You've been doing that since the day we met. Even Uncle William and Aunt Sophia don't do that. Why do you think you can? You're the only one who talks down to me."

He was surprised to hear this. She thought he talked down to her? "I'm not talking down to you. I would've done the same thing if I saw Katherine here. You shouldn't be here."

"Don't tell me where I should be or should not be. You don't know the first thing about me. I'm not Katherine and all those princesses you know. I don't need you to protect me. I can take care of myself."

They stood staring at each other. He couldn't understand why they were arguing. He was only looking out for her safety. Yet, the way Tessa was asserting herself, with her strong will and defiant attitude, he felt unsure how to deal with her.

"Let's just go home. Please?" He started toward his car.

Grudgingly, she followed him, but she refused to talk while they drove.

"You're going to stay grumpy the whole night?"

She ignored him and looked out the window.

"Your birthday's next week?"

She remained silent.

"Fine. Be that way." He gave up. He had never met anyone more difficult and irritating.

When they reached home, she got out of the car and quietly shut the car door. In silent anger, she walked toward the house. He got out of the car and followed her.

"Why are you coming? Can't you leave me alone? Don't you have to go back to your dorm?" she asked.

"I have to tell Mother and Father what happened."

She stopped walking. "You know something, Anthony? You're a real pantywaist. Must you consult with your parents about everything? Can't you resolve anything on your own? What is so serious that we have to summon the whole house?"

"Don't call me a pantywaist."

"You're being a pantywaist. Go. Go tell Uncle William and Aunt Sophia. Oh dear. Tessa went to a bar, and now she's home safe. But let's make your parents upset and worried over nothing. You can be the goody-two-shoes tattletale, and I'll be the troublemaker. Then we can both be like little children and see what your parents have to say about this. Who is the immature one now? Pantywaist."

"Stop calling me that!"

"Pantywaist, pantywaist, pantywaist," she said and walked toward the house until she reached the front door. "You coming in?"

He stood in place, trying to decide what to do. She had a point. It made little sense to alarm his parents now. But shouldn't he let them know what she was doing? But, what did she say? Did he always consult with his parents on everything? What did he do to make her think he was a pantywaist?

She went inside and closed the door.

"Damn it, Tessa," he mumbled under his breath and went back to his car. No one ever accused him of being a pantywaist before. He couldn't remember the last time anyone made him lose his composure like this.

# # #

In his dorm room the next morning, Anthony tried to study, but he couldn't stop thinking about his argument with Tessa the night before.

— *You are the only one who talks down to me like that.* Did he always talk down to her like she said? He wasn't aware that he did. She had looked so frustrated with him when she said that.

— *You've been doing that since the day we met.* He thought of the first time they met. He chided her in the rose garden, but she was making a mess of it. They had a pool party for her after that. She didn't even appreciate it, so he had told her she must stay. When she took a summer job, he tried to talk to her about responsibility and that didn't go so well. Was he talking down to her all those times? Had he been rude any other time without knowing it?

— *You're a pantywaist. Pantywaist, pantywaist, pantywaist.* How could she insult him like that? Whatever flaws he had, he certainly was no weakling. She was the one who was rude. All he did was try to look out for her.

— *You don't know the first thing about me. I don't need you to protect me.*

He didn't do anything wrong to get her out of the bar. But then he remembered the redheaded boy who stood up to him. Come to think of it, that boy was actually trying to protect her from him. And the bartender who rushed to check up on her when they left, she must've been watching over Tessa the whole time. Was Tessa truly able to take care of herself like she said?

He knew so little about her. How did she end up at the tavern? What did she do on her own? What kind of people did she spend her time with? How much more about her did he not know?

— Sixteen. I'll be sixteen next week.

It only now occurred to him that although she had lived with his family for two years, he didn't even know her birthday. Perhaps that was excusable. He had been away at school most of the time after she arrived, but he never did bother to find out, either.

And then it struck him. Their argument last night was the first real conversation they had ever had with each other.

She was right. He didn't know the first thing about her.

— Must you consult with your parents about everything? Can't you resolve anything on your own? What is so serious that we have to summon the whole house?

All right, we'll do it your way, he thought to himself. We'll resolve this on our own.

He closed his book, put on a light jacket, and left his room.

Chapter 27

Downtown, Anthony strolled about the streets looking for a place to shop. He had no idea what would make a good birthday present for a teenage girl. For Katherine's birthdays, his mother always picked out a gift and they would give it to her as a family.

He went into a gift shop and aimlessly looked around. The shop sold nothing but dolls, small toys, and stationery and pens. Nothing appealed to him. He left and wandered down the block, passing by several more shops until he came upon a small jewelry store. It was a very small store hidden on a side street. "Unique, handcrafted jewelry," said the sign hung on the door. He scanned the items shown in the display window. A small, pretty necklace caught his eye. A pink rose made of coral hung on its simple gold chain. It reminded him of the flowers in their rose garden. Maybe Tessa would like that. It could be a nice memento to remind her of their home. He smiled and went inside.

The storeowner, a thin, middle-aged woman, greeted him immediately. "Welcome. How may I help you? Are you looking for a gift?"

"Yes. I'm looking for a birthday gift."

"For your mother? Or for your girlfriend, maybe?"

"Oh no." He laughed. "For…" He didn't know how to describe who Tessa was to him. He started saying sister, but that wasn't right. He never thought of her as a sibling and she certainly didn't treat him like one. He could say they were cousins, but they weren't that either. They weren't close the way Katherine and Alexander were with him. Were they friends? Not exactly. They sort of coexisted, and generally stayed out of each other's way. How awful was that? She lived in his house.

"For a family friend, I guess." He couldn't think of what else she could be.

"I see," said the store owner. "Is she a young woman or an older lady?"

"A girl. It's for her sixteenth birthday."

"That's easy." The store owner walked to one of the counters and gestured for him to come over. "Come look at these. What do you think?" She brought out a velvet tray of gold and silver necklaces. Some were adorned with rhinestones, others with crystals. "You can get her something made with her birthstone. What month is her birthday?"

"Actually," he said, "can I take a look at the rose necklace in the display window?"

"Sure." She took the necklace out from the display window and showed it to him for a closer look.

Close up, the rose's detailed carving was even more impressive. "I'll take this."

"Good choice," she said. "Would you like it gift-wrapped?"

"Yes, please." While she took it away to wrap it, he checked his watch. Three o'clock. He had time to take it home and return to school before dinner.

#

When he arrived home, his mother was surprised to see him.

"Anthony, this is unexpected." Sophia gave him a hug. "What are you doing home?"

"I came back to drop off something. Is Tessa around?"

"No. I haven't seen her since breakfast. She went out with her friends. They're doing a metal scraps drive for the army at the community center."

"Is her birthday next week?"

"You remembered?"

He was too ashamed to tell her he hadn't known it in the first place.

"Yes, her birthday's next week," Sophia said. "I asked her if she would like us to throw her a sweet sixteen party. When Katherine turned sixteen back in March, Leon and Anna hosted a very nice lunch party for her at the Sienna Country Club. I didn't want Tessa to feel like she deserved anything less. Your father said Tessa wouldn't want it, and he was right, as usual. Tessa said no. She said she didn't like parties and didn't want all that attention."

He thought back to last night when he found her at the tavern and smiled to himself. He had a better idea of how she would rather spend her birthday. Anyway, too bad she wasn't here. He looked at his watch. He didn't have time to wait for her to come home.

"I need to drop off something upstairs. Then I'll have to be off," he said.

"So soon? Won't you stay for dinner?"

"I can't. Exams are coming up. I have to study." He kissed Sophia on the cheek and went upstairs to Tessa's room.

He hadn't been in this room since she moved in. It looked almost exactly like the guest room that it was before she came to live with them. That was odd. She had lived here for two years, but one could not have known this was her room. She did nothing to make it her own. It didn't even look like a girl's room. No collection of mementos anywhere. No soft and pretty pillows on the bed like Katherine's. No accessories and jewelry scattered on the dresser. The dresser top was almost clear except for a hairbrush and a bottle of perfume.

The country landscape paintings on the wall, the clock next to the bed, the vase on the chest of drawers, everything had been there before she arrived. She changed nothing and added nothing. The only things in the room that gave any clue to it being hers were her schoolbooks on the bookshelf and a few necessary items like her school bag and her umbrella. It made him a bit sad that she felt so unattached to this place. Two years, and it was as though she was still a temporary visitor.

There were fresh roses in the vase. He wondered if Tessa had put them there herself, or if his mother or their housemaid had.

And there was a framed photograph of her parents on the nightstand. It was the most personal item in here except for her clothes. In the photograph, her parents looked very happy.

He put his gift on the desk and scribbled a short note.

"Dear Tessa,

Happy sixteenth birthday. Sorry about last night. Would you agree not to visit bars and taverns again? I don't want anything bad to happen to you. — Anthony"

He hoped this would make up for what happened last night. On his way out, he noticed a scarlet red dress on her bed. While the dress looked stylish and elegant, it seemed too mature for a young girl. He couldn't remember ever seeing her dressed up. When did she wear this? Where did she go dressed like that, he wondered.

But he had no time to think about this anymore. He had to meet Mary Winters for dinner. If he stalled any longer, he would be late. He didn't want to keep her waiting.

#

When Tessa saw the birthday present Anthony had left her, she regretted being so rude to him last night. It would've been easier if he had stayed disagreeable. In that case, she could've shut him out like the way she did with Katherine and her friends. A thoughtful gesture on his part made things harder. She wasn't used to backing down and reconciling from a conflict.

She opened the gift box. Inside was a very pretty rose necklace. She held it up and examined it. The rose looked like some of the ones in the memorial garden. It looked handmade, with intricate, skillfully carved details of the petals.

When he returned home this summer, she would have to thank him.

She read once more the note he left her.

Would you agree not to visit bars and taverns again? I don't want anything bad to happen to you.

He worried about her? If he had spoken to her the way he wrote this note instead of telling her she should leave because she was too young or that she was a girl, they wouldn't have bickered the way they did last night. Why did he always have to talk at her like she was a child?

Would she stop going to Murphy's? The truth was, even without him asking, she had been thinking she might stop going. She wasn't worried that something bad might happen to her, but the place had changed. Like Nadine said, the regulars were gone. Jack was gone. The people who made Murphy's fun for her had been replaced by soldiers passing through in transit. Being at Murphy's no longer felt the same. The only reason she still went there was Nadine, but Nadine had her hands full these days with the waves of servicemen frequenting the bar. As for Henry, she saw him often enough when she visited Ruby on the weekends.

She looked at the rose necklace again.

Pink. A little girl's color. Too bad it wasn't another color. Something more daring, like red. Or something unusual like black or purple. She couldn't immediately think of any occasion when she would wear anything pink. Carefully, she put it back into the jewelry box and placed it in her dresser drawer.

PART NINE
Mary Winters

Chapter 28

Tessa never had a chance to thank Anthony for her birthday present when he returned home for the summer. She never got to tell him she had stopped going to Murphy's either. The right moment never came up. For one thing, he started his summer job with Uncle Leon and wasn't around during the day. Whenever he came home, he was too busy planning for Mary Winters' upcoming visit. He never had time, so she stopped bothering.

Mary Winters was the young woman Anthony had been seeing at school since they met at the student center on campus last fall. He asked her to visit him at his home during summer while her parents vacationed in Palm Springs. She hesitated at first, but eventually agreed. Her parents had spoken to William, and all the proper arrangements had been made for her stay with the Ardleys. Anthony had waited anxiously for her to arrive since summer began. He planned a series of activities for them for the week she would be here.

Because her visit was a big event for him, it became a big event for the entire Ardley household. Instructions went around to all the help to make sure every part of the house was in perfect order. The gardens and the yards were groomed. Daytime outings, evening entertainment, and dinners with William and Sophia were all meticulously planned. Tessa watched everything from the sidelines, amused by all the fuss and commotion. The best thing about Mary's visit was that everyone was so preoccupied, they largely left her alone. She only wished Katherine's friends could be here to see this. With the way they always gushed about Anthony, she wondered how they would react.

When Mary finally made her appearance, she was as remarkable as everyone expected. A classic, statuesque beauty with porcelain skin and sharp, brown eyes, she was dressed to perfection. From her elegantly coiffed blonde hair to her neatly done make-up, her entire look complemented her face. Not that she flaunted herself in any way. Her suit dress, finely tailored and understated, showed she had class.

The daughter of a steel magnate, Mary's family had established itself in Illinois for three generations. People deferred to her father in the business community and revered her mother as a pillar of Chicago's elite class. Mary herself was the president of the Chicago Junior League and one of the most sought-after young ladies in her social circle. Young women wanted to befriend her, and young men wanted to court her, but she chose her friends carefully, and her suitors even more selectively.

And yet, even she was flattered when Anthony Ardley showed an interest in her. As many young men as there were who wanted to court her, there were just as many young women who wanted to date him. It had always seemed obvious to her that he and she should meet. The fact that they started dating surprised no one. It was almost expected. From family backgrounds, to looks, to accomplishments, they were a good match in every way. As good manners required, she did not immediately let on that she cared when they first began seeing each other. But from the moment he introduced himself, she knew their pairing was an obvious matter of course.

She arrived at the Ardley residence early in the afternoon and was pleased with everything she saw. Her first meeting with Anthony's parents had gone well. William and Sophia Ardley were delightful people. As always, she handled herself beautifully. Afterward, Anthony took her outside for a walk. He had planned for them to spend the day at the beach the next day, followed by dinner with his parents and his aunt and uncle at the Cliff Dwellers, a private club that supported the performing arts. Later in the weekend, there would be a luncheon at the Ardleys' home for her to become more acquainted with the rest of his family. Everything was going along smoothly, and her visit was an absolute success.

Until she saw that girl for the first time.

The girl first showed up when she and the Ardleys gathered for dinner. Her appearance surprised Mary, as she didn't expect anyone else to join them. No one had told her about this girl until they met that night. They introduced her as Tessa Graham. She came from England and would be staying here until the war in Europe was over.

The first thing Mary noticed about Tessa Graham was her extraordinary beauty. When it came to the matter of beauty, Mary considered herself an expert. Everyone thought she was one of the most beautiful young ladies in the Chicago upper class. They didn't come to that conclusion by accident. She worked at it. Her achievements in the way she looked took careful, disciplined effort in dressing right, applying make-up just right, regimented visits to hair salons, and years of diligent practice to master proper social grace and etiquette.

Tessa Graham's beauty was something else. Her beauty was wild and unconventional. Her hair, which she didn't bother to curl, fell untamed down her shoulders. Mary knew of no woman or girl who was so careless with her hair. She must admit though, Tessa looked very attractive that way, so natural and free.

And the way she dressed! Who dressed like that? Her blouse, not even tucked in, hung loosely on her as if she had put it on as a lazy afterthought. The thin, airy fabric subtly revealed the lightness of her body and the lissome way she moved. Combined with the suggestive but not obviously low neckline, she appeared…desirable. Whether Tessa Graham was unaware of this, or was aware but did not care, Mary could not tell.

Suddenly, Mary found her own beauty too constrained and contrived. Tessa Graham was beautiful without trying at all, and she dared to show her sensuality in a way Mary herself never would.

But hardest to forget was Tessa's face. So soft and yet so striking. Her grayish eyes so hard to read.

For the first time in her life, Mary felt someone had eclipsed her.

Just then, Tessa looked up from the dinner table and caught Mary staring at her. Their eyes met, and Tessa smiled at her. It was a courteous smile that caught Mary off guard. No other girl ever reacted this way to her. The few whose beauty and qualities could rival her were competitive with her. The ones who didn't compare to her would either want her friendship and approval or would be intimidated by her. Tessa's smile showed none of these reactions. Her smile showed only cool disinterest, an obligatory gesture of politeness. Tessa neither cared to please her nor challenge her.

How disappointing. While she was observing Tessa and trying to figure out where they stood against one another, Tessa took her as inconsequential. This had never happened before. She had never been so insignificant to anyone.

She glanced at Anthony. His beaming smile reassured her somewhat, and she smiled back. At least, Anthony's affection was only for her. But for the first time since they met, she began to have doubts.

In her own world, she was always the winner. Sharing the spotlight with another girl, one possibly more extraordinary than herself, was not in her plans.

Chapter 29

Despite the unexpected presence of Tessa Graham the night before, Mary enjoyed the pleasant and relaxing afternoon with Anthony on the beach. It was good to finally be able to spend their time together away from the university without the stress of schoolwork. She looked forward to dinner at the Cliff Dwellers later on in the evening.

They returned home with plenty of time to dress for the night. Before leaving the guest room, she checked herself. Hair, lipstick, skirt, purse, shoes. Everything was in order.

Wait. One more thing. Smile. And grace too. Can't forget grace. Now she was ready to go downstairs to wait for Anthony and his family.

As she approached the ground floor, the intense and powerful performance of Rachmaninoff drew her to the parlor. Tessa Graham was at the piano. Fully immersed in the music, she did not notice Mary's presence at the door.

The expertise with which Tessa performed the piece amazed Mary. Mary herself could play the piano too. She had taken lessons for ten years. But her skills, while excellent, remained in the realm of an amateur. She cultivated her musical skills for the sole purpose of becoming an educated and refined lady. She performed for entertainment on social occasions and volunteered often as an accompanist for charity functions and school events.

What she could do on the piano was nothing like the music she was hearing now. Tessa's performance was that of a true artist. When Tessa played, she did not produce mere pleasing melodies. She manipulated the musical notes for the most dramatic effect intended by the composer and seized the listener's heart.

When Tessa finished, Mary could not help but applaud. Tessa looked up, surprised to see her.

"That was outstanding." Mary came next to the piano.

"Thank you," Tessa said, her tone remained distant and reserved. "I still can't compare to my father. He can play so much better than me."

"Then he must be a virtuoso," Mary said. Her praises were sincere, but she was troubled by the feeling that Tessa had surpassed her yet again.

The doorbell rang. The maid opened the door and in came the Caldwells and Alexander's private tutor. Sophia and Anthony both came downstairs to greet them.

"You must be Mary. I'm Anna Caldwell, Anthony's aunt." Anna came into the parlor. Katherine followed right behind her.

Before Mary could answer, Katherine chimed in. "Mary! I've been so looking forward to meeting you. I'm Katherine, Anthony's cousin. I joined the Junior League last summer. I have so many questions to ask you. What are you doing tomorrow? My friends and I will be meeting for lunch at the Drake Hotel. Would you like to join us?"

"Sorry, Katherine." Anthony put his arm around Mary. "We've got plans tomorrow, and every day after that. And right now, we've got to get going." He looked at both Katherine and Tessa. "Sorry to leave you kids, but Father's waiting at the Club." He started to lead Mary away. "Come on," he said to her. "I'll introduce you to Uncle Leon." He glanced over at Leon, who was lecturing Alexander to get started with his French lesson while Sophia showed the tutor to the study.

Before they walked away, Mary looked back and smiled at Katherine. "I'll be here for the rest of the week. We can talk more next time I see you."

"Yes!" Katherine said and pumped her fist after Anthony led Mary away.

"You kids will be okay by yourselves for tonight?" Anna asked before leaving.

"We'll be fine, Mother," Katherine said, annoyed. "I'm going to call my friends." She left for the den to use the telephone, leaving Tessa alone in the parlor again.

On their way out of the door, Mary turned back and looked into the parlor at Tessa. Tessa had already turned her attention back to the piano. The music of Debussy filled the air, surrounding her with an ethereal aura that separated her from the rest and took her someplace where no one else could reach.

I could never do that, Mary thought to herself. She would never be able to take music to such a high level where it could embody her feelings or who she was.

# # #

Outside, Sophia had gone ahead with Leon and Anna in their car, leaving Anthony and Mary to drive to the Cliff Dwellers on their own. While they drove, Mary could not stop hearing Tessa's music in her mind.

"Tessa. She's unusual," she said to Anthony.

"Unusual how?" he asked.

"There's something very distant about her."

He stopped at the crosswalk to let an old lady and her dog pass. "Maybe it's the British in her. Her father is Dean Graham."

"The British actor?"

"That's him."

No wonder, Mary thought. That was where Tessa got her striking good looks. "I heard her play the piano. She's very gifted."

"She is. You play piano too, don't you? Want to play something for me tomorrow?"

She let out a laugh of disbelief as if he had suggested something preposterous. How could she play for him now? She was not about to draw attention to her own comparative weakness.

"How come you never told me about her?"

"What's there to tell? She's a kid living at my home. Don't mind her. I'll make sure she and Katherine won't get in your way." He looked ahead to the road and moved into another lane, oblivious to the probing tone in her voice.

"What do you think of her?"

"Tessa?" He answered as if he had never given the subject much thought. "She's kind of reckless and irresponsible. I try to give her advice sometimes but she argues and never listens. I would like to reach out to her more, but no one ever knows what's on her mind. She doesn't talk much."

Mary thought of the way Tessa played the piano. "She speaks through her music."

"What?"

"That's how she expresses herself. She's a true artist."

"You're giving her too much credit. She's an excellent piano player, yes. Maybe she'll grow up to be a true artist, but now she's just a kid. What deep thoughts could she have that she has to convey through music?"

Mary didn't say anything more. Obviously, Anthony didn't see Tessa for who she was. If he didn't see, there was no point in drawing his attention to another girl. But for the rest of the way, she weighed in her mind whether being Anthony Ardley's girlfriend was worth it.

Was she jealous of Tessa? No. Not at all. She was too well brought up for that. However, that did not mean she wanted to share the stage or be upstaged. In her own world at least, she meant to be the center of attention. Tessa Graham was someone she would rather keep far away from her own sphere. The problem was, if Anthony and the Ardleys were to become an important part of her life, Tessa would be there too.

Sure, Tessa would return to England one day, but when? What if she did not leave at all? She had already been here for two years. What if she stayed here long enough and became rooted here? What then?

She watched Anthony as he drove. Her doubts about their future together continued to widen.

Chapter 30

While Anthony showed her his family albums the next afternoon, Mary's mind drifted back to Tessa. Tessa was having more effect on her than she should allow. Her own thoughts clouded what should be a wonderful and successful visit. Her doubts were lightened only by the sweet affections Anthony showed her each day.

He opened the album to pictures of him camping when he was ten, and told her how he and his friend Brandon sneaked out of their tent at night and pretended to be ghosts to scare the others. He flipped through the pages, telling her about his adventures and misadventures while growing up.

They came to the photos of him in high school. Many were photos of him in swimming competitions.

"You won all these?" She pointed to the pictures of him taken during medal and trophy presentations.

"Yes."

"Where are your championship medals? Can I see them?" It was her intention to flatter him.

"They're no big deal." He softened his voice, slightly embarrassed.

"No, really. I want to see them. Do you still have them?" She insisted.

"All right," he said, his eyes now beaming with pride. "Wait right here." He left the den to go to the storage room on the third floor where he had put away some of his personal belongings before he left for college.

#

When he opened the door to the storage room on the third floor, Anthony found to his surprise the entire room had changed. His swimming competition medals, which he had packed away safely in a box, were no longer on top of the desk where he had left them. The room itself was a mess. A big pile of stuff covered in a large white cloth overtook one side of the room. A rainbow of colors, red, blue, purple, orange, all created by accidental smearing of paint, splattered over every part of the cloth. Canvases and half-finished paintings lay here and there all over the room. In the center, Tessa worked feverishly on a painting with her shirt sleeves half rolled up. Dabs of paint had marked her forearms and jeans. A loose lock of her hair had fallen in front of her face from her ponytail.

"What's happening here?" he asked.

"I'm painting," she said without looking up.

"I can see that." He walked in. "I mean what happened to this room?"

"Uncle William and Aunt Sophia said I can use it as my studio. They said no one uses this room anymore."

"Where are my medals?" He took the white cloth off the pile and searched through the heap of books, old souvenirs, and collectible items that had long been forgotten.

"I don't know. What medals?" She paid no attention to what he was doing.

"My medals that were here." He pointed to the desk, where paint tubes and paintbrushes lay scattered on top.

"Maybe they're in that pile next to the bookshelf. Why don't you look there?" She still did not look up.

"Who put them there?"

"I did."

He went over to the pile, irritated she did not even offer to help him after admitting she had messed his things up.

He found his box among a stack of old books and a mound of old, worthless figurines his father had brought back from his trip to Egypt some years ago. His box had tipped to the side and some of his medals had fallen out onto the floor. Annoyed, he put the medals back into the box, picked it up, and started to leave the room. As he did, he looked at her back and grumbled to himself until he saw what she was painting. He walked up next to her by the easel. On closer look, he saw he was not mistaken. She was painting a man and a woman with long red hair in a naked embrace.

"What in the world are you painting?!"

She barely registered a reaction to him. "You can't see? Or you don't know?" She added another touch of gray color to the man's nether region to create an impression of a shade. "They're two people making love."

"This is unacceptable!"

"Why?"

"It's pornographic."

"You have a dirty mind."

"You are the one painting this and I have a dirty mind? Where did you get this idea anyway? You haven't...you haven't..."

"I haven't what?" She looked up from the painting. He looked back at her, unable to say out loud the question that had sprung to his mind.

She must have guessed what he wanted to say. "How dare you even think that?" she asked, indignant.

"Sorry," he apologized. That was over the line. How could he have asked her that? He felt his face burning.

She turned back to the painting. "I've seen photos and magazines. Nudity is often shown in fine arts too, you know."

Yes. But not nude people in the act, he thought.

"And I've seen my parents."

"Your parents?" He couldn't believe what he heard. "You spied on your parents?"

"Of course not! Why would I do that?" She leaned slightly away from him, aghast at the suggestion. "I lived in the same house with them all my life. I couldn't help seeing what was going on. Haven't you ever seen your parents?"

"Stop! Stop right there. I am not having this conversation." He took a step back.

"You sound disgusted," she said. "There's nothing disgusting about what my parents did. I've never seen anyone more passionately in love than my parents." Her eyes turned tender and dreamy. "When I fall in love, I want to be just like them," she said softly, more to herself than to him.

He broke into laughter.

"What's so funny?"

"Who's going to fall in love with a moody wild child like you?" He couldn't resist teasing her. This was the first time he had ever seen her act like a normal girl. Before she could answer, he walked out of the room. "See you later."

Furious, she threw a paintbrush at him, but he had already closed the door. The paintbrush hit the door and fell to the ground, leaving her alone in the room, livid.

Chapter 31

"You have to come with me tomorrow night," Ruby said to Tessa over the phone. Tessa could hear through the receiver the background noises of people at the USO Center where Ruby was. "It'll be fun. I promise." She wanted Tessa to go swing dancing with her and two soldiers she had met.

"I'm not sure." Swing dancing no longer occupied her life like last summer. For one thing, Jack was gone. The dance halls weren't the same without him. Other things had changed too. Baseball games threatened to cease as more and more players went off to war. With the gas ration in effect, people went to fewer places. Sugar was rationed too, and the Montmartre no longer served their delicious mousse and tarts.

This summer was nothing like the last. Henry took a bussing job at Murphy's again, except now he took on more shifts. Tessa was immersed in her new passion for painting. Ruby volunteered at the USO Center. It started as a sincere effort on her part to support the armed servicemen, but these days, she mainly went there to meet boys. The USO held parties and dances. She had asked Tessa to join her many times, but Tessa always declined. This time, she thought Tessa might say yes if they went to the Melody Mill.

"Henry's coming too," Ruby said. "Please, Tessa. You have to come with me. I don't want to be the only girl."

"What about your other friends you usually go to the USO with? Why don't you ask one of them instead?"

"Because I want you to come."

Tessa smiled to herself. She figured Ruby wanted to impress those two soldiers by bringing along a friend who could dance well.

"You should come," Ruby urged. "You haven't gone dancing at all this summer."

Yes. It had been a long time. "It feels strange to go without Jack."

"I bet you he's dancing up a storm at a USO center somewhere right now, wherever he is. He likes it too much not to. Don't you want to keep up so you can dance with him again when he comes back?"

When Jack comes back…

Could she keep up with him if he did?

"All right. I'll go."

"That's great. We'll pick you up at nine o'clock tomorrow night. Be ready."

Tessa hung up the phone. Tomorrow would be a good night. Uncle William and Aunt Sophia had a special black-tie fundraiser to attend for the Chicago Hospital and they would be out until late. Anthony had invited his friends over for some kind of special dinner for Mary. No one would be paying attention to her. If she didn't tell anyone, they wouldn't even know she was gone and she could return home whenever she wanted. The timing was perfect.

# # #

Tonight was a special evening. Anthony had spent weeks planning this dinner to introduce Mary to all of his friends who did not attend UC. He had invited his old classmates from before college, fellow members at the local swim club, and several neighbors. By introducing her to them, he wanted her to know he would openly acknowledge who she was to him to everyone he knew. Formalities like this mattered to her.

As he expected, Mary charmed and impressed all of their guests. She was knowledgeable and well versed on every subject that came up, from music, to art, to current events. After dinner, they brought their lively conversations to the parlor. The atmosphere of the evening became relaxed and Matthew, one of Anthony's high school friends who was home for the summer from Princeton, suggested they should have some music.

Having been to the Ardleys' home before, Matthew took it upon himself to pick out a selection of music from the album collection in the den for everyone to enjoy. On his way back to the parlor, a young woman coming down the stairs ran smack into him and almost knocked him over. The stack of records he was holding dropped onto the floor.

"I'm sorry," she said as they both bent down to pick up the records. Her beautiful voice rang like wind chimes. He looked up. The most beautiful girl he had ever seen was right before his eyes. Her hair, tied in a ponytail, brought out the delicate but striking features of her face. Her scarlet red dress revealed the softness of her figure, and he couldn't help stealing a quick glance at her chest beneath the low neckline. So captivated by her, he could only look at her, speechless.

"There." The girl picked up all the albums and put them back in his hands. Then she got up, gave him a quick smile, and hurried out the front door.

He walked back to the parlor, dazed. "Anthony," he said. "Who was that raving beauty I just saw? Why isn't she here with us? Dang! You could've at least introduced her to me."

"What raving beauty?" Anthony didn't know whom he was talking about.

"The one who just ran out." He pointed to the large window facing the Ardleys' driveway. "Who is she?"

Anthony looked out the window and saw Tessa running up to a car in their circular driveway. The same redheaded boy he had seen at Murphy's a few months ago leaned out the window of the driver's seat as Tessa got in.

It was now late in the evening. Where was she going? She hadn't told anyone she had planned to go out.

Two other men and a girl sat inside the car. He couldn't make out who they were in the dim nightlight. The men appeared to be in military uniforms.

Who were these people? Why couldn't she keep better company than running around with strange men?

As he tried to decide what to do, the car started pulling out of the driveway. Alarmed, he got up from his seat.

"Excuse me. I'll be right back." He rushed out of the house to his own car parked in the driveway and followed, hoping to catch up with them before they drove too far away.

On the road, he tried to overtake their car but other vehicles kept getting in his way. He hoped she was not going to the tavern again. He had asked her to stay away and would be quite disappointed if she had chosen not to listen. The way they were heading though was not the way to the tavern. He wondered where they were going. Instead of stopping them, he decided to follow behind to find out.

They arrived at a dance hall called the Melody Mill Ballroom. Near the entrance, he lost sight of them. He parked his car and went inside. The place was crowded and he walked around searching for her. He finally found her when he heard a wave of loud cheers from the dance floor. There she was, swinging and stepping to the beats with total abandon in the middle of a pack of spectators who had circled around her. In the heat of the dance, she looked nothing like the lonely, arrogant teenager he had come to know.

And she was good. More than good. She was fantastic. He could not believe his eyes.

Her dance partner repeatedly pulled her in and released her. Each time, her skirt swirled. His heart jumped every time her legs were revealed. When her partner threw her up into the air, her skirts flew so high he could see what she wore underneath. He almost lost his breath.

When the music ended, she bowed over laughing. He had never seen her in such a state of exhilaration. This was not the Tessa he knew at home.

The music started again and another dancer cut in. She had no shortage of people who wanted to dance with her.

Watching on the side, he was no longer sure whether he needed to be here. He did not expect this. He came to watch over a rash and vulnerable young girl, one whom his family had a responsibility to protect. Should he stop her? She looked so in her element. She belonged here.

He checked his watch. A voice in the back of his mind told him he should go home to Mary and his friends. They must be wondering where he had gone, but he felt no urge to get moving. He liked watching Tessa dance. He wanted to keep watching.

Unaware of Anthony's presence, Tessa rotated from one dance partner to another. It had been so long since the last time she came here, she had forgotten how much she loved this.

She was thoroughly enjoying herself until, out of the corner of her eye, she saw Henry in a dispute. A confrontation had broken out between him and a pair of thugs. She recognized those two. They were Don and Lester from the amusement park last summer. Lester made a sneering face at Henry, and Henry yelled back. They pushed each other while Ruby yelled at them to stop.

She could not stand for those two to pick on her friend. She stopped dancing and walked over to them.

"Lay off him, creep," she told Lester.

"Hey sugar, it's you again." Lester turned his attention to her. "You want me to lay off him? Tell you what. I'll lay off him if you come lay with me." He reached his hand out to her. Before he touched her, she slapped him in the face.

"Oh now you've done it," Lester scowled. "You little…"

"Get your hands off her!" Henry stepped in between them, but Don punched him and he fell.

"Henry!" Ruby ran over to him.

Laughing, Lester grabbed Tessa's arm. "What are you going to do now? Your little boyfriend can't protect you."

"Let go of me." She jerked her arm back to shake him off.

Horrified by what was happening, Anthony came forward. He pulled Lester's shoulder and arm away from Tessa and twisted his arm around to pin it against his back. Lester squealed in pain.

"Don't you dare ever touch her again." He pushed Lester onto the floor.

Tessa had no idea where Anthony came from and was stunned to see him. But before she could say anything, Don pulled out a knife and pointed it at Anthony.

"Anthony! Watch out!" She lunged toward Don to try to stop him. Anthony turned around just in time to see Don's knife and Tessa pushing Don away. The knife sliced Anthony's arm and Ruby shrieked. Everyone around them stopped dancing and fled.

Tessa grappled with Don and tried to snatch his knife away from him. Quickly, Anthony grabbed Don's wrist and squeezed until he howled and dropped the knife. Anthony calmly picked up the knife and looked Don in the eyes. Don backed away, then turned around and disappeared into the crowd. Lester crawled up from the floor and ran after him. He looked back at Tessa and Anthony as he ran. His face was still scrunched up in pain.

With those two gone, Tessa stood waiting for Anthony to get riled up. She was sure he would lecture her again, but he only said, "Are you done yet? Ready to come home now?"

She looked over at Henry and Ruby. "My friends…"

By this time, Ruby had helped Henry up onto his feet. Henry's nose was bleeding. Tessa went over to him. "Are you okay?"

"He sprained his ankle," Ruby said. "He can't drive us home."

Tessa glanced sheepishly at Anthony. Anthony had no choice but to offer to help. "You're all coming with me then?"

"What about Peter and Roger?" Ruby asked, referring to the two soldiers who had come with them. "They went to the cocktail lounge. Shall I go find them?"

Tessa stole another look at Anthony, afraid to ask him to do any more favors.

"I am leaving. So either you all come with me or you can stay and go with them," he said, then looked pointedly at Tessa. "Except you."

Tessa took Henry by the arm. Henry hadn't said anything, but she could tell from his expression he was in pain. "Forget them, Ruby. Henry's hurt. Let's go."

They followed Anthony out of the dance club back to his car.

# # #

While driving, Anthony checked the rearview mirror to take a better look at Tessa's friends. "So, you're Ruby?"

"Yes," Ruby answered.

"And you're Henry?"

"Yes," Henry said. "Thank you for helping us and driving us home."

"Sure." Anthony looked back onto the road.

Tessa turned around from the front passenger seat. "Anthony's Uncle William's son," she said to Ruby and Henry.

When they arrived, Ruby helped Henry out and they thanked Anthony again. Anthony and Tessa remained in the car and watched them go inside. While they sat, Anthony looked around at the old, run-down buildings where they lived. Henry and Ruby came from such a different place than Tessa. But from the little he had seen of them, he could sense they cared very much about each other. The first time he saw Henry with Tessa at Murphy's, he had thought Henry looked rough and uncouth. Now, he saw that Henry was not a delinquent. Both times he had seen him, Henry had tried to protect and defend Tessa, and Tessa readily stood up for him too. Their willingness to look out for each other was very touching.

He looked at Tessa staring out the window on the passenger side. Why did she keep so many things to herself? Away from his home, in places she chose to be, with people she chose to be with, she was an entirely different person. Why was she so different around him? Who was this girl, really?

After Ruby closed the front door of her building, Tessa sat back in her seat. When she saw Anthony looking at her, she said, "I'm sorry. I really am."

"It's all right," he said quietly.

"What were you doing at the dance hall? Were you following me?"

"Would you rather I didn't?"

She lowered her eyes. The situation might've been very bad if he hadn't come.

"I saw you leave the house with those soldiers. I was worried you might get yourself into trouble." He turned on the ignition and started the car.

"Wait," she said. "Your arm's hurt." She took a handkerchief out of her purse and tied it around his wound. While she did that, he thought of her pushing Don and the knife away from him. How reckless of her to put herself in danger like that. She came frighteningly close to being injured herself. The thought of the knife hurting her made him cringe.

And yet, she did that for him. She risked herself for him.

He looked at the handkerchief wrapped around his arm. A sweet warmth rose in his heart knowing that she cared about him. "Thanks."

She looked away and sat quietly in her seat.

They drove on home. Cars were sparse on the expressway this time of the night. The highway lamps gleamed and the building lights shone like jewels out of the windows of the buildings in the view ahead. Inside their car, all remained quiet except for the occasional swooshes of another car driving by.

"I stopped going to Murphy's." She broke the silence. "I haven't gone there since the last time you saw me there."

He gave her a quick glance. He ought to tell her she shouldn't have come out so late alone without telling anyone, but he couldn't even convince himself of that. He saw her dance. How could it be right to stop her from doing something she did so well?

In any case, he was in no mood to open up another argument with her. He needed to think of how to explain to Mary why he had left her and their party so suddenly and disappeared when he was supposed to show everyone she was special. What would he tell her when he got home?

He should be furious with Tessa for ruining his night, except he wasn't. His heart skipped a beat every time he thought of her swirling on the dance floor, her skirt flying high and her legs moving fast, her bright smile livening up the entire place as she danced the night away.

In the passenger seat, Tessa stole worried glances at Anthony. She felt terrible about what happened tonight. She wished he would scold her and argue with her, but he remained quiet. This silence was worse. Maybe he was upset he got injured. What about Mary? What happened to her and all his friends? Did he leave them behind all evening? Mary must be angry.

She scratched her head. She wondered what she should do. It wasn't her fault if Mary was angry with him. She didn't ask him to come after her. But what if this time he was so upset at her antics, he told Uncle William and Aunt Sophia everything? She didn't want to have to explain how she got into a fight and how Anthony got injured because of her.

Maybe this time, she was in real trouble.

When he finally spoke, she was expecting the worst. Instead, he said, "You look very nice tonight." He said this while looking straight ahead at the road.

Dumbfounded, she widened her eyes. "Oh…thank you." She didn't know what else to say. Why wasn't he riled up? "You're not upset?"

He didn't answer. She figured she had better not push her luck. As long as he didn't alarm everyone when they returned home, she was fine with letting things be.

Chapter 32

When they arrived home, it was close to eleven p.m. All of Anthony's friends had left. Feeling guiltier than ever, Tessa went back to her room as soon as they came inside. She could do nothing to help Anthony now. The best she could do was to hide her face, get out of their way, and let him and Mary talk on their own.

Anthony went into the parlor and found Mary waiting for him alone on the couch.

"I'm sorry. I can explain," he said. His voice halted when she turned her sharp eyes on him. He felt like a guilty party on the stand under interrogation, even though she hadn't said anything. Her eyes landed on the handkerchief wrapped around his arm.

"I saw Tessa going off," he tried to tell her. "I thought she might get into trouble." No. This was coming out all wrong. He needed to explain himself better. "I only wanted to make sure she was okay. Then she and her friends got into a fight. Someone tried to hurt her and I had to intervene. After that, I drove her friends home."

Mary sat watching him. Her stare made him feel completely uncomfortable.

"Is everyone okay then?" she asked.

"Yes."

"Are you all right?" She glanced at his arm. "You should clean your wound."

"I will," he said. She was asking all the right questions, but nothing felt right. Beyond the concern on the surface of her voice, there was a tone of coldness he found unsettling. "What happened after I left?"

"Well, it was very awkward." She didn't hide her resentment. "It's somewhat embarrassing when your boyfriend invites all his friends over, then leaves you to run after a raving beauty and doesn't come back."

"A raving beauty?" He laughed. Her accusatory tone about Tessa annoyed him. "It was just Tessa. You know that. I didn't run after any raving beauty."

"Your friend Matthew thought otherwise. He couldn't stop talking about her after you left."

"Mary, you can't possibly think I…"

"No. Of course not." She cut him off. "It's late." She smiled. "We should call it a night." She got up and left the parlor.

He meant to go after her and to say something to make it up to her, but it was all too difficult. Clearly, a mere apology and explanation would not do.

Exhausted, he plopped down on the sofa and closed his eyes. The vision of Tessa twirling on the dance floor came to him again.

#

The next morning, Mary told Anthony she had decided to leave early to join her parents at their summer home in Palm Springs. By the time he saw her, she had already made her plans to depart.

"If it was about last night, I apologize again." He tried to convince her to stay. "I am very, very sorry. I should not have left you like that. I promise it won't happen again."

She would not change her mind. She couldn't explain to him that last night was not the only reason for her decision to leave. It was humiliating for her, of course, but she could forgive him even for that. To a point, his action was justified. He thought he was looking out for a vulnerable young girl. He didn't know that if he hadn't been there, plenty of other men would have stepped in and done what he did. Tessa was too attractive for no one to come to her rescue. Only he couldn't see that. Besides, she had a feeling Tessa wasn't someone who wanted anyone to rescue her.

None of this mattered now. She wanted to leave because she didn't want to occupy the same space with Tessa. No matter what they were doing, Tessa was always there, always threatening to outshine her. Tessa got everyone's attention. Like Matthew's reaction to her, and the way Anthony ran after her. Last night was a good indication of how things might be with Tessa Graham around.

No, she thought. She could not allow someone to overshadow her. Not in her own world. She had worked too hard to become who she was.

"We'll see each other again when school begins." She touched Anthony gently on his arm, knowing the whole time her words were hollow. She had already decided it was over between them. "I've had a very pleasant stay. Your parents are wonderful. I enjoyed meeting them very much."

He put his hand on hers, his face still troubled. "You're still upset, aren't you?"

"No. I'm not angry about last night at all. Honest." She pulled her hand away. "I'll go say goodbye to your mother. Please tell your father I'm sorry I didn't have a chance to say goodbye in person since he went off to work. I'll say goodbye to Tessa too."

"To Tessa? Why? This is all because of her."

Mary only smiled. "About Tessa, don't you find her attractive? Not at all?" She couldn't resist asking.

"Tessa?" He looked at her as if it was the most ridiculous idea in the world. "Right. If you mean she attracts trouble like a magnet."

She let the subject drop. None of this concerned her anymore.

From the door of the small storage room on the third floor, Mary watched Tessa add dabs of color onto her painting. She could not help but admire the way Tessa focused so fully on her work. Tessa looked beautiful with her mind deep in concentration like that.

Leaving was the right decision. Mary was sure of that now. She cleared her throat and knocked on the door.

Tessa looked up. "Please come in."

"Hello, Tessa. I've come to say goodbye." Mary gave her a warm smile. "I'm leaving for California today. My ride's waiting for me outside."

"You're leaving? So soon? I thought you would be here until the end of the week."

"I've had a change of plans." She noticed Tessa's painting depicting a man and a woman with long red hair, naked in a passionate embrace. "Your painting…" she said in amazement. "Such exquisite use of color. Beautiful form and style too."

"Thank you."

Mary studied the painting more closely. The boldness of its subject matter impressed her. No one she knew would dare to draw something like this. She herself would not dare. For a fleeting moment, she almost felt Tessa's sense of freedom and lack of restraint. The feeling was breathtaking. Liberating.

But, it was not a life she knew how to live. She stepped away from the easel. "Maybe we'll meet again someday."

Tessa smiled. It was the same polite but reserved smile as the first day they met. "I hope you're not leaving because of what happened last night. I'm sorry if I caused any trouble."

"Don't worry about last night."

"It's great that you came. Anthony's very lucky."

"Yes." She looked at Tessa. Her eyes conveyed a meaning deeper than what she would openly say. "Perhaps he is."

PART TEN
Moonlight

Chapter 33

Everything came to a standstill after Mary's sudden early departure. Most of the remaining activities Anthony had planned for her were canceled. Uncle Leon and his family still came for the weekend luncheon, but it turned into a simple family affair instead of a meaningful occasion.

The failure of Mary's visit put Anthony in an uncharacteristically dour state. Tessa didn't think much of it at first, but when his wistful mood continued for days, she genuinely felt sorry for him. Mary's visit was the highlight of his summer, and she felt partly responsible for what happened. If she hadn't gone out dancing without telling anyone, he wouldn't have worried and come after her. If she hadn't provoked Lester into a fight, he wouldn't have been delayed all night and would have returned to Mary before the evening ended.

Not only that, he didn't even get her into trouble for what she had done. At lunch the day Mary left, Aunt Sophia asked him about the bandages wrapped around his arm. "What happened to you?" she said to him.

Tessa held her breath. She looked at her plate and kept her head down, waiting for the worst.

"I had an accident," Anthony said. "I hurt myself at the gym."

She sneaked a glance at him. She couldn't believe her ears.

"What could you have done at the gym to hurt yourself like that? Is it serious?"

"I'm fine, Mother. Don't worry about it."

Tessa looked at him, but he kept eating and didn't look back at her.

But he blames me all the same, she thought and made a face at herself. The next day, he went back to work at his summer job with Uncle Leon and never said a word to anyone about what happened.

What bothered her, though, was seeing him do nothing else besides going to work. Before Mary arrived, he had planned a full week off to spend time with her. Now that Mary was gone, he would go to work, then come home at night and hole himself up in the den and read. His reading didn't advance very far. Most of the time, she noticed he only stared at the pages.

He had tried to telephone Mary all week, but Mary was always unavailable. When he couldn't reach her, he would look even more depressed.

Tessa never thought Anthony could be sad. He always seemed so in control, so organized and unassailable. She thought nothing could ever shake him and nothing bad could ever happen to him unless he was drafted to war.

Maybe that wasn't a fair judgment. Perhaps there were times when he, too, could be vulnerable to things beyond his control. But how would she know that? She never knew what went on with him. He came and went between summers and holidays, and occasionally dropped in at home whenever it pleased him. When he did bother with her, it was always to tell her not to do this or not to do that. How curious it was to see there was a sensitive person with feelings behind all that.

And for all his troubles, she hadn't even thanked him for saving them that night at the Melody Mill. She owed it to him to let him know she appreciated his help.

When he retreated to the den again after dinner, she went in after him and sat down on the sofa across from him.

"Hello," she said.

Lying on the couch, he barely stirred. "Hey," he said and returned to his book.

"Are you going to do anything else besides read?"

"There's nothing else I want to do," he said without looking at her.

"You'll see Mary again when you go back to school in the fall."

He frowned at the mention of Mary's name. "I know."

"Then why are you so morose?"

"I'm not morose."

"Yes, you are. You've been sulking for days since she left."

"No, I haven't."

"Yes, you have. You don't go anywhere or do anything. All you do is go to work. Then you come home and brood in the den."

"I swim."

"That doesn't count."

"What's all this sudden interest in how I spend my time?" He plopped down his book.

"You saved me and my friends. I want to treat you to a movie to thank you, but I can't do that if you won't leave the house."

Amused, he said, "I don't want to see a movie." He picked up his book again, although at least now he was smiling.

"You'll want to see this one. My father starred in it. He rarely does films. He prefers stage acting, so it'll be a treat."

"Your father?" His interest piqued. "What's the movie?"

"*Julius Caesar*. It was released four years ago. It was the first time he made a film and he did it only because it was Shakespeare, and because Mother wanted very much to see him in one. My father's not too fond of movie acting."

"Why is that?"

247

"He thinks stage acting is more artistic. Still, his movie was very well received. He has a legion of fans and they all came to see him on opening night. My mother went too. She looked so beautiful and proud. She even blended a special rose perfume to commemorate the night and gave it to all the actresses in the cast. Well, she didn't blend it herself, it was the perfume lady she found who knows how to take extracts from our roses and make perfumes with them."

"Yes, I heard you have a rose garden at your home in London too."

Tessa nodded. "My mother planted our garden to commemorate my grandmother, and Anthony Browning and Mrs. Browning. Back home, we plant different species of roses every summer. My mother and I would take most of the flowers to the hospital for her patients, but she would set aside some for making perfumes. She gives them as gifts to her co-workers and the actresses my father works with, and she gives me a bottle every summer. In fact, she just sent me a new bottle. Our garden must be blooming now."

"Tessa." Anthony sat up. "You said, 'back home' and 'our garden'. Do you not feel at home here? You don't even have a lot of your own things in your room."

His question surprised her. She hadn't given much thought to whether she considered the Ardleys' house as her home. "I guess I always hoped my stay here would not be very long. If I get too attached to this place, then my home, my parents, my whole life back in London would feel even farther away from me."

He looked at her for a moment, his eyes softened. "You'll always have a second home here. You should know that."

She felt a lump in her throat. "Thank you," she said in a low voice and looked down. Not wanting to show her feelings, she changed the subject. "You've never seen my father's work, have you?"

"No."

248

"So how about it? Want to see the movie with me? The Biograph is showing a rerun tomorrow night."

"I can't say no, can I? That would be disrespectful to your father."

"I would take it that way," she joked. "We're going then. The movie's at eight o'clock. We can go after an early dinner?"

"All right."

Satisfied, she got up to leave.

"Tessa?"

"Yes?" She turned around at the door.

"You miss home very much, don't you?"

She looked away. The lump was back in her throat again. Without answering, she smiled and closed the door behind her.

Chapter 34

On their way to the cinema, Tessa fidgeted in the passenger's seat while they slowed down with the heavy traffic. As they got closer, she leaned eagerly forward, as if doing so would help them reach the Biograph sooner. She stared out the window, straining to see the first sight of the theater's sign beyond the cars in front of them. Seeing her so excited, Anthony couldn't help catching some of her enthusiasm. He cut off the car in the next lane to get them a few spots ahead. He wouldn't have done that normally, but he was glad he did when she gave him a huge smile.

They arrived more than fifteen minutes before the film began, but her impatience already got the best of her. "Come on! Hurry up." She hustled him along and went ahead of him. "You're so slow."

"Do you want some popcorn?" He started toward the concession stand.

"No!" She turned back and dragged him by the arm back toward the theater. "We have no time. We don't want to miss the opening scene. And who eats popcorn when watching Shakespeare?"

The movie began with Caesar's triumphant return to Rome after the Battle of Munda. Right away, the audience was treated to an elaborate set depicting the ancient city. The cast, too, impressed by delivering strong performances worthy of the Bard's beloved masterpiece. The film would have been superb on these strengths alone, but when Dean Graham made his first appearance as Brutus, he took the production to a whole different level. His acting skills surpassed all the others. His magnetic presence kept the audience's eyes firmly fixed on the screen.

Anthony had never seen Dean Graham before except in the photo in Tessa's room. The actor exuded a passionate and intense energy, but at the same time, exhibited an air of reservation. For Anthony, these qualities felt oddly familiar. He looked at Tessa in the next seat and began to understand how she got to be the way she was.

He turned his eyes back to the screen. Dean Graham was without a doubt an attractive man. His soulful eyes, full of depth and emotions, drew the viewers in like an enigma. When he smiled, he seemed to be hiding a secret.

Anthony watched in awe. This unusual man was Tessa's father? He looked at her again. She definitely inherited her father's looks. From her hair, to her eyes, to her smile, which always carried a hint of mischief, she resembled her father in so many ways.

As if she felt she was being watched, she turned toward him and gave him a quizzical look. "What?" She mouthed the word.

"Nothing," he whispered and returned to the movie. His mind was no longer on the film.

About Tessa, don't you find her attractive? Not at all? Mary had asked him.

At the time, the thought hadn't crossed his mind. But if Tessa was like her father, then surely she would grow up to be a stunning beauty.

#

"Did you enjoy that?" Tessa asked Anthony as they drove home after the movie.

"I did. Thanks for inviting me."

"I'm glad it took you away from moping around the house. You've taken over the den. I can't even go in there to listen to music because I'm afraid I would bother you."

"I haven't been moping."

She stifled a smile. "Okay. If you say so."

"What about you? Did you enjoy it?" he asked.

She didn't answer at first. He took a quick glance at her.

"I haven't seen my father in two years. This was as close as I could get to seeing him in person."

He wished he could say something to console her, but he knew nothing could. He tried to divert her mind to something else instead. "You stopped going to Murphy's?"

"Yes."

"Did you go there a lot?"

"I did. For a while."

"Why did you like going there anyway?"

She gazed out the front window. They had driven out of the city and were cruising along the Gold Coast by the lake. From the car, she could see the Edgewater Hotel towering over the beach and the other buildings nearby. She thought about last summer when she had gone to Murphy's to give her winning ticket to Jack so he could take Carmina to the Edgewater instead of her.

She thought about why she went to Murphy's. Mainly, she went because Jack was there. Then Jack left. She kept going anyway and she never asked herself why. Now, thinking about it, she thought she probably kept going because of Nadine. Nadine was the only adult here who understood her.

"A lot of reasons." She rested her elbow on the rim of the passenger's side window and held her head in her hand. "It's fun to go to a place that I know would shock the sensibilities of the nuns at St. Mary's."

"It's not the safest place for a girl to be. What if something terrible had happened to you?"

"Are you planning to lecture me again? I told you I can take care of myself."

"Like you took care of yourself at the dance hall?" He laughed.

She pouted and looked out her side of the window. "Nothing would happen to me. Nadine watches out for me."

"Nadine?"

"She's the head bartender there. Everyone at Murphy's listens to her."

Anthony thought back to the night at the tavern. "Is she the woman with red hair?"

"Yes."

He remembered her. That woman had come up to him and Tessa when they left the bar and insinuated he was causing Tessa trouble.

"Why do you have that look on your face?" Tessa asked.

"What look?"

"You're scowling. Your forehead and eyebrows were all scrunched up when I mentioned Nadine. Why?"

He wasn't aware he was doing that. "I don't know. I guess she probably isn't the type of woman you should associate with."

"And what type of woman is that?" she asked, her voice wary and guarded.

"I...it's...she's..." The word he was thinking of was "loose," but he couldn't bring himself to say something derogatory about a woman.

Tessa watched as he struggled to explain himself. She had an idea of what he wanted to say. People, "good people," always made assumptions about women like Nadine. It disappointed her that Anthony was no exception, but she was glad he at least still showed respect. He was so decent, he couldn't even say aloud what he thought. She wondered how much it would shock his mind if he knew the types of women she had grown up seeing, like the two-bit actresses who flaunted their sex appeal to try to get roles, and the shameless women who trotted before her father hoping to catch his attention. Compared to those women, Nadine was as pure as a vestal virgin. Amused by his simplistic view of right and wrong, she sat back and enjoyed watching the strained expression on his face.

In the end, he only said, "I'm glad you're not around her so much now."

She shrugged and looked out the window.

But then he added, "You're too young. She might not be a good influence on you."

She glowered at him. The way he treated her like a child and always had an opinion on what she should or should not do annoyed her to no end. She started to talk back, but the sight of the small beach area ahead gave her a better idea.

"Anthony, look!" she said, pointing to the beach. "Can we please pull over and stop there for a moment? Let's get out for a breath of fresh air."

"It's late."

"Please? Just a quick stop? Look at the beautiful moonlight reflecting off the lake."

He glanced over to the spot where she was pointing. The view of the beach was indeed very nice. She looked at him with pleading eyes. Not wanting to be too disagreeable after a pleasant night, he conceded. "Okay, a quick stop. Then we have to get on home because it's late."

"Of course." She gave him a big smile.

He stopped the car at the parking area behind the beach. No other car was there besides theirs. At this hour of the night, the beach was deserted.

She got out, took a deep breath, and walked toward the secluded side of the beach concealed from the road by a cluster of trees. He followed. The ambiance of the night and the soft sounds of the waves soothed him. The night air blowing in from the water was cool and crisp. He could see the clear view of the reflection of the moon glowing on the dark, calm water.

Tessa had gone on ahead of him. Halfway to the edge of the beach, she turned around. "It's a beautiful night, isn't it?"

He smiled. She walked a few more steps ahead, then started to take off her dress.

Confused, he squinted his eyes. When he realized she was undressing, he asked, "What are you doing?"

"I'm going for a swim," she said, nonchalantly as if she had said she was going to take a walk. She dropped her dress on the ground and took off her underwear.

"Tessa!" he stopped and shouted. "Put your clothes back on!"

"I can't. I want to swim and I don't want to get my clothes wet."

"Tessa!" He shouted again, frantic. "You're out of your mind!"

She ignored him and started toward the water. He looked away. He didn't know where to look.

"Tessa, come on! That's enough. This is not funny. Get back here and put your clothes back on. Please! I'm begging you."

She stepped into the water. She could hear him shouting and hollering behind her. She bit her lip and snickered to herself. She wondered what type of girl he thought she was now, or, would he still dare to talk to her as if she was some naive child. *No matter,* she thought. *Serves him right.* She waded in deeper and slid into the lake.

On the beach, Anthony couldn't decide if he should walk any further. He was afraid if he went any closer, he might see more of her. He turned his back to the beach, but they were out here alone and it was dark. He feared something might happen to her. He turned back toward the water and watched her continue her nonsense. Before she immersed her body into the water, he could see her naked silhouette under the shining moonlight. His breath quickened.

He watched her swim back and forth, sliding through the soft waves like an ethereal sylph in the water.

"Don't you want to come in too?" she called out from the water. "Isn't swimming your forté?"

Flustered, he tightened his fists and walked a few steps forward. "Enough, Tessa. It's dangerous swimming in the lake in the dark. Please! Come back already," he shouted. "If you don't come out now I'll tell Father you got us into a fight. I'll tell him everything!"

She stood up from the water and reveled at the sight of him standing there agitated and not knowing what to do. It made her laugh so hard, her stomach hurt.

When she recovered herself, she got out of the water and picked up her clothes. Still naked, she walked toward him. He took a step back and turned his face away from her.

"Would you please relax?" she said. "What's wrong with you? Have you never seen a naked woman before?"

"Stop playing around," he said, his head still turned away. "You're sixteen. You're not a woman."

"How would you know? You aren't even looking at me." She put her dress back on and went back to the car.

Entirely embarrassed, he returned to the car and drove away.

Heading home, he held tight onto the steering wheel. He could not believe she would trick him this way. He wanted to tell her what she did was reckless and reprehensible, but her dress was soaked and he could see the curves of her body and her undergarments beneath the wet, clinging fabric. Her hair was drenched too. His heartbeat quickened every time he glanced at her. As the night wind blew through the car windows, he could smell a faint scent of sweet rose perfume from her dress flowing in the air.

When they arrived home, all the lights of the house were off except for the porch light. His parents must have already gone to sleep. He breathed a sigh of relief. He didn't want them to see him coming in with Tessa all wet and her dress practically transparent.

He parked on the circular driveway and they got out. Before heading inside, she came up close to him and whispered to his ear, "Will you tell Uncle William about tonight too?"

She walked away with a devilish smile on her face.

How could she? He stood by his car for a long while after she had gone back into the house.

Chapter 35

At breakfast the next morning, Anthony had every intention of letting Tessa know he was displeased. Her behavior last night was out of line beyond words. The girl had no concept of the boundaries between right and wrong. She had made him lose all sense of decency. This could not be. She must understand she could not do this to him again.

Good thing his mother had gone to a ladies' breakfast. He couldn't face his mother this morning with Tessa there.

His father had just finished eating and opened the newspaper to enjoy his coffee when Tessa walked in.

"Good morning, Uncle William," she said, bright and cheerful as if nothing out of the ordinary had happened.

"'G'morning, Tessa." William greeted her and returned to his newspaper.

She took a seat across from Anthony and stared straight at him. "Good morning, Anthony." She made a point of talking directly to him, all the while taunting him with a smug, winner's look on her face.

He was about to give her a stern look of admonishment. But the moment he looked at her, only one thought remained in his head.

I saw her naked...He wanted to dig a hole and bury himself in it.

"Is everything okay, Anthony?" William asked. "You look flushed. Are you ill?"

Anthony stared down at his plate. "I'm fine."

William looked at Tessa. She looked back at him and shrugged, her expression innocent.

Anthony stuffed the rest of his breakfast down. "Excuse me," he muttered and hurried out of the room. He could feel Tessa's eyes following him, still smirking as if this was all a funny joke.

#

He could no longer look directly at her. For days after the night at the beach, Anthony could not look at Tessa without thinking thoughts he knew he shouldn't. Whenever he saw her, the memory of her standing on the beach would return. He felt paralyzed at the thought of her silhouette under the moonlight as she turned around and smiled. The fragrance of the faint scent of her perfume lingered in his mind, refusing to let him forget.

Stop. He told himself. This was not right. He shouldn't think about her this way.

But he couldn't stop. When he closed his eyes, he could see her on the dance floor, her skirt swirling and flying up high. The fast movements of her legs sent his heart racing.

As if drawn by an invisible force, he came to the room on the third floor that was now her studio. Her artwork lay around all over in no discernible order. Most visible was the large canvas drying on the table against the wall on the left side of the room. It showed the West End bustling with people crowding a theater entrance.

The smaller painting next to it provided a diametrical contrast. In it, William and Sophia were strolling down the quiet, idyllic street outside of their home. He smiled when he saw that she had painted his parents, and came in closer to take a better look. She did a fine job depicting his father and mother.

In the back of the room, he found her less successful creations. Abandoned pieces of half-finished illustrations and failed attempts at abstract cubism spread on the floor on top of each other. He smiled again. He could imagine the grudging look on her face when she couldn't achieve the results she had wanted.

On the floor on the right side leaning against the old bookshelf was the painting he saw last time, the one with the redheaded woman and her lover entwined in an erotic embrace. The painting was finished. He recognized the woman now. Nadine. The bartender at Murphy's.

What went through Tessa's mind when she painted this? Did the woman named Nadine tell her about these things? Did Tessa truly understand what she had painted? He studied the two people in the painting again. There was so much passion in the way they looked at each other. How was she able to so artfully capture their emotions?

As his eyes traced the curves of Nadine's body in the painting, his thoughts returned to the lines of Tessa's body that night at the beach.

No. He turned away from the illicit image in the painting. What was she working on now? He looked to the center of the room. On the easel was a painting of waves. Not large or violent waves, but gentle, soft waves that appeared to be moving, beckoning him to come closer and reach out to touch the water's smooth, slippery surface. Below it, a deep, seductive undercurrent tumbled and flowed, pulling him in. He touched the foam of the waves with his fingertip. He could almost feel the water enveloping him, whirling and gliding around every part of him. He closed his eyes. The image of the waves and water in his mind transformed into Tessa herself. He could almost feel the smoothness of her skin as she embraced him and her legs slid down his body.

He snapped his eyes open. What was he thinking? How could he think of her that way?

Quickly, he left the room. This was not right. His family had a duty to guard her and he must respect her. He could not lose control of himself. He hurried downstairs to get away, but it was useless. The speck of desire within him was growing and it wouldn't stop tapping at his heart.

# # #

For Tessa, being around Anthony had become absolutely impossible.

He wouldn't talk to her. He avoided her when he saw her. If they must be in the same room, he would stay as far away as he could from her.

Did he think that badly of her? All she did was play a prank on him. She only meant to shake him off his high horse and mess with his mind. It was high time someone showed him what a prude he was. Besides, he deserved it, after his criticism of Nadine and the way he kept telling her what was or was not good for her. She showed him she knew how to break the rules of decency on her own without Nadine. She showed him he didn't know anything.

But she never meant for things to become this awkward. Not only did he keep his distance, the way he looked at her was so odd. Sometimes she would catch him staring at her. If she looked back at him, he would frown and look away.

Did seeing her without her clothes on traumatize him that much?

By God. Maybe he really hadn't ever seen a girl naked before.

Or maybe he now thought she was one of "those" women. The type of women who, as he said, one "shouldn't associate with."

If he thought that, then he was the one with the problem. Good thing her own friends, Ruby, Nadine, Henry, and Jack and his friends weren't close-minded and judgmental like him.

# # #

Returning from his jog, Anthony slowed down in front of the driveway entrance to his home to rest his legs. Saturday mornings were the best. The streets were quiet and devoid of people. A warm summer breeze blew past him, carrying with it the fragrance of the roses in their garden. He took a deep breath and soaked up the sweet, pleasant scent.

In the memorial garden, Tessa was kneeling on the ground picking flowers to take to the hospital again. His mind told him to stay away and go back to the house, but the sight of her compelled him to walk toward her. She looked so different now than the child he saw the first time they met. She had grown taller. All hints of her juvenile awkwardness had disappeared. When she tucked her hair back behind her ear, she moved with such graceful softness, he couldn't take his eyes off her.

She looked so beautiful.

He came up next to her. "Do you want some help?"

She looked up. Her cheeks, flushed from the work and the summer heat, looked so ripe, he wanted to reach out and touch her face.

"Sure." She looked slightly surprised that he was talking to her, then smiled. She even looked happy to see him. "Here." She picked up a bundle of flowers off the ground. "I already scraped the thorns off these. Would you wrap them up? Five stems in each bundle?"

"Okay." He began wrapping up the flowers with the tissue papers she had laid on the ground. His heart raced being so close to her. Unable to look her in the face, he kept his eyes on the flowers.

"Ouch!" she cried out and startled him. "I pricked myself."

She held up her finger. A drop of blood oozed from where the thorn had pricked her. Without thinking, he took her hand, wiped off the blood, and put her finger in his mouth. He only meant to help her clean her wound, but in that instant, he felt as if he had just kissed her. Shocked at what he had done, he froze, unaware he was tightening his grip on her hand.

"What?" she asked, her voice confused and worried. "What's the matter? Why are you looking at me like that?"

He let go of her hand. An awkward silence hung between them. Her face reddened and she looked away from him. "I'm almost done. I'll finish up inside." She picked up all the flowers and started to walk away.

"Tessa, wait!" He grabbed her arm and pulled her back. She stared at him, but he had no idea what to say. He had an urge to pull her into his arms, but he was afraid of what might happen if he did. He might frighten her, or…she might laugh at him.

Still holding his breath, he let go of her arm. She took an uncertain step back, her eyes confused.

"I'll see you later." She turned to leave.

He watched her rush away with the batch of roses in her arms. Could this really be happening, the way he felt? Would she ever accept him?

Could it be possible, the two of them?

#

The uncomfortable silence between them continued at dinner that evening. Anthony could not bring himself to look at Tessa again. Tessa, too, avoided direct eye contact with him. He wished his father wasn't out at a business dinner. With just him, Tessa, and his mother at the dining table, the awkwardness between Tessa and him was too obvious. But if his mother had noticed anything, she didn't let on that she knew.

"Katherine's preparing for the Passavant Cotillion." Sophia passed the dish of green beans around the table. "The Passavant Cotillion is Chicago's annual debutante ball, Tessa, in case you haven't heard. Katherine plans to enroll in ballroom dancing classes. She and her friends are talking about signing up for etiquette classes too."

"Hmm." Tessa mumbled and reached for a piece of bread.

"Anna wanted me to ask you if you might be interested in joining them."

"Joining them for what? Ballroom dancing class or etiquette class?" She asked Sophia, still avoiding any eye contact with Anthony. "I already know how to dance. My father taught me. I can do the tango and the foxtrot. I don't know about etiquette class, although I'm sure Uncle Leon and Aunt Anna probably think I should enter and stay there until I turn thirty."

Anthony smiled. He noticed she didn't mention the jitterbug.

"Join them to go to the debutante ball," Sophia said.

Tessa put her hand over her mouth, nearly choking on her food.

"Katherine has started looking for her dress. It could be a fun experience."

Anthony glanced up from his plate. Would Tessa go? He wondered. If she went, would someone she knew from her swing dancing escort her? The thought was enough for him to hope she would say no.

"No," Tessa said firmly without a second thought. "No, I have no interest."

He smiled again, but then disappointment hit him. What if she had decided to go and needed someone to escort her? Now she didn't need an escort.

"Well, let me know if you change your mind," Sophia said, but didn't push her any further.

"I'm sure Katherine will look beautiful at the Ball," Tessa said.

"I think you would look better." Sophia poured herself more water. "You have your father's stage presence. I think you would make a grand entrance like no one else."

She would look better. He imagined Tessa walking into the Cotillion in a formal evening gown. What a shame they wouldn't have a chance to see her that way.

"And we would have some wonderful photos to send to your parents," Sophia continued.

"Oh, no. That would be the last thing I want. If my father sees me all dressed up in a frilly ball gown like a socialite, he would laugh at me."

But she looks so stunning when she dresses up. Anthony thought. He remembered again how alluring she looked in the red dress she wore at the Melody Mill.

Perhaps feeling his eyes on her, she glanced at him. This time, he dared to look back, but she didn't seem to understand. She lowered her eyes and turned her face away.

Could it be possible, the two of us? he thought again. From the way she reacted, he didn't think he had much hope.

After dinner, Sophia pulled Anthony aside to speak alone with him. "Is everything all right with you and Tessa? Are you two bickering again?"

"No." Anthony denied. "We're not bickering."

"Then why are you two acting so strange around each other?"

"We're not." He put on as honest a face as he could.

"You're sure nothing's wrong?"

"I'm sure."

Sophia studied his face. "Okay. If you say so, I'll believe you. But if something is wrong, you should resolve it quickly. I don't want her to feel uncomfortable living here."

"Yes, Mother," he said and left without giving her any more chance to ask questions.

Back in his room, he lay down on his bed with his hands clasped behind his head. His mother was right. He couldn't take chances with Tessa. She lived here. It would not do if she felt uncomfortable living with them because of him.

He looked at his door. Her room was only a few feet behind it across the hallway.

So close and yet there was nothing he could do.

PART ELEVEN
Cadet Nurse

Chapter 36

Tessa knew something was wrong when Aunt Sophia told her Ruby was on the phone. Ruby didn't have a telephone at her home, and it was too early in the day for her to be at work or at the USO club where she usually made her calls.

"Hello?" Tessa said into the receiver.

"Tessa…" Ruby's voice was shaking.

"Ruby? Are you all right? Where are you calling from?"

"I'm calling from the Chicago Veterans Hospital. Jack's back."

"Jack's back?" Tessa didn't understand. "What do you mean Jack's back?"

"He's back and he's at the Veterans Hospital."

"The Veteran's Hospital…" The implications of what Ruby said dawned on her and she felt a chill shooting up her spine. "Is he okay?" She was afraid to ask.

"He's…" Ruby's voice trailed off and she could hear Ruby crying on the other end of the phone.

"Ruby? Ruby?" she cried into the receiver. "Wait for me. I'm coming." She hung up the phone, grabbed her purse, and ran out of the house to head to the hospital.

#

Tessa rushed to the Veterans Hospital as fast as she could. Once inside, she slowed her steps. The closer she came to where Jack was, the less she was able to move forward. Her heart palpitated and each step became harder and heavier. She feared finding out what had happened to him.

She came to a large room filled with patients. For a moment, her mind went into a state of confusion and she could not immediately process what she saw. As she looked at all the disabled patients with arms and legs amputated lying on the rows of beds, she felt an odd dissociation from the scene. This could not be real. This was not real. How could it be that someone she cared so deeply about was here? There must have been a mistake. She clutched her purse. She couldn't recognize anyone here. The noises around her buzzed and her vision blurred. She felt dizzy. She wanted to turn around and leave, to run and make this all go away.

She closed her eyes and counted to five. When she opened her eyes again, she felt slightly more grounded. She looked around, searching until she saw Henry's bushy red hair on the far left side of the room. His mother and Ruby were with him. Janie, the girlfriend of Jack's friend Fred, was there too. Janie had her arm around Mrs. Morrissey.

Tessa stood frozen in the middle of the room. She could not take another step ahead. Thankfully, Ruby saw her and came to her. "Tessa!"

"When did he come back?"

"Yesterday. I only found out myself this morning that he had gotten back. Henry came and told me. Then I told Janie and we rushed over here. I called you as soon as I could."

"How is he?" Tessa asked in a small voice. "What happened?"

"He was severely wounded." Ruby turned around and looked at the bed where Jack lay. "His left leg is all messed up and shredded by shrapnel. They operated on him again earlier. The nurses said he had operations on site where he got hurt but they couldn't complete all the surgeries he needed because the Americans had to evacuate the Philippines. That's all I know. Henry and his mother are so upset, I don't want to ask them any more questions."

"So he'll be fine, right? He's fine and everything will be fine, right?" Tessa asked.

Ruby pressed down her lips. "His other wounds and injuries will heal. His leg though…the doctor said he'll probably have to use a brace for the rest of his life. If he's lucky, he might recover enough and he'll only have to use a cane. They said they won't know for certain. Not for a long time."

Tessa felt dizzy again.

"Are you all right?" Ruby took hold of her arm.

"Yes," Tessa inhaled to steady herself. "Can I see him?"

Ruby nodded. "He's asleep."

They walked to his bed. Tessa's eyes immediately trained on Jack. Seeing him peacefully asleep, she felt slightly better. Henry glanced up at her, too sad to say a word. Next to him, Mrs. Morrissey sobbed. The older woman, normally tough and sturdy after years of hard work, now looked small and frail as Janie tried to comfort her. Janie didn't look much better. Fred was drafted three months ago. Jack's return this way surely must have added to her worries.

"He's such a good boy," Mrs. Morrissey wiped her tears with a handkerchief. "He's been through so much already. Why? Why does this have to happen to him? It's so unfair."

Janie pulled Mrs. Morrissey closer and stroked her arm, trying to soothe her. Mrs. Morrissey leaned her weakened body against Janie.

Tessa couldn't bear to look at them. She felt tears welling in her own eyes.

In the bed, Jack stirred and opened his eyes.

"Jack!" Mrs. Morrissey grabbed hold of his arm.

"Jack! Jack!" Henry cried out.

Groggy from the sedative, Jack nonetheless smiled. "Why do you all look so somber?" He pushed himself to sit up on the bed.

"Jack." Mrs. Morrissey sat down next to him. "What have they done to you?" She hugged him close to her chest.

Jack raised his arm and hugged her back. Weak from his medication, he couldn't hold her for long. "Don't cry, Mom. I'm fine. I'm fine."

Henry, too, had tears rolling down his face. Tessa turned her face away.

"Why are you all crying? I'm alive, and I'm back."

Mrs. Morrissey sniffled and calmed down a little.

"He's right, Mrs. Morrissey." Janie put her hand on the older woman's shoulder. "We should all be glad for that."

"He's only twenty years old," Mrs. Morrissey cried again. "He'll be crippled for the rest of his life. Why? They've ruined him."

"Mom, please don't," Jack said. "I still have my leg. See?" He pulled off his blanket to show his leg wrapped in a cast. Tessa looked around the room. At least half the patients in there had amputated limbs.

"This injury saved me." Jack rubbed the cast on his leg. "We lost the Philippines. The Japs took Manila. In May, our entire battalion surrendered in Bataan. Seventy-five thousand people—Americans, Filipinos, men, women, didn't matter. Everyone became their prisoners of war. No one knows what happened to them. I got hurt just before that. The army treated me on the field and sent me to an evacuation hospital. Then I was on my way back here." He took his mother's hand. "I got out just in time. If I hadn't gotten injured and been sent back, I would've been taken prisoner along with the rest of them."

Tessa felt her skin crawl. She hugged herself to rub the goosebumps off her arms.

"See, Mrs. Morrissey?" Janie said. "There is a blessing in all of this. Everything will be okay." A tear dropped down Mrs. Morrissey's tightened lips. It was a good thing Janie was here and could comfort the poor woman. Tessa couldn't think of anything to say to make anyone feel better.

"I won't go away again, Mom. I promise," Jack said.

Two nurses came in to make their rounds. They started hustling families and friends out. Visitors' hours were over.

"You should go home and get some rest, Mrs. Morrissey." Janie patted the old woman's back and steered her to leave.

"Yes, Mom. Go home. I'll be fine." Jack put on a cheery smile.

"I'm sorry, Jack." Mrs. Morrissey dabbed her eyes. "You're the one injured and you have to turn around and console me. I don't know what's wrong with me."

"That's all right. I'll be home soon and everything will be just as it used to be. Hey, Henry." He eyed his younger brother to signal him to look out for their mother. "Why are you so quiet? Did you drive here? Take Mom home and make sure she gets some rest."

Shame-faced, Henry answered, "Yes."

"Oh, Jack, I wanted to tell you," Janie said before they left. "Fred and I got married." She held out her left hand to show him the gold ring on her finger.

"You two got hitched? That's great news! Congratulations."

"We wrote to tell you but you probably didn't get the letter."

"I'm thrilled. Say, where is he?"

Janie gave him a bittersweet smile. "He was drafted three months ago. We got married before he left for basic training."

Jack's face fell. But quickly, he brightened up again. "Don't worry. He's a tough guy. He'll make it out okay."

The nurses were now yelling at everyone to leave. Henry and Ruby helped Mrs. Morrissey gather her things and Janie led Mrs. Morrissey out. The poor woman had lost all her strength.

Quickly, Tessa came to Jack's bedside. "I'll be back tomorrow to see you."

He nodded. She glanced at his leg in the cast, then reluctantly walked out of the room.

After saying goodbye to everyone in the lobby, Tessa couldn't hold herself together anymore. The reality of what had happened finally set in. Her legs felt weak and she leaned her back against the wall for support. The thought of how close Jack had come to being taken prisoner made her tremble. She bowed her head and put her wrist on her forehead. Tears fell uncontrollably down her face.

She thought of all the good times they had together. How quick and smooth he was when they danced. Now, his body was broken and would never be the same. He was crippled for life.

...He will never dance again...

A sharp pain seared through her heart. She could do nothing but cry and hyperventilate between her tears.

When she got a hold of herself again, she went to the restroom and splashed water on her face. Looking into the mirror, she vowed she would help Jack any way she could, except she didn't know how.

Slowly, she walked back into the hospital lobby toward the exit. She felt drained and wooden. On the hospital bulletin board, a large poster showing a young woman in military uniform bore down at her.

"Join the U.S. Cadet Nurse Corps."

She stared at the poster.

Written in smaller print below, "Enlist in a proud profession. Your country needs you."

While she stared at the poster, a nurse and a medic pushed a patient on a rolling hospital bed toward her. She moved out of the way to let them pass. The patient, sedated, had no arms. She looked on at the ghastly sight.

After they were gone, she looked at the poster again.

"We can use more recruits," someone said to her from behind. She turned around. A young nurse with blonde hair and warm, gentle eyes came up to her. She looked about twenty. "I'm Ellie Swanson. I'm a student nurse here. I'm in my last year of training." Ellie held out her hand. Tessa took it, but felt unsure.

"Every hospital in the country is experiencing an acute shortage of nurses. A lot of experienced nurses have gone overseas since the war started. There aren't enough nurses at home. The injured veterans are returning, and civilian patients still need help. Student nurses are covering most of the work at home. We can use a lot more volunteers." Ellie pulled a flyer from a stack on the shelf under the bulletin board and gave it to Tessa. "Take this. Go home and think about it." The young nurse smiled and walked away.

Tessa held the flyer in her hand.

A group of young nurse trainees in military uniforms passed by the lobby on their way out of the hospital. They looked so sharp, so purposeful.

She looked at the flyer. The training program at the Veterans Hospital would begin next month. If she worked here, she could see Jack every day. Maybe even take care of him.

A dozen thoughts ran through her mind. As she stepped out of the hospital, the world seemed different. The city no longer felt like a transient stop where she waited for time to pass. Something new had found her, calling to her. If she would only reach out, she could grasp it.

Chapter 37

In the week that followed, Tessa visited Jack every day, but she never had a chance to talk to him alone. Someone else was always there. His mother came every day. Henry changed his shifts at Murphy's so he could come with his mother. Ruby and Janie came as often as they could too. They brought him all his favorite foods and magazines. Mr. Murphy sent him several bottles of beer. Henry even brought Monopoly and they played the board game with him. Tessa brought him a new deck of cards to play with the other patients. All in all, Jack seemed to be in high spirits.

While visiting him, Tessa could not help noticing the other patients around them. A few had such horrific, disfiguring injuries, she couldn't look directly at them. At least they had friends or families. No one ever visited the one with bandages wrapped around his head covering his eyes. She wondered if his injuries had blinded him, but she dared not ask. As for the rest, a number of them needed wheelchairs and crutches to move around. She had never seen so many people with lost limbs in one room, and all the patients looked not much older than her.

Thank goodness Jack still had his leg, but even he would never be the same as before.

So many healthy bodies blown apart. So many young men permanently scarred. Why didn't anyone talk about this? For all the talk of war she had heard at home or on the radio, she could not recall anyone ever discussing the wounded. Even her own mother, who must have seen numerous injured British soldiers in the last two years, hadn't said a thing about this in her letters. Did her mother avoid the subject so as not to scare and upset her? Was her mother still trying to shield her from the horrors of war? She didn't want to be shielded anymore.

Back in her room, Tessa sat at her desk with the Cadet Nurse Corps flyer in front of her. She must have read it twenty, maybe thirty times.

When she was a little girl, she used to play dress-up as a nurse to imitate her mother, but the idea of actually becoming one herself never entered her mind. She never had her mother's natural warmth and sympathetic touch toward strangers. The occupation required constant interaction with too many people and she liked her solitude too much.

But what else would she want to do? She couldn't be an actor like her father either. She didn't have an ounce of acting talent in her. St. Mary's offered no guidance on the matter. For all its prestige and reputation, she couldn't think of anything she was learning there that could be useful for anything. Of course, people didn't attend a school like St. Mary's to prepare themselves for work. The girls went there to learn to become suitable wives of men that society deemed to be of great importance. When she thought of that, a cynical smile crept up her face.

Immediately, she felt ashamed. What entitled her to harbor such disdain for her school and classmates? Beyond helping out with a few metal scrap drives, what had she done that she could regard herself better than the other St. Mary's girls? She looked down on them, and yet, when she considered what she was doing with her life, she was one of them in every way except for her attitude.

She thought of her parents. While they had spared her from the terror of the Blitz, her mother had volunteered with several groups to rebuild London. Her father toured the country and beyond for the British troops. Jack had already made a huge sacrifice having gone off to fight. And Ellie Swanson, the young nurse who gave her the flyer, was helping those like him who had come back.

What was she doing still wasting time at St. Mary's?

She read the flyer again. Maybe she would never be as great a nurse as her mother, but if she could help all the people like the ones she saw at the Veterans Hospital, surely it was a more worthwhile way to live than hiding in the protective shell where everyone had placed her.

Once she made up her mind, she took her stationery out of her drawer and wrote a letter to her parents.

Downstairs, she found Uncle William and Aunt Sophia in the den. Uncle William was reading the evening newspaper while Aunt Sophia listened to her favorite mystery detective program.

"Want to join us, Tessa?" Sophia asked. Tessa took a seat across from them while trying to think of the best way to broach the subject.

"What is it?" William asked. "Is there something you want to tell us?"

She mustered her nerves and said. "I don't want to go back to St. Mary's this fall."

"You want to stop going to school?" Sophia turned off the radio.

"Not exactly." Tessa handed her the nurse recruitment flyer. "I want to join the Cadet Nurse Corps instead. They offer a training program for nurses at the Veterans Hospital."

Sophia scanned the flyer, then gave it to William. Although Sophia looked surprised and worried, William smiled. When he looked up, a nostalgic spark lit up his eyes. "Your mother always had her own ideas of what she wanted to do too," he said. "So you want to follow in your mother's footsteps?"

Tessa closed her hands. "I can only hope to ever be as good a nurse as she is."

"What brought on this idea?" Sophia gave her husband a reproachful look. There was still concern in her voice.

"I've been visiting the Veterans Hospital. I saw a lot of returning soldiers who need help. A student nurse there told me about this program. She said there's a dire shortage of nurses across the country because of the war. I want to do something to help."

William took his time and read the flyer. Tessa clasped her hands tighter, trying to read his expression.

"Knowing your mother, I don't see why she wouldn't approve," William said. Tessa's eyes lit up with hope. "But we should write to your parents first and ask for their opinion and permission."

"There's no time, Uncle William." Tessa leaned forward in her seat. "It's already mid-August. The next training program starts in September. I need to decide and apply now. I already wrote a letter to my parents. I'll post it tomorrow. I'm hoping you'll both approve."

Sophia took the flyer from her husband and read it again. "Are you sure this is what you want? Being a nurse is a serious commitment."

"I've thought about it all week. As long as you approve, this is what I want to do."

Sophia still had doubts. "But…"

William touched her lightly on her arm and stopped her. "We will have to make some inquiries about the program first," he said. "We want to make sure the program is worthwhile and you'll be working in an environment we feel comfortable with."

"You approve then?" Tessa asked, excited and relieved.

"Not so fast. Assuming the program is sound, I still have to discuss it with your Aunt Sophia. I will not allow it if she disagrees." He glanced at his wife with a teasing smile, clearly with the intention of inciting her reaction.

"William! You're putting me on the spot!"

He smiled at Tessa. She saw from his eyes he was already on her side.

"But even if Sophie agrees, we cannot allow it if your parents object in any way. If they disapprove, you will have to return to St. Mary's."

Tessa couldn't ask for more. "Thank you, Uncle William. Thank you, Aunt Sophia." She got up and gave Sophia a hug. Tessa never hugged anyone. Her unusual gesture of affection took Sophia by surprise and Sophia could only relent. "Of course."

Having achieved her aim, Tessa left the room quickly before Aunt Sophia could change her mind.

# # #

For Anthony, it was a welcome break when for once, discussions at home about the military didn't revolve around him. What he never expected was that their talk would center on Tessa. More than that, everyone left him entirely out of the conversation as if the matter was of no concern to him, like he had no part in Tessa's life. No one thought to ask his opinion. Nobody noticed how much that annoyed him either.

Tessa, especially, seemed to have all but forgotten about their night on the beach and everything that had happened between them since. Her new plan to become a cadet nurse occupied all her attention. How disappointing it was to know she thought so little of him, but her goal was noble. It would be petty to dwell on his own disappointment. Moreover, he couldn't very well begrudge it when, after so many discussions about him joining the military, Tessa became the one who actually ended up in service.

It was amazing to watch her. Since she made her decision, she had taken on a whole new persona. She had grown more thoughtful and serious. Her determination, her enthusiasm to serve, and her excitement about choosing her own path and following her own will, all made her look more attractive than ever. He wished he could tell her how much he admired what she was doing, except she and everyone else treated him like an afterthought in this whole matter. Why did everyone think he cared so little about her?

After Tessa left for the Veterans Hospital to submit her application, his mother brought up the subject of Tessa's departure from St. Mary's for the Cadet Nurse Corps again.

"Are you sure Dean and Juliet won't mind?" Sophia asked William.

"I don't see why they would," William said. "Juliet's a nurse herself. I don't think she ever thought Tessa would follow in her footsteps. She told me she thought Tessa might do something involving the theater since she and her father are so close."

Anthony stopped reading but didn't say anything, partly because he wanted to hear what his parents had to say, and partly because he was still annoyed no one had asked for his thoughts since this whole matter started.

"Maybe we should've enrolled her in another school instead of St. Mary's. I don't think she ever liked it there."

"We all knew it would be a difficult adjustment for her when she came," William said. "It was a good plan at the time. St. Mary's is academically superb, and she and Katherine are close in age. We thought they could be friends. Besides, we all thought she would be like Juliet, outgoing and sociable. We didn't know Tessa would be so different and so much like her father."

"Yes. Tessa can be a handful, that's for sure."

You don't know the half of it. Anthony thought to himself.

"And you," his mother jokingly reprimanded his father, "you indulge her. All those times she sneaked out of the house at night to go dancing, you never even tried to stop her. If something bad had happened to her, how would we ever explain ourselves to Dean and Juliet?"

Anthony put down his book. "How'd you know she went dancing?"

"We overheard her talking to her friend Ruby on the phone a few times," his mother said. "I wanted to ask her more about it but your father didn't want us to do that."

"You worry too much, Sophie." William stroked her back to comfort her. "Tessa's a very independent girl. She wouldn't stop doing something because someone told her not to. It's better we gain her trust and let her come to us if she's ever in trouble. Knowing Dean and Juliet, they wouldn't want their daughter to be over-protected."

Anthony thought back to all the times when he had told Tessa how she should conduct herself. How presumptuous he had been. He could've been more thoughtful like his parents in how he dealt with her.

"The dancing's harmless fun," William said. "It's what young people do. She's finding things she likes. If we restrict her from that, she'll be very unhappy here."

Why hadn't he considered that before? Anthony smiled to himself. What would make Tessa happy? What could he do to make her happy?

"Is that what you think? Harmless fun?" his mother said to his father. "Well, one day some boy's going to fall in love with her while she's having her harmless fun. Then you go ahead and explain to Dean what happened."

Anthony stopped smiling. Without saying anything, he picked up his book and left the room.

Chapter 38

After submitting her application for the Cadet Nurse Corps, Tessa went to the hospital room where Jack was staying. Visitors' hours wouldn't start for another hour, but no one was paying attention to her. She couldn't wait to tell Jack what she had just done.

She dallied near the patients' room until the hallway emptied, then scurried inside. Even though she was not authorized to be here, none of the patients minded her. She looked to the far end of the room toward Jack. Excited to see him awake and sitting up in his bed, she approached him. Her joy vanished when she saw the look on his face. Staring out the window, he looked as sad and lonely as she had ever seen him. His body lay deflated as if he had no strength or spirit. All last week, he had looked so cheerful in front of everyone. Was it all a facade?

She walked up quietly next to his bed.

"Tessa!" He looked up, surprised to see her. His expression quickly turned upbeat. "What are you doing here?"

It's all for show, she thought to herself. *He's acting happy so we won't worry about him.*

"I came to submit my application to become a cadet nurse." She sat down next to his bed. "I've decided to become one."

"Seriously? You didn't tell us."

283

"I only found out about the program last week, and I was undecided until a few days ago. So guess what? Starting in two weeks, I'll be coming here for classes and work." She looked at the door to check that no hospital staff or nurses were coming in, then she leaned closer to him and whispered, "I was on my way out but I took a detour to come see you."

"Thanks."

"How are you feeling?" She put her hand lightly on his injured leg.

"I'm getting better."

She looked silently at him. She had so many questions for him. He stared back at her, then lowered his eyes. "Don't look at me like that. I don't know how to take it."

She couldn't help herself. Her eyes still on him, she gathered up her nerve and asked, "When you were away, did you think about me?"

He hesitated, then looked her in the eyes. "All the time."

She tightened her hand on his cast.

"How could I not think about you after what happened the night before I left?" His voice softened. "Over there, I saw things I can't even talk about. When things got really bad, when everything got to be too much, it always helped me to think of you."

His answer was more than she had hoped for. She didn't think he felt the same way about her at all.

Just as her hopes were raised, he said, "But I can't think about any of that. Especially not now." He glanced at his wounded leg.

"It doesn't bother me," she said.

"It bothers me." His terse response and firm tone dashed her hopes. "If I'm with someone, I want to be able to take her to a better place and show her a better world. I couldn't have done that for you even before, and I definitely can't do that for you now. All I would do is drag you down. I'm sorry, Tessa. I can't give you what you want."

Tessa looked away from him to the floor. Why was it so important to him to take someone he loved to a better place? "Did you think about her?" She was afraid to ask, but she wanted to know.

"Sometimes. I tried not to." He looked at his leg in the cast again. "Some wounds never heal."

Her heart hurt, both for him and for herself.

"She's married now," he said. "She wrote and told me. I was the only one in my entire company to get a Dear John letter from an ex-girlfriend. It was like she broke up with me twice, and the second time I wasn't even her boyfriend anymore."

She tried to laugh with him, but couldn't. With his attempted joke fallen flat, he finally dropped all pretenses. "It doesn't matter anymore. I can't think about any of these things now. What I actually need to do is to figure out how I'm going to find a job when I leave the hospital. I won't be able to move around all that easily. I'm worried I won't find anyone to hire me. We might have to move too. I can't climb up and down three flights of stairs. With me not working, it'll be tough to find a new place for my family to live."

"Jack…" She felt horrible. He had serious life worries, and she didn't even think of that. All she thought about was her own feelings for him, her silly schoolgirl dreams. At last, she began to understand what he meant when he told her a year ago they were in different worlds. How stupid and insensitive she had been.

"Don't look so sad, Tessa." His smile returned.

She took his hand. She realized then that if she truly cared for him, she had to put aside her feelings for now and not add more burden to his already troubled mind.

"I'll be all right," he said. "I only told you all this because, I don't know why, you're the only one I can tell these things to."

She knew why. It was because his problems had no real impact on her life, whereas for his family, or even Janie and Ruby, his problems

285

would become their problems as they all depended on each other one way or another.

"Don't tell anyone what I told you," he said.

"I won't." She was glad he trusted her.

"Are we still good friends?"

"Of course, Jack!" she squeezed his hand. "Always."

Chapter 39

At orientation on the first day of class, Tessa sat quietly by herself in the back row and read the information packet given to each attendee. While she waited for the orientation program to begin, a new trainee, slightly chubby with curly hair, sat down next to her. "Hi. I'm Sarah Brinkman. What's your name?"

"Tessa Graham." Tessa wondered what she should say to the new girl. She never liked small talk with strangers.

Her worries turned out to be unnecessary as Sarah continued talking. "Nice to meet you. Where are you from? I was born in Chicago. I'm twenty years old. I have three brothers in the military. Dale is the oldest and in the Marines. Donald is a paratrooper, and David is in the army anti-aircraft unit. It didn't feel right for me to sit at home while they serve, so I joined the Cadet Nurse Corps. I love to bake. Especially pies. I can make a mean pecan pie. Do you like pecan pie?" she asked but never gave Tessa a chance to answer. "My mother's a school teacher and my father works for an advertising agency…"

Could this girl ever stop talking? Tessa wondered. In less than five minutes, Sarah had told her entire personal and family history. Thankfully, the hospital administrator entered the room and everyone quieted down as the orientation began.

Several nurse trainees entered the room with the hospital administrator. Tessa recognized one of them as Ellie Swanson, the young nurse she met a few weeks ago. When the administrator's welcome speech was over, Ellie surprised her by coming to the back of the room to greet her. She didn't think Ellie would remember her.

"I'm so glad you decided to join," Ellie said as she took hold of Tessa's hand. "What's your name?"

"Tessa. I'm Tessa Graham."

"I'm Sarah Brinkman," Sarah introduced herself. "How long have you been a trainee?" she asked Ellie. "Do you like it? Are the hours very long? I heard the hours may be very long. Well, as long as I still have time to bake, I don't mind. Do you plan to sign up for overseas assignment…"

"We'll get to all that," Ellie said and laughed. "First, let me take you around and show you the rest of the hospital. Come and follow me." Ellie brought them to the front of the room where all the new trainees were divided into groups to be taken on a tour of the facilities. Tessa was relieved to move on, but Sarah stuck by her side the entire time. When the tour ended, Tessa realized to her dismay that Sarah Brinkman had somehow decided they were new best friends. By the end of the morning, she had learned everything there was to learn about Dale, Donald, and David. She could write their biographies. She wondered how she could extract herself without being too rude.

At lunch time, Tessa changed her mind. She found herself seated among a group of new people, except here, keeping to herself like she always did at St. Mary's was not an option. At the hospital, she had to work with everyone. Having Sarah with her turned out to be a life-saving convenience. As long as Sarah kept talking, she didn't have to. Sarah relieved her from having to bear the suffering of being superficially social. Having Sarah by her side wasn't such a bad thing after all.

A few weeks later, the hospital staff had come to think of them as inseparable. People referred to them as the talkative one and the quiet one. Tessa didn't mind. By then, she had gotten used to Sarah's incessant talking. It had become background noise to her. The good thing about Sarah was, she never pried. She didn't seem to mind that Tessa, on her part, never told her anything. Or maybe she was too busy talking to notice Tessa never said much. Either way, the arrangement worked for Tessa.

The new environment suited her too. Here, no one gave a second thought to who she was or was not as long as she did her work. She even liked some of the people here, like Ellie Swanson. The way Ellie handled the patients reminded her of her mother. Ellie knew how to comfort the injured ones in pain and console the broken ones in sorrow. She could even appreciate Sarah. The veterans loved listening to Sarah's stories, especially when she brought them her famous pies.

The best thing was, being here, she could check in on Jack and make sure he had everything he needed.

She had made the right decision. She had finally found her purpose in Chicago.

PART TWELVE

Dream of Love

Chapter 40

Lying on the field of browning grass outside of his dorm, Anthony opened his text book on his lap and rested his head and back on his book bag. A fall breeze blew past and flipped the pages, breaking his concentration on his book. He looked up out at the sun shining on the field. Ordinarily on a day like this, male students would be out playing a game of pick-up football. Today, only female students strolled by when they took walks between classes.

Sometimes, he wondered what he was still doing here. Last winter, he had resolved to enlist after Pearl Harbor. His father had persuaded him to wait until the overcapacity at the Army training camps eased. Since the summer, the glut of volunteers for enlistment had dropped. If he wanted, now would be a sensible time to follow through, except for one thing that was holding him back.

The autumn wind blew again and the tree branches around him swayed. The yellowing tree leaves fluttered and fell to the ground. He closed his eyes and thought of the night when he and Tessa drove home after the beach, when the summer breeze blew through the car windows, carrying with it the faint scent of rose perfume.

He had left home to return to school without even saying a proper goodbye to her. At the time, he felt as awkward as ever around her. If she was someone he had just met, it would be so much easier. He wished they could start over and he could introduce himself anew. As it was now, she would probably laugh at him. She probably thought he was a close-minded prig.

Or worse, she didn't think of him. She certainly didn't seem like she did. The two weeks before he returned to school, all she could talk about was becoming a cadet nurse at the Veterans Hospital.

What if he told her how he felt?

His mother had warned him not to make her feel uncomfortable living with them.

What if he told her how he felt and enlisted and went away? If he was gone, she wouldn't have to feel uncomfortable. If she laughed at him and he made a fool of himself, then at least he could go off to do something honorable and regain some dignity. And if by some miracle, she didn't laugh at him…

Across the field, two military vehicles parked alongside the road. The army officers exited the cars and entered their campus.

He opened the cover of his book. The small torn piece of paper with the address and phone number of the enlistment office stared back at him.

How much longer would he have until his draft number came up?

If it did, would she be there to send him off and promise to wait for him to return? If he had to go to war, could he have that small piece of happiness?

Maybe he could. After all, she chose to become a cadet nurse. Chances were, he would have to enter service at some point whether by enlisting or by conscription. Maybe she would think more highly of him if he were off to serve too.

In his heart, he knew he could not let this rest without at least trying. He wanted her. He had never wanted something and not acted on it. Besides, with conscription looming, he would regret it if he didn't let her know. If only he could find some way to let her know how much he wanted her to be the one waiting for him.

#

When Anthony returned for fall break in October, Tessa was glad he was acting normal around her again. He didn't avoid her or keep far away from her the way he had after that night at the beach. That was a relief. After all, he was Uncle William and Aunt Sophia's son. She had worried he might resent her presence in his own home. She didn't exactly want him to think she was some kind of abomination.

But then he started acting strange in another way. Now he was around her all weekend. Normally, he liked to study alone in his own room. When he saw her studying in the den, he came in there to study too. He even offered to drive her to class Friday morning. She told him she didn't need a ride and took the bus, which she did every day. When she started training to become a nurse at the hospital, Uncle William had offered to have his chauffeur drive her too, but she turned him down. All the other trainees came by public transportation. She didn't want to appear pompous.

The best news for her that weekend came from her parents. They wrote back and praised her decision to join the Cadet Nurse Corps.

"Father wished me good luck," she told everyone at dinner. "He said if he ever gets ill, he would now have two nurses to look after him. But Mother! Good Lord. She sent me ten pages' worth of advice. She sent medical books too, and she wants me to send her photos of me in my uniform."

"We can take photos," William said. "Let's make your mother happy."

"Ugh." Tessa made a face. "I don't want to make a big fuss."

"You can't deprive your mother of the chance to see you in a nurse's uniform," Sophia said. "She must be overjoyed you decided to take up her profession."

"Okay. One photo, maybe. I'll think about it, but I just know she will show it to all her friends at the hospital. It'll be so embarrassing with everyone talking about me."

Sophia smiled. Then, changing the subject, she turned to her son. "Anthony, how is Mary? Is she in Chicago this weekend? If she is, why don't you invite her here for dinner tomorrow night?"

"Mary?" He almost knocked over his water glass. "I'm not seeing her anymore." He steadied his glass and looked directly at Tessa.

He still blames me for that. Tessa twisted her lips and looked away.

"Oh," Sophia said, a bit surprised. "That's too bad. She's a nice girl."

Chapter 41

Fall break was over all too quickly. Anthony wished he had more time. All weekend long, Tessa remained oblivious to him and everything he did. If he could be around her longer, maybe he could find some way to make her see him differently. That, however, was not to be. The weekend had ended and he had to return to school. When he said goodbye to her before leaving, she barely raised her head.

He drove along the road. His mind wandered from thoughts of her, to classes, and to the next swimming competition, when he realized he had forgotten to take his Economics textbook back to school with him. He was already halfway to school. Although annoyed, he had no choice but to turn the car around back to his house.

The house was quiet when he returned. His parents had gone out for their Sunday afternoon walk. He picked up his book from his room and was coming down the stairs when the piano music flowed out of the parlor. Chopin. "Fantaisie Impromptu." As if under a spell, he sat down on the stairs to listen.

The music started off with the dramatic rush of fast notes, fiery and full of angst. It sounded like Tessa herself, brooding yet raging and wild. The next segment of softer and more delicate notes followed. That was like her too, when on occasion she showed her more sensitive side.

I want to treat you to a movie to thank you, but I can't do that if you won't leave the house. He smiled at the memory. She could be so sweet sometimes.

Then it dawned on him. It was all so obvious now. She wasn't nearly as hard to understand as she appeared. Everything about her, her feelings and who she was, were all in her artistic talents. She expressed herself not by words but by her music and her paintings.

The Chopin piece ended with dramatic fury like its beginning. After a brief pause, she moved on to another piece. He recognized the wondrous, tender opening notes at once. Franz Liszt. "Liebestraum."

He leaned on the stair rails and closed his eyes. The mesmerizing sound of the music drew him in. He got up and came to the entrance of the parlor. The rising dreamlike notes sailed across the air, each cadenza reached deeper and deeper into his soul.

Unaware that anyone was listening, Tessa played the piece with total abandon. "Liebestraum," also known as "Dream of Love." She had learned to play this when she was nine, but it took her quite some years before she was able to properly interpret it and make something distinctive out of it. In fact, her idea of how she wanted to convey this music had come to her only recently. During the hours when she made her painting of Nadine and Laurent, her perceptions and understanding of the music began to form. Once she discovered how she wanted to play it, she fell more in love with it than ever. It captured every fantasy she had about love.

She set her fingers on the keys, imagining the first cadenza as a serenade of two lovers during their first encounter. The soft, dreamlike beginning and the buildup of excitement symbolized their realization of falling in love. After the romantic beginning, a flurry of fast, dancing notes cascaded across the keyboard, creating what sounded like the flutters of a butterfly's wings and dazzling stars swirling in the new lovers' jubilant hearts.

The second cadenza repeated the same melodies. This time, the romantic opening sounds portrayed the lovers' embrace. The volume of the music grew, signifying their deepening kisses and caresses. The music intensified like lovers making heated, passionate love. Each string of melodies represented a movement of their bodies. The tempo surged with the escalating force of each beat until their passion ascended to a dramatic height, followed by a release of fast, tumbling notes which brought the lovers down from the pinnacle of rapture as they fell into a cloud of euphoric bliss. The third cadenza ended with delicate, loving tenderness like their gentle and radiant afterglow, and the lovers' whispers of eternal love.

Was passionate love really like that? She hoped that it was.

When she finished, she emerged from her concentration. This was as well as she had ever played this piece. Satisfied, she looked up. The unexpected sight of Anthony standing at the parlor entrance watching her startled her.

"I thought you left!" Her face burned at the thought of him listening to the way she had played this song.

"I did, but I forgot my book so I had to come back and get it." He threw his jacket down on the couch, held up his Economics textbook to show her, and walked over to her. "I was on my way out again and I heard you playing, so I stayed and listened."

She bowed her head, embarrassed by his unexpected intrusion. She felt as though she had accidentally exposed her most private thoughts.

"That last piece you played, 'Liebestraum,' I like it a lot. Would you play it again?" he asked.

Play this for him? Was he mad? Why would he want her to play the "Dream of Love" for him? She most certainly would not.

But something about the way he asked her, something in his voice and the way he was looking at her gave her second thoughts. Yearning. It was written all over his face. Could her music have had such an impact? Did she finally play it well enough to make the listeners feel the music to such an extent? She wanted to know.

She laid her hands on the keyboard. A bit hesitant at first, she began to play again the slow, soft beginning of the first cadenza. Curious, she glanced up to see his reaction. She had never seen him so close. He had beautiful eyes, deep blue like the ocean. She never noticed them before. His eyes looked so tender too. Was this the effect from listening to her music? He must really love this music, or she must be playing it even better than she had thought.

Seeing how the first cadenza had achieved its intended effect, she let go of her hesitation and seized each note with her full heart and feelings. She let her emotions guide each key. The music moved and flowed until it rose and unleashed into a crescendo.

She looked at him again. He was watching her, transfixed. Could the music be all there was to it? Was he confusing the music with the person making it? He almost looked as if he was yearning for her. What a mad idea to think that. What a mad idea it was that he even asked her to play this for him. The "Dream of Love."

He wasn't the only one who was mad. She must have gone mad herself, because she liked the way he was looking at her. No one ever looked at her like this. A sweet, paralyzing sensation crept into her heart. Was this what it felt like to be wanted?

He looked so drawn in. Could he hear the love and passion in the melodies and rhythms? Did he understand all that she meant to express in the way she played? If he did, what would he think? Would it shock his sensibilities, or would he find it enthralling?

She continued to manipulate the keys. Every time she looked up at the sheet music, she could catch glimpses of his quickening breath from the subtle heaving of his chest. It was hard not to notice his toned physique. She was used to seeing his athletic form and never paid much attention to it. Only now, with him so near her, did she realize that he exuded strength. And she had to admit, it made him very attractive.

It wasn't only his strength. With the way he stood, so near her and so without inhibition, she could feel keenly his presence. What an inexplicably pleasant feeling it was, to be so close to someone who was so strong. Her heart softened.

When she finished, the room fell silent. For a moment, they stared at each other. She didn't know if she expected him to applaud, or praise her, or do something else altogether. The longing on his face had deepened. She tightened her hands and fingers resting on the keyboard. Her chest stiffened and her breath felt constricted. The room needed more air. There was not enough air.

Abruptly, he backed away. "Thanks. I'll see you next time." That was all he said. In no time, he was gone, taking with him the intimate feeling they had just shared.

In shock, she watched him leave. Was that all? *Thanks? I'll see you next time?* He didn't even tell her whether he liked how she played or not. Was he really as mesmerized as she thought while she played, or did she imagine everything? She felt so stupid.

Tone deaf. He was definitely tone deaf. She would never ever play this or anything else for him again.

Hurrying away from the parlor, Anthony could only breathe again after he left the house. The way Tessa stared back at him after she finished playing almost convinced him she understood how he felt, but he wasn't entirely sure. With a great effort, he tore himself away. He had to leave. Immediately. Or else he might do something he would regret, like taking her into his arms and kissing her, and then frightening the hell out of her.

"Thanks. I'll see you next time." He blurted out the words while all he could think of was to get away. He forgot to even give her the courtesy of a compliment on how she played. What could he have said anyway? He couldn't tell her how the emotional tones roused in him a deep, latent passion, or that the fast frenzied beats brought him to an elated state of excitement.

He couldn't possibly tell her how the flush on her cheeks as she played sent his heart racing.

On the other hand, he knew now what he could do. If she could only express herself through her music, then he must find a way to do the same. He had a vague idea of how he might do it. In any case, he had to try.

#

All Anthony wanted to find was a poster featuring "Liebestraum." Why was that so hard? He had gone to nearly every music shop and poster store he knew near school and downtown but had no luck at all. Of the few he did find, he didn't like any of them. They all showed enlarged photos of the performing artist. He wanted a poster that featured the music, not the performer. He walked out of one store after another. He didn't want to give up, but he was losing hope.

As a last-ditch attempt, he went to the little souvenir shop around the corner from the Chicago Symphony Orchestra Hall. Browsing through the posters offered for sale, he found it at last. *A Celebration of Franz Liszt*. Below it, the song title "Liebestraum, Dream of Love" printed in bold as the highlight performance along with a list of other musical selections in much smaller print. The concert had taken place three years ago in the spring of 1939. An illustration of a swirling piano keyboard served as the poster's background. It was perfect.

Excited, he bought the poster and returned to campus. He would have to get it framed. It should be ready in time for when he went home for his father's birthday during Halloween weekend.

Lost in his thoughts and walking in haste, he ran into another student who was herself in a hurry. One of the folders she carried dropped to the ground.

"Excuse me," he apologized and picked up the fallen folder and papers.

"I'm sorry. I was in a rush," the other student also apologized. He recognized her voice.

"Gretchen!"

"Anthony! My goodness. It's been a long time."

"Yes it has." He hadn't seen her since Brandon left. "How are you?"

"I'm good. And yourself?"

"Good. You going somewhere in a hurry?"

"To a CDA meeting."

He handed the papers and folder back to her. As he did, he noticed he had picked up a photo of a group of people crammed inside the cars of an old train. The passengers' lost, apprehensive eyes and gaunt faces stared out at him. "What is this?" he asked.

"I'm not really sure." She took back the folder, the papers, and the photo. "There have been some rumors. We think they are Jewish people being rounded up by the German Nazis."

"Rounded up for what? Are they criminals? Prisoners?"

"We don't know. We don't think so. Look." She pointed to a face staring out of a small train window. "This looks like a child. If they were prisoners, there shouldn't be any children with them."

The image was disturbing. He didn't know what to make of it.

"I've seen more photos like this one. My father's working with the underground resistance movement in Poland. These photos are some of what he's been able to obtain, but we have no concrete information about what's happening. There are rumors the Nazis are rounding up Jewish people and sending them to labor camps. They're just rumors. I'm heading to a CDA meeting now to try to find out what's going on." She put the photo back into the folder. "It's good to see you again." She started to leave.

"Gretchen, wait," he called out to her. "Have you heard from Brandon?"

She turned back. "Yes. He's a naval lieutenant now. He can't tell anyone where he's stationed but from some of the things he wrote about, I think he's stationed somewhere in the East. If he is, I'm very worried. The battles on that front are vicious."

He couldn't say anything sympathetic without sounding hypocritical, not when he had remained in the safety of home while Brandon had selflessly gone off and put himself at such great risk.

Thankfully, she didn't hold this against him. "I'll see you around." She smiled and took off.

With a heavier mind, Anthony walked on. The war. The atrocities that it brought. All of it was never far from him. Every time something good happened, the war would come back to the forefront and remind him there were things that mattered more than himself.

What happened to his resolve to enlist after Pearl Harbor?

Everywhere he went, more and more men had taken up the uniform. If this continued, pretty soon, he would have to explain why he was not in one.

Till the end of this year, he told himself. He would give himself until the end of this year, unless fate called upon him sooner and he got drafted. There was one more thing he wanted to do. He tightened his grip on the poster tube and walked on down the path.

Chapter 42

On the weekend of his father's birthday, Anthony returned home full of anticipation, only to have his hopes crushed. Tessa would be gone the entire time. The Veterans Hospital was short-staffed and she had to work through the weekend until Monday. By then, he would be gone.

How disappointing.

When he arrived home, his mother watched him make several trips in and out of the house, carrying with him his duffle bag of books and clothes first, then a large framed poster all wrapped up.

"Is that a birthday present for your father?" she asked.

"No. I've got his presents in my bag." He carried the poster upstairs. "This poster's for Tessa."

"For Tessa?"

"Yes," he said and went up to the second floor. She watched him from the bottom of the staircase, puzzled.

Saturday passed, completely uneventful with no Tessa and no children coming by to collect candy. The sugar ration had put a stop to the Halloween tradition. Nonetheless, his mother and their housemaid had still managed to bake his father a birthday cake. They had been saving up sugar for the last three months to make sure they had enough.

On Sunday afternoon, Uncle Leon and his family came to join them for the birthday lunch.

"Katherine," Sophia asked, "how is the preparation for the debutante ball coming along? It's in two weeks, isn't it? Are you excited?"

"I rather am," Katherine said. "Charlie Cranston will be my escort. He's a junior at Stonefield Academy."

"Cranston?" William asked. "Is his father on the board of the Merc?"

"Um-hmm. All my friends are jealous. Not only because of Charlie, but because some of them still don't have anyone to take them. They're panicking. A few of them are thinking of not going because their boyfriends have been commissioned." She looked across the table. "Anthony, I have friends who still need an escort. Would you like to go with one of them?"

"No!" He couldn't answer fast enough. "I can't go. I have too much homework. Sorry."

Looking peeved, Katherine said no more on the matter. Sophia glanced at her son, intrigued.

When they finished their food, everyone brought out their gifts. William delighted in all the presents he received, from the cashmere scarf and watch his wife had bought for him, to the bottle of vintage bourbon from the Caldwells. Leon even made a generous donation to the Chicago Hospital in his name.

When he got to the presents Anthony gave him, he broke into a huge smile. "Binoculars!"

Thrilled that his father liked the gift, Anthony said, "I thought you could use them for bird watching. It's the latest model. The glass is coated with magnesium so more light can come through the lenses."

"Yes." William held it up to his eyes. "They'll definitely come in handy when we go camping again in the summer."

Anthony didn't answer. He hadn't thought of that when he bought the binoculars. He couldn't tell his father that there would be no camping next summer. By then, he would in all likelihood be gone.

"You're going camping?" asked Alexander who was sitting next to him. "Can I go too if you go?" He turned to Anthony. "I've asked Father to take me so many times but he said he didn't want to sleep outside."

"Certainly," Anthony said, feeling uneasy with his lie. "Wouldn't think of going without you."

"And this. I love it." William held up the book on David Livingstone's explorations in Africa in the 1800s. "I've been meaning to get a copy of this myself. I've been too busy and haven't gotten around to it. It feels like a lifetime ago since I last traveled to Africa." He smiled at his son. "I will enjoy reading this. Thank you."

"And last but not least," Sophia said, "Tessa has something for you too." She left the dining room and returned with a small, framed portrait of him drinking brandy and reading the evening newspaper on the sofa by the antique lamp in the den.

"When did she do this?" He looked at the painting in awe.

"I don't know," Sophia said. "She doesn't like anyone poking around in her studio. It's very nicely done, don't you think? I told her so when she showed it to me."

William passed the painting to Leon. "She's got loads of talent," Leon said. "Maybe she shouldn't have gone into nursing. She could've been an artist instead."

"Can I see?" Anthony asked. Leon handed him the painting. Anthony looked at it, pleased. The drawing closely resembled his father and captured his peaceful countenance when he relaxed at home in the evening. Tessa must care a great deal for his father to be so observant and to paint him like this.

"We'll have to find a nice place to display this," William said. "Thank you, everyone. What a wonderful birthday."

"We're not finished yet," Sophia said. The housemaid took the cue and brought out his birthday cake. Everyone had been waiting for this. They had not had a piece of homemade cake for months. Desserts with real sugar were rare nowadays. Of course, they could always go to the black market. The Ardleys and the Caldwells would have no problem paying the higher prices. However, in the spirit of supporting the men fighting overseas, they had chosen to follow the rules for rations.

"It's too bad Tessa isn't here to have a piece too," Anna said.

"We'll save one for her," Sophia said.

"It'll become dry and stale overnight."

"I'll take it to her," Anthony offered. Sophia looked curiously at him again. "I'll go by her hospital on my way back to school."

"The Veterans' Hospital is out of your way, isn't it?" Leon said off-handedly as he dug into his piece of cake. "Now you're pushing your gas ration limit."

Anthony smiled and didn't answer. Gas ration or not, he finally had an excuse to go see her. That was the only thing that mattered.

Chapter 43

Before he left home after his father's birthday lunch, Anthony went to Tessa's room and took down the countryside painting hanging on the wall across from her bed and replaced it with the framed poster of the "Liebestraum" concert. Satisfied, he tore a small piece of paper from the stationery notebook on her desk and wrote her a note, then folded it and inserted it in the slit behind the rim of the frame in the lower right corner.

He tried to imagine what she would think when she saw the poster. He wished he could be here to see her reaction when she returned. Well, at least, he would see her later at the hospital when he brought her the cake.

The Veterans Hospital was one confusing compound. He had to take several detours after being given the wrong directions before he finally got the correct information where Tessa was. A nurse at the reception desk on the third floor told him she had taken a patient to the loading area at the south exit. Exhausted, he went back down the corridor and down three flights again.

Approaching the south exit, he saw Tessa outside the doorway with two other people. The one standing next to her was her friend Henry.

He wondered why Henry was here. The other person was a few years older and in a wheelchair. Excited to see her, he was about to call out her name but stopped when he saw Tessa with that person. She placed her hand on his shoulder and talked gently to him. He didn't know why, but the way she was talking to him bothered him. He had never seen her behave so tenderly toward anyone.

He watched Tessa and Henry help the patient out of the wheelchair. The patient leaned on his crutches as they helped him into Henry's old car. Henry gave Tessa a friendly hug before he got into the driver's seat. Tessa said goodbye to him, but most of the time, her attention remained on the patient who was now in the backseat. She waved to them and watched them as they drove off.

When they were gone, Anthony came closer. She did not notice him standing behind her until she turned around after Henry's car disappeared down the road out of her sight.

"Anthony?"

Her surprised reaction pleased him, but he couldn't help being curious. "Who was that you just helped into Henry's car?"

Sadness filled her face. "That was Jack. Henry's older brother."

"Henry's brother?" She never told him Henry had a brother. "You look like you care about him a lot."

She gazed down the road where Henry and Jack had gone. "I do. He's a very dear friend to me."

His heart eased when she said the word "friend." "What happened to him?"

She looked at him as if he had asked the most ridiculous question. "You're at the Veterans Hospital. What do you think happened to him?"

She was right. What a stupid question. He felt like a fool in front of her.

"He was injured in the war," she said, her voice turned serious and solemn. "He came back from the Philippines a few months ago. He didn't lose his leg, but he's crippled and will be limping for the rest of his life."

Now he felt even worse than a fool. That poor guy Jack had become disabled after fighting in the war. It was more than what he himself had done. How awful was it of him to feel vexed by Tessa talking gently to a war veteran? After all, she was a nurse. She had a duty to be kind and compassionate to her patients, especially a patient who was also her friend. He felt so ashamed.

"He's very worried he won't find work," Tessa said. At least she hadn't noticed how insensitive he was just now. "He thinks no one will hire him because he's crippled. I don't know how Henry will get him home. They live on the third floor. Their building is a walk-up with no elevator. I feel terrible thinking of him having to climb up all those stairs."

Anthony took another step closer to her. Seeing her sad made him sad.

"What are you doing here anyway?" she asked.

"Me? I came to give you some birthday cake," he said with a bashful smile. "You missed Father's birthday lunch today."

"You came all the way here to bring me a piece of cake?"

Unable to explain himself, he said, "Mother really wanted you to have it." He handed her the small box with the piece of cake inside. "I'll be off now. See you." He rushed off while she stared at him, perplexed and baffled.

# # #

Tessa returned home Monday afternoon, utterly worn out. Her weekend shift came right on the heels of a full week of classes. The shortage of nurses had stressed the hospital's staff and resources to its breaking point.

Even as a first-year nurse trainee, her help was needed everywhere by the doctors.

She came into the house in sore need of rest, but as her Aunt Sophia was reading in the parlor, she stopped to greet her and to let her know she was back.

"How was your weekend?" Aunt Sophia asked her first.

"Long." Tessa let out a deep breath. "I'm dead tired. I'm going off to bed if that's okay."

"Do you want to have lunch before you go to sleep?"

"No. I'm too tired to eat." She covered her mouth to stifle a yawn. "Did Uncle William like my painting?"

"Absolutely. He hung it in his study."

She was glad to hear he liked it. When she woke up, she would have to see where he had chosen to display it. "Oh, by the way, Aunt Sophia, thank you for sending me a piece of the birthday cake."

"No need to thank me." Sophia turned the page of her magazine. "It was Anthony's idea. I meant to keep a piece for you when you come home. Anna said it'd be stale by the time you got back, so Anthony volunteered to bring it to you."

Confused, Tessa wondered if she remembered wrong. She could've sworn Anthony had said Aunt Sophia wanted him to bring her the cake, but she was too exhausted to try to remember. She had been on her feet for hours. All she wanted now was her bed. Everything else could wait.

She dragged her tired body up to her room. As soon as she saw her bed, she kicked off her shoes, threw herself face down on it, and let its softness soothe her body.

When the aching of her feet and muscles subsided, she turned around and lay on her back, debating to herself whether to change her clothes or to simply fall asleep. The unfamiliar look of the wall distracted her. Something had changed. What was it?

The painting. It was the painting. The country landscape was gone, replaced by a music concert poster. She got up to take a closer look.

A poster for a piano concert performance of "Liebestraum, Dream of Love" now hung on the wall. Even though she couldn't believe it, she knew immediately who put it there. A rush of warmth surged up within her.

A small folded piece of paper stuck out from the lower right corner of the frame. She took it and unfolded it.

Tessa.

It's about time you have something that belongs to you in your room. Hope you like this. — Anthony

The way he smiled when he brought her the cake yesterday sprang to her mind.

Anthony...

The warmth she felt inside her turned into a tingling tenderness in her heart. She smiled and ran her fingers across the words "Dream of Love."

Not tone deaf after all.

PART THIRTEEN
New Year's Eve, 1942

Chapter 44

The Monday before Thanksgiving, Tessa arrived at the hospital and found herself deluged with pies. Sarah Brinkman had brought six pies to work as gifts for her and Ellie Swanson.

Sarah was not to be stopped by a mere obstacle like the sugar ration. "I made two of each kind. There are two pecan, two apple, and two pumpkin. For the pecan, I used honey. For the apple, I used maple syrup, and for the pumpkin, I used brown molasses and cinnamon with just a touch of brown sugar I was able to spare. The pecan is still the best, I think. I told you I can make a mean pecan pie. I wanted you both to have these. They're my Thanksgiving gifts to you, to thank you for being so kind to me. I actually wanted to give them to you on Wednesday so you could have them for Thanksgiving dinner on Thursday, but I have to work today and Tuesday, and on Wednesday I'll have to help my mom with cooking our Thanksgiving dinner. Mom and Pop are super excited because Dale will be coming home for Thanksgiving. He got furloughed! Mom and I brainstormed on our Thanksgiving dinner menu all weekend. We'll make beef stew and a turkey, because Dale loves beef stew. And Uncle Oliver and Aunt Martha will be coming with my little nieces Nikki and Jenny, and…"

Tessa had stopped listening. Although, even for her, it was hard not to want to laugh at the sight of all the pies before them. Sarah must have baked all weekend long. She really shouldn't have. Tessa didn't think she had been particularly nice to Sarah to warrant Sarah making such a huge effort for her. She accepted Sarah being around her to relieve herself from having to engage in small talk and pointless socializing at work. If she and Sarah had met elsewhere under different circumstances, she wouldn't have been so tolerant of her incessant yapping. They probably wouldn't have become friends.

"Sarah, this is so very thoughtful of you," Ellie said, "but Tessa and I can't possibly eat all these pies by ourselves. It's too much even if we bring them home to our families."

"I know." Sarah stared at the pies, distraught. "I get these urges to bake, and I couldn't decide which kind of pie to make, so I made all the flavors that inspired me at the moment. Besides, I wanted to experiment with the different sugar substitutes."

Ellie picked one up. "How about we share them with some of the patients who don't have family visitors? We can give them out to those patients in our ward during visitors' hours."

"That's a great idea," Tessa said. "I'll share mine too, although I'd like to keep the pecan pie if that's okay."

Sarah seemed satisfied with the suggestion.

"All right then. Let's do that." Ellie picked up the pies and put them away for serving later, except for the pecan pie that Tessa wanted to reserve for herself.

Actually, Tessa didn't want it for herself. She wanted to take it to Jack and Henry after work. The last time she had seen them was the day when Jack was released from the hospital, and that was weeks ago. She had meant to visit him, but work had been so demanding. New veterans arrived everyday and they required all her attention. Someone somewhere always needed her help. Often, she stayed overtime for them.

It had been too long. Today, she would make time to go see them.

Chapter 45

After work, Tessa went to Canaryville as she had planned. The chilly winter wind had returned for another season. The dreary streets reminded her of the first time she had come here two years ago. The weather that day was just like today's, but so much had happened since then. So much had changed.

She hadn't told Jack or Henry she was coming. She wanted to surprise them. Jack, at least, would be home. He couldn't move around or go anywhere easily. Mrs. Morrissey should be home from work too.

When she arrived, Henry was the one who opened the door.

"Henry," she greeted him. "Good afternoon, Jack, Mrs. Morrissey." She entered their apartment. "Look what I brought you. It's a homemade pecan pie." She held up the box with the pie inside to show them.

Unable to contain himself, Henry threw her a big hug. "Tessa! Thank you! Thank you! Thank you!"

Tessa didn't expect this overwhelming response.

"Tessa, thank you." Mrs. Morrissey too gave her a hug. "Thank you so much. You're such a good friend to my sons." She wiped the happy tears from her face.

"Um…it's only a pie…" Their outpouring of gratitude was too much.

Seated on their old couch, Jack, too teared up. "I can't thank you enough in a million years, Tessa. You have no idea how much this means to us."

She put the pie down on the table. "I'm not sure what you're all talking about."

"Come on, Tessa," Henry said. "You don't have to pretend anymore. We're talking about Jack's new job."

"Jack's new job?"

"We really appreciate you getting Anthony to arrange it for Jack."

"I got Anthony to arrange it?"

"That's what Anthony said. He came by three weeks ago. He met Jack and told him about the Ardleys' residential properties over at Lincoln Park. He said the property manager, Mr. Mason, was looking for an assistant. Then he took Jack to meet Mr. Mason, and they offered him a job as assistant property manager."

That was news to her. "Assistant property manager…what will you be doing?" she asked Jack.

"It's mostly a desk job," Jack said. "Mr. Mason already has a staff of people who takes care of the property. He needs help to manage them, schedule maintenance and repairs, answer tenants' complaints, handle bills and rental payments, that sort of stuff. I've never worked a desk job before. He did me a huge favor to hire me."

"The job comes with housing too!" Henry said. She couldn't remember ever seeing him this excited. "Mr. Mason said all the property managers have to live on site because emergencies come up all the time. We'll be moving to a unit in one of the rental buildings over there. Anthony came by two days ago and took us to see the unit reserved for us. It's three times bigger than this place."

"The best thing is," Jack said, "the unit's on the first floor. It'll be very convenient for me." He glanced at his crutches. "It won't be difficult for me to get around the Ardley properties anyway. Every building has elevators. Those places your family owns are very nice."

Still stunned by the news, Tessa remained speechless. Anthony hadn't said anything to her about this.

"I wanted to come and thank you when Jack got the job," Henry said to her, "but Anthony told me not to. He said you wouldn't want us to make a big fuss and feel beholden to you. He told us to wait until we've moved into our new home and then to invite you for a house warming dinner."

Mrs. Morrissey took her hands. "Tessa, I thank you and your family from the bottom of my heart. We have so much to be thankful for now. We'll have a true Thanksgiving this year."

Tessa squeezed her hands. She decided not to tell them she had nothing to do with arranging Jack's new job. She had no wish to take credit for something she didn't do, but she was still trying to understand what had happened and it was too difficult to try to explain. The most important thing was, they were happy and Jack no longer had to worry about how to find work.

"When will you start your job?" she asked Jack. "When will you all be moving?"

"I'll start work after the new year," he said. "Mr. Mason is so kind. He told me to rest through the winter holidays, but we're moving the weekend right after Thanksgiving. Mr. Mason will be sending his people to help us with the move." He took his crutches and got up to walk over to her. Quickly, she went to him. He held her arm, his eyes full of gratitude. "Thank you for everything. I know this wouldn't have happened if it weren't for you." He was close to tears again.

She hugged him to lend him her support. This was all wonderful news. A happy ending for Jack after all. And it was all because…

Anthony…

# # #

After she left the Morrissey's home, Tessa took the bus to the University of Chicago campus instead of going home. She had to thank Anthony for what he had done.

She had never visited the UC campus before. Its stately and traditional environment reminded her very much of him. Walking past the school buildings, she tried to imagine what living here might be like for him. He had a whole life in this place that she didn't know a thing about.

Following the directions given to her by passing students, she came to Breckinridge Hall, the Palladian-style brick and stone building Anthony had chosen as his dorm.

So this is where he lives. She hoped he was here.

The student working at the reception desk recognized Anthony's name right away and telephoned his floor. Luckily, Anthony was in.

"Tessa?" He looked overjoyed when he came downstairs. That warm, tender sensation ran through her heart again when she saw how happy he was to see her.

"I didn't expect you to come see me." He looked down and smiled at her. He was so close to her and his voice was so intimate, her heart tingled. But she must be imagining this. She had to be imagining this. Why would Anthony treat her any differently than before?

"What brought you here?" he asked.

"I went to see Jack and Henry earlier," she said. "Why didn't you tell me what you did?"

From the way he smiled, it was obvious he had been waiting for this moment. "I wanted to surprise you."

She looked at him in disbelief.

"Seriously though, I'm glad we can help them. I don't want you to worry about your friends. I asked Father for a list of all the job openings at our companies that might be suitable for someone with his kind of disabilities, then all I did was introduce him to Mr. Mason. From there on, it was all up to Jack. Mr. Mason wouldn't have hired him if he didn't like Jack or if he didn't think Jack was up to the job."

Even so, being introduced by Anthony must have helped. She smiled at the thought. It was so nice of Anthony to have done what he did.

"It wasn't much effort on my part," he said. "I'm just a pantywaist who goes to my father for everything, remember?"

"No." She touched his arm. He stared at her hand and she pulled it back. She didn't know why but suddenly she felt embarrassed. "I take it back. I take it all back. You're not a pantywaist. You did a very wonderful thing. I came to say thank you. Thank you for helping Jack."

"It's my pleasure. I got to know Jack too. He makes me feel so humbled. You were right. I have my parents and I'm never in want of anything. He's younger than me and he's been taking care of his family for years. On top of that, he's already fought in the war. And here I am." His tone changed to one of frustration. "I should enlist. It's getting humiliating. Me being an able body and staying at home."

"No!" she said. Her sharp tone surprised him and some of the students nearby.

She drew back and clasped her hands. "I don't want you to go." Her voice was barely audible but she couldn't bring herself to say this any louder. Still, he heard her and gave her a warm smile. She lowered her eyes, too embarrassed even to look at him, but she honestly didn't want him to be in danger.

"Have you had dinner yet?" he asked.

"No," she said without raising her head. "I just came to say thank you. I should probably go home."

"Why don't you stay and eat with me then? I can drive you home later. There's a great place I know for Italian beef called Marconi's. Have you ever had Italian beef? It's a Chicago specialty."

She didn't want to leave so soon either. "Okay."

His face lit up. "Wait here. I'll call Mother and let her know." Excited, he hurried back upstairs.

She felt excited too. In fact, it surprised her how happy she was to see him. He didn't let her wait long. When they walked outside, he flashed her a bright smile that made her think of a ray of sunshine.

On the way, she stole silent glances at him. He did have a positive energy about him that cheered up everyone around him. He wasn't as terrible as she thought after all.

Chapter 46

Another four weeks passed. Soon, it would be Christmas again. This would be Tessa's third Christmas in America. The bloody war had no end in sight. But for the first time, she didn't feel a hole of deep sadness that came with the arrival of the holiday season since coming to America. The reason was because Anthony would be coming home.

Since the time she had visited him at his school after learning of what he had done for Jack, they made a pact to go to Marconi's for Italian beef every Saturday for lunch. Marconi's made the best Italian beef sandwiches, and they both agreed it would be an atrocity if they didn't go there for a beef sandwich at least once a week. Like he said, the Italian beef sandwiches there were delicious. Neither of them could stop raving about them.

What she couldn't say was that she didn't come to see him every week only for the food. She couldn't explain what had changed, but it was now fun being with him. Every time she saw him, she would play a prank on him. It was easy because he was always so straight and sincere. He didn't seem to mind that. He had stopped his annoying way of telling her what she should or should not do. If he hadn't done that and had been more like how he was now, they would've gotten along much better before. They could've been better friends.

Friends…Sometimes, she couldn't help feeling they were more than that. There were times when she felt he didn't think of her only as a friend. The gentle way he talked to her and the entranced way he looked at her sometimes made her wonder if he might have a different kind of feeling for her. That couldn't be, could it? For him, she had always been a difficult problem child. Why would he take that kind of interest in her now after all this time? She must be imagining things. It annoyed her that she would have such ridiculous imaginings. How humiliating it would be if she were wrong.

And yet, that feeling would not go away. It was there too the last time they went to Marconi's.

They had just sat down with their food and he was telling her all about the swimming championship final. It was fun watching him. He got so excited every time he talked about swimming.

"So after Roland fell behind, we thought it was over. There was no way we could catch up to the guys from Northwestern," he was telling her about the last relay competition. "But Kyle went for it and caught up with them just enough to give us a shot. A long shot, but still a shot. I was up next and the last to go…" His enthusiasm made her chuckle.

"And then! Unbelievable. The last guy up on their team slipped! He slipped and fell butt first into the pool. I wish I could've watched the rest of his team's reaction but I had to dive right in. We were winning for sure now…" She couldn't help laughing now. He got even more animated because he thought she was laughing at what he had said, except the real reason she was laughing was because he looked so endearing when he got so excited.

He carried on. As she listened, she found herself admiring his toned physique again. What would it be like to be held by arms that were so strong?

He had a very nice grin too.

"Is there something on my face?" he asked.

327

"No." She didn't realize she was staring at him. Quickly, she changed the subject. "Do you always order your sandwich sweet dry? It tastes better with toppings on it." She had tried all the different varieties already, but he never ordered his any other way.

"I like it sweet dry." He took another bite of his sandwich.

This was why he was an open invitation for pranks. She drank her entire glass of juice and said, "Would you please get me another glass?"

"Sure." Without a doubt as to her intentions, he went to the ordering counter. He was so trusting of her, it made her chuckle again. While he was at the counter, she put all the toppings of carrots, peppers, and celery from her sandwich on top of his sandwich. Watching him from the back, she put her hand over her mouth to hide her laugh. When he returned to the table, she put on a straight face and bit into her own sandwich.

"Here you go." He put down the glass of juice he bought for her and sat down. She watched him bite into his sandwich again. "Hey! Why'd you do that? You messed up my sandwich."

She laughed. "I am going to mess up your life like you won't believe."

As soon as she said it, she realized her words came out differently than she intended and they fell into an awkward silence. The awkwardness was only broken when he stared at her with an intriguing smile that made her feel self-conscious and embarrassed. She grabbed her glass of juice. "Give me that." She looked away and sipped on her straw.

He resumed talking about the swimming championship, but now it felt to her as if he was only trying to use the words to fill the air. Why did it feel so uncertain when they were together? Like they were always holding something back. What was that something? She still couldn't understand or explain it to herself.

#

The day before Christmas, Anthony suggested they go ice-skating. Tessa didn't know how to skate, but he said he would teach her.

"I played ice hockey when I was a kid. Let's not be cooped up inside all day," he said.

He didn't have to try very hard to convince her. She had been looking forward to him coming home. Only she didn't want to admit that to anyone, or herself.

He took her to a skating rink not far from where they lived. At first, she wobbled all over and couldn't stop laughing. He skated backward, circling around her, laughing with her and trying to lead her. She didn't know he was such a good skater.

Two laps around the rink later, she felt steadier on her feet and she started to skate a bit faster. The rush of head wind felt so refreshing. She hadn't felt so free in a long time.

Gliding along, he abruptly pulled her close, startling her. For a moment, he held her against him. His arms wrapped protectively around her. Two large teenage boys hurtled past her at high speed. They would've knocked her over if he hadn't pulled her out of their path. The boys sped away and he released her.

Did she imagine it, or did he hold her much closer to him than he needed to get her out of the boys' way?

When he had his arms around her, her heart skipped a beat.

"Are you all right?" he asked. "You look dazed."

"I'm fine." She tried to shake off her thoughts.

"Come on." He took her hand and led her forward.

With the way he had his arm around her, and now with him holding her hand, she realized again how strong he was. Not only was he physically strong, he exhibited such strength the way he carried himself.

She watched him as she followed him from behind and saw for the first time what made him so attractive to all the girls around him. His commanding presence and his gallant attitude were irresistible.

She wondered what it felt like for Mary Winters to walk hand-in-hand with him. To have him look at her with adoration in his eyes. To be held by him in his arms as someone he loved. To be kissed by him. She wondered why she was wondering about all this. She wondered if she had lost her mind.

Around and around the rink they skated. She wished they could go on and on. She wished this day would never end.

Skating in front of Tessa, Anthony dared not turn and look back. If he did, he might look like a fool. In the brief seconds when he held her in his arms, his heart jumped. It was beating rapidly still. Before he released her, he caught a whiff of her perfume. Like an elixir casting a spell over him, it made him want to pull her even closer, to embrace her and bury his face in her hair and her neck and to breathe in deeply that sweet rose scent.

In all his life, he had never felt such mad desire for any girl. And never before had he been so maddeningly lost for a way to let a girl know how he felt about her. How could he tell someone to whom he had paid so little attention to and with whom he did nothing much but bicker that he was madly in love with her? He had no idea.

For the first time in his life, he was afraid he might be turned down. He feared she might reject him. This never worried him before. Girls didn't usually turn him down. The times when they did, well, he must not have been that attracted, because he didn't remember being bothered by it. But Tessa might turn him down. In fact, she would probably laugh in his face. What would he do then? He would look like a fool in front of her. He didn't want to look like a fool in front of her.

But at the rink, he could hold her hand and pretend he was keeping her from falling. He could hold on to her and feel for a moment what it would be like if they were together the way he wanted them to be.

Not wanting to let her go, he skated on until he started to worry her legs might be tired and she wouldn't be able to keep going. Amazingly, she didn't ask to stop until he stopped. Reluctantly, he drew his hand back from her.

Afterward, he suggested they go to the Museum of Science and Industry. "They put up a Christmas tree dedicated to the Allied troops. I heard it's magnificent."

He couldn't be happier when she readily agreed.

When they got to the Museum, they learned that the Christmas tree had a theme, "Christmas Around the World." Volunteers from twelve different countries had decorated it as a symbol of peace.

He watched Tessa admire in awe the Christmas lights and ornaments. Silently, he said a prayer in front of the tree. He hadn't told anyone, but his time was running out. He had given himself until the end of this year, and the end was fast approaching. When she wasn't looking, he crossed his heart. No matter what the future might hold, he wished that for the many Christmases ahead, they could be happy again like today.

A photographer came by. "Would you like me to take a picture of you two in front of the tree?"

Uncertain, Anthony looked at the photographer, then at Tessa. Tessa smiled and gestured to him to come next to her. Gladly, he said to the photographer, "Yes. Thank you."

Standing next to her, he put his arm lightly around her. She glanced over at his hand on her shoulder. Unsure, he almost took his arm off her, but she looked up at him and smiled. Relieved, he let his arm remain and pulled her a bit closer to him. The flash went off, capturing a moment in time that he wished would last.

331

Maybe, he thought to himself as he watched her walk around the tree. Maybe there could be more for both of them.

Chapter 47

That week that followed Christmas was all about the Fur Ball.

Tessa wasn't thrilled about it, but she had to go along. The Fur Ball was a pet event dreamt up by Uncle Leon. The war had cast such shadow everywhere, hosting any kind of usual New Year's Eve celebration became impossible. A black-tie gala would appear too indulgent and extravagant. A private family affair didn't feel festive enough for everyone who craved distraction and entertainment for a release from the gloom. The idea of the Fur Ball was to include a private war bond drive and a rally to collect donated fur for making coats and jackets for American soldiers fighting overseas.

Instantly after its announcement, the Fur Ball, which would be held at the Caldwells' home, became the most highly anticipated New Year's Eve event for all of Chicago's elite. Everyone in town coveted one of the invitations with the print of a Persian cat wearing a string of pearls. This lavish event was the only one everyone could attend without feeling guilty for celebrating while soldiers fought abroad. The tie-in with war support efforts was a stroke of genius. The war bond drive would make everyone feel good and patriotic for giving the troops their support. The fur drive even gave the wealthy a chance to show off the fur they owned.

There would be special guests too. Uncle Leon had invited an army colonel and a soldier to attend to help drum up the war bond sales. Rumor also had it, the glamorous actress Celeste Le Vonne would make a special appearance and sing for the guests. Whether this was true or not, Uncle Leon would not disclose even to his family.

"I don't blame Leon," Uncle William said. "Life at home has to go on. Regardless of everyone's motives, he would be raising a lot of money for the army. This will be a good night."

A good night? Tessa didn't think so. Mingling with strangers pretending to be social was not the way she wished to spend New Year's Eve. She had no choice though. Everyone had to go to support Uncle Leon.

Not that the rest of the family had any complaints. On Christmas day when the Caldwells came to their house for the Ardleys' annual Christmas luncheon, Katherine could not stop talking about how excited all her friends were to have a reason to dress up again. Everyone she knew and their parents were looking forward to attending the Fur Ball.

Unlike Katherine, Tessa remained blasé. Aunt Sophia practically had to drag her to shop for a dress suitable for the occasion. Not wanting to draw attention to herself at the event, Tessa chose a simple black velvet evening dress with ruche shoulders, half sleeves, and a full A-lined skirt that reached just below her knees. Its only adornments were the black rose designs sewn on the skirt, which were hardly visible.

"A bit plain," was Aunt Sophia's opinion.

Nonetheless, on the night of the event, the joyous mood and commotion lifted everyone's spirits. Even Tessa's. She watched in amazement how stunningly beautiful her Aunt Sophia looked in her sleek, elegant silver evening gown. Her Aunt Sophia's taste was impeccable. No flashy jewelry, just a simple but exquisite necklace matched with a pair of diamond earrings. She and Uncle William made such a handsome pair, Tessa was sure they would be the best looking couple at the Ball.

While she admired them, Anthony came up to her and said quietly to her, "You look beautiful."

His compliment made her heart flip. "I'm trying not to," she said to deflect his attention. She didn't know what to make of her own reaction to him. To escape, she followed Uncle William and Aunt Sophia to the door where the housemaid was helping them with their outerwear. Behind her, Anthony watched her put on her coat as if she was putting on an armor bracing for battle. Her mind preoccupied, she did not see the way he was looking at her.

When they arrived at the Caldwells', other guests were already filing in. At a table at the front entrance, Aunt Anna and Katherine, along with two ladies, greeted the arriving guests while they collected the furs the guests brought for donation.

Aunt Anna gave them a warm welcome. "Leon is around somewhere. The colonel and the lieutenant have arrived too."

They entered the main parlor. The furniture had been cleared to accommodate the long buffet tables. On one side, a string quartet in white tuxedo jackets and black pants performed on a stage temporarily set up for the night. A standing microphone stood before them, a sign that there would be a vocal performance later on. Maybe Celeste Le Vonne really was coming.

The room started to fill up. Uncle Leon could be seen making the rounds soliciting the guests to purchase war bonds. A group of girls Tessa knew from St. Mary's had gathered around the punch bowl, talking to each other while looking over at the young lieutenant here for the war bond drive and the handful of young men who had come.

"Let's go say hi to Senator Reinhardt," Uncle William said.

Having no desire to follow them around and not seeing anyone she wanted to talk to, Tessa asked, "Uncle William, may I go help Aunt Anna with the fur collection instead?"

"Of course."

She returned to the fur collection table while Anthony watched her walk away.

"Katherine," Tessa said.

Katherine, who was helping with the fur drive, looked miserable for missing out on the party going on in the parlor.

"Want some relief?" Tessa asked. "I can take it from here."

"Yes!" Katherine held her hands up in prayer. "You don't mind?"

Tessa shook her head.

"Thank you!" Katherine squeezed Tessa's arm and took off.

Tessa busied herself with the fur collection, hoping to pass the night without having to do much else. When most of the guests had arrived, the ladies who were helping them left to join the Ball. Anna suggested that Tessa return to the party to enjoy herself, but Tessa declined. "You're the hostess, Aunt Anna. You should go inside and talk with the guests. I'll manage."

"Are you sure?"

"Yes, I'm sure."

"Okay, dear, but you don't have to stay here long. When all the guests are here, you come in too and join us."

"I will," she reassured her.

After Anna left, Tessa sat down behind the table. She wouldn't mind spending the whole evening here instead.

She looked around her. Furs of different kinds, from big coats to small scarves, now filled the boxes next to the table. A sample vest for the Merchant Marines for which the furs would be used was on display on a coat rack. A banner which said, "United We Stand," hung on the wall behind the table.

"Hi, Tessa." Alexander came up to her. In a mini-tuxedo, he looked like a smart little gentleman.

"You're looking handsome," she said.

"I brought you a fruit punch." He handed her a glass.

"Thank you." She took a big sip. She hadn't realized how thirsty she was. "Are you enjoying yourself?"

"No." He put his hands on his waist. "This is boring. It's all old people and they're all just talking. I'm going back to my room. I'll see you later."

Tessa laughed. "Happy New Year," she called out to him. He waved without looking back. Tessa held up the glass in her hand. What a caring gesture on his part to think of bringing her a drink. Come to think of it, even Katherine had warmed up to her somewhat, now that she no longer attended St. Mary's and had no more impact on Katherine's social standing. There was no denying it. The Ardleys and the Caldwells were now her family. They all treated her like family, and she was one of them.

Except Anthony. What was she to him? And what was he to her?

When everyone on the guest list had arrived, there was nothing more for her to do and she returned to the parlor. Feeling no desire to join in on any conversation, she went to one of the large windows facing the front of the house. The courtyard looked quiet and peaceful with the shining night lights. A light flurry of snow danced in the air.

Where was Anthony? she wondered. She turned around to look at the room. The group of girls at the long table by the punch bowl had surrounded him.

As if he felt her watching him, he looked up. Their eyes met.

Seeing the girls around him amused her. Surely, he would be plenty occupied tonight. She smiled, then turned back to look outside. Although cold, the air seemed crisp. She loved the stillness of winter nights like this one. She put her hand on the window and felt the icy surface of the windowpanes. Perhaps she could go out and take a walk around the courtyard.

Over by the punch bowl, Anthony caught sight of Tessa by herself at the window. She had finally come in, and to his surprise, she was watching him. He wished she didn't see him talking to all these girls. He didn't invite this. They started talking to him, and he was talking to them only to be polite. Their parents and his parents were friends and business associates. He was ready to extract himself, but Tessa smiled as though she saw something funny and turned away. What kind of reaction was that? he thought, feeling miffed. A different string of thoughts then went through his mind. Was she not upset to see all these girls around him? Did she feel no disappointment at all? Couldn't she have looked a little jealous?

Nonetheless, he didn't want her to misunderstand. "Excuse me," he said to everyone and walked over to her. She was looking out the window and did not noticed him behind her. He tugged at her elbow and spoke softly to her ear. "Want to get out of here?"

She turned her eyes away from the window and looked up at him. "And go where? Home?"

"No. I know of a better place."

She gave him a suspicious smile. "All right."

"Go get our coats. I'll tell Mother and Father we're leaving."

She gave the party one last look and left. After she was gone, he scanned the room for his parents. They were seated at a table with Senator Reinhardt and several other guests at the table. He came up behind his parents. "Tessa and I are leaving."

"Leaving?" William turned around in his seat. "Where are you going..." Sophia put her hand on his arm and stopped him. "You kids go and have fun," she said to Anthony. "Just be sure you look after her and make sure she's okay."

"I will, Mother." Anthony said goodbye and took his leave.

"What was that all about?" William asked Sophia as Anthony walked away.

"You have no idea, do you?"

"No idea of what?"

"Your son. He's infatuated with Tessa."

"What?" William asked. "How long has this been going on?"

"Since this summer."

"This summer?"

"Yes. This summer."

"But I thought he was seeing Mary Winters this summer."

Sophia shook her head and sighed.

After overcoming his initial shock, he asked, "And Tessa? What does she think?"

"That, I don't know," Sophia said. "I'm not even sure she knows how Anthony feels. With her, it's always hard to tell, but it looks like he has at least convinced her to go somewhere with him tonight."

William looked over at the parlor entrance. There, Tessa was already waiting with her hat and coat on. She handed Anthony his coat, hat, and scarf. He put them on and they both exited the parlor.

On stage, the actress Celeste Le Vonne had arrived. Her grand entrance was causing a commotion among the guests. "Ladies and Gentlemen," the Master of Ceremonies announced. "May I present to you, the ever lovely Miss Celeste Le Vonne."

Thunderous applause filled the room, but William was still looking at the door. Sophia clapped her hands with the rest of the guests, but she, too, was watching the parlor entrance where Anthony and Tessa had just left.

"I see." William watched his son and Tessa leave, as if the idea of Anthony and Tessa had finally sunk in. He turned to his wife. "Well, we've wanted Dean and Juliet to come to America. I think Dean might finally brave those U-boats and come now, to kill me."

Sophia laughed. The band started to play. The enchanting voice of Celeste Le Vonne singing soon filled the room and captured everyone's attention.

Chapter 48

Anthony and Tessa left the Caldwells' and stepped out into the crisp, wintry night. Behind them back in the house, Celeste Le Vonne had started to sing.

"She's really here!" Tessa said. "We're missing her live performance."

"Oh well," Anthony said. He hardly cared. He had finally got Tessa alone with him. "Come on." He led her across the Caldwells' courtyard out onto the surrounding streets. The entire neighborhood was quiet and empty. They were the only two outside. Every time the wind blew, specks of snow would drift past them.

Without a car, they caught the bus just in time when it arrived at a bus stop down the road. The festive atmosphere inside the vehicle dramatically differed from the quiet stillness outside. The passengers were all laughing and in a party mood. Many of them had dressed up for a night out on the town.

Tessa didn't know where she was going and Anthony wouldn't say, but she was glad they had left the Fur Ball. She had felt so out of place there. She wondered what he had in mind for them.

The bus approached the Michigan Avenue Bridge and she gazed out the side window. A light layer of snow had covered the ground. The street lamps along the sides of the bridge illuminated the night and their lights reflected off the frozen river.

"What a beautiful view." She turned to Anthony. "So romantic."

She covered her mouth with her hand as soon as she said those words. She didn't mean to say these words to him. She was only commenting on the scenery. "I didn't mean…What I meant was…I…" she tried to explain. She felt so embarrassed sprouting out fanciful notions like a silly girl.

"Do you want to get off and take a look?" he asked. "We can walk across the bridge."

She couldn't believe him. It was a crazy suggestion. The temperature had already dropped to below freezing. Walking across the bridge over the water would chill them to the bone. Even more amazing was that Anthony would propose such a wild idea. He didn't usually act on impulse, and he wasn't one to do something wild and outrageous.

"Let's go." He got up when the bus came to a stop. She had no choice but to follow him. At the same time, she loved it that he was acting on impulse for her.

Unlike the Caldwell's neighborhood, downtown Chicago was buzzing. She didn't expect the streets to be this lively. The city had cancelled its fireworks celebrations because of the lighting restriction at night across the country since Pearl Harbor. She thought that would have kept people home. Instead, people were still out, searching for fun. Rowdy people and groups of servicemen passing through town roamed the streets.

Walking in front of her, Anthony led their way to the bridge where an icy wind blasted. "Oh no," she said.

"What?" he asked.

"I left my scarf on the bus."

He took his own scarf off and wrapped it around her neck.

"What about you?" she asked. "You'll freeze."

"I'll be fine." He stopped and gazed out at the river. "What do you think?"

"Cold," she said. Her teeth chattered and she pulled the scarf tighter around her. Each time she breathed, she could smell his scent. Oddly, she liked it. She held the scarf against her face and inhaled.

"Let's keep moving then," he said.

When they got to the other side of the bridge, he hailed a taxicab to take them to the Allerton Hotel. He pointed to the top of the hotel building where a sign lit with the words "Tip Top Tap."

"Is that where we're going?" she asked.

"Yes."

Coming into the busy hotel lobby, he told her to wait while he took their coats and outerwear to the hotel concierge. Despite the line of people waiting to be helped, the concierge chose to assist him first. She didn't know why, as they weren't guests here. The concierge took their coats and other articles, then made a phone call and nodded to him. He seemed to know his way around here well.

When he came back, they took the elevator to the top floor. The Tip Top Tap, she found out, was a posh, stylish rooftop lounge. He took her hand and led her in past the crowds and groups of people.

"May I see your tickets, sir?" the host at the lounge entrance asked.

"We don't have any," Anthony said.

"I'm sorry but you need tickets…"

Before the host could finish, the lounge manager came to greet them. "Mr. Ardley! Happy New Year! So wonderful to see you joining us tonight. Please come in. I have your seats ready."

The host looked at them, bewildered. Tessa felt as confused as he looked. She was sure Anthony hadn't planned this. She didn't know how he got everyone here to cater to him, but she had no chance to ask questions as he led her inside.

The lounge itself covered only a small area, but it was packed. The rolling music from the jazz band brought out a much more rambunctious mood than the classical quartet that played at the Fur Ball. Tessa felt exhilarated just looking at the people swinging on the dance floor. She had never been out to a lounge or a club on New Year's Eve before.

The manager took them to a table with two seats by the floor-to-ceiling windows which showed a panoramic view of downtown Chicago from up high. Without taking her seat, she went over to the nearest window.

"How do you like this view?" Anthony asked behind her.

She looked at yellow streetlights glowing from the snow-covered streets below. "It's gorgeous."

A waiter came by and gave them their cocktails.

"How were you able to get us in here? The lounge manager knows you."

He took a sip of his drink. "Our family owns a stake in this hotel."

That solved the mystery, she thought. They leaned by the window and watched the crowd.

"Do you like it here more than at the Fur Ball?" he asked.

"I would feel bad if I said that," she said. "Uncle Leon put in so much work planning the Fur Ball, and he's very proud of it. The fur drive and the war bond drive were great causes to support." She wiped the condensation off her glass. "I just never know what to do with myself at parties like that. I guess I'm like my father that way. He always loathed parties and receptions for the theater patrons too, although he never had a choice but to go and pretend to enjoy himself."

They stood silently side-by-side as the crowd danced and laughed. The hour of midnight was approaching and many had put on the 1943 paper party hats the hotel had left on the tables. Some started blowing whistles. The band stopped. The lead singer began the countdown. Everyone followed, cheering with each count. "Ten! Nine! Eight..."

The exuberant atmosphere could burst through the roof. Tessa whispered along to the count, unaware of Anthony watching her while she was watching everyone else.

"Seven! Six! Five! Four..."

The noises of kazoos, clappers, and party horns nearly drowned out the singer's voice. Thrilled, Tessa picked up a clapper from their table and joined in on the fun.

"Three! Two! One!" She waved the clapper in her hand and counted along. The next thing she knew, Anthony had pulled her into his arms and kissed her on her lips.

When he let her go, she felt as if her heart nearly stopped.

It all happened so fast. *What was that?* she thought. A New Year's tradition? Unsure and bewildered, she looked at him. The band had begun playing again and the crowd was singing to the music of "Auld Lang Syne." Confetti and streamers fell down from the ceiling. Everything was so loud and confusing, she could not understand what just happened, or if it even happened at all. She almost thought she imagined it, but that couldn't be. He still had her in his arms.

He erased her doubts when he kissed her again, this time more tenderly and longer.

She felt herself weakening in his arms. Her heart was beating so fast. She wasn't sure if it was because she was caught up in the excitement of the party or something else, but his warm lips on her own stirred a yearning within her. Whatever this might be, she didn't care whether she understood it anymore. She only knew she liked the feeling and she wanted to kiss him back.

"I've wanted to do this for so long," he whispered to her.

She took a deep breath and raised her hand to touch his face. Softly, he brushed his cheek against her hand, then put his own hand on hers and turned to plant a kiss in her palm. Her heart melted. She understood now. This was what people meant when they said their heart melted.

How did she not see this? How did she not know her own feelings for him all this time?

The noises in the room had calmed. The band was now playing a slow song. The familiar melodies of "I'm Confessin' that I Love You" beckoned.

He looked her in the eye. "Tessa, I don't know how to swing dance, and I wouldn't be very good at it if I tried. But if you care, I'd like to do a different kind of dance with you."

A stirring sensation rose in her heart. She held up her hand. He took it and led her out to the dance floor into a slow dance.

On the dance floor, he held her waist. She gasped when he pulled her body against him. Lightly, she raised her free hand to his arm and looked at his chest. There it was again, the force of his strength and his presence. She could give herself completely over to it.

Slowly, they moved to the music. She raised her eyes. He gazed at her and leaned down to kiss her again. She felt light-headed and slightly short of breath. Again and again they kissed, timidly at first, then closer and more and more intimately. The stirring sensation continued to rise within her, and at last, she understood what it was. Desire. The feeling of wanting to be physically closer to him. With that feeling, she kissed him back, more passionately each time as the night went on.

He held her closer. His kisses too became deeper and more and more demanding.

They held onto each other. If only they could hold onto this night, onto time. If only this moment in time could stand still and last forever.

— To be continued —

Post an Amazon Review!

I hope you enjoyed this book.

If you would like to leave a review on Amazon
Please go to:

http://bit.ly/RoseOfAnzio-Moonlight

Thank you!!

Rose of Anzio
Book Two ~ Jalousie

is

Now Available on Amazon!

http://bit.ly/RoseOfAnzio-Jalousie

———————

The second book of the Rose of Anzio series, this sequel to *Moonlight* tells a tale of love that transcends the tide of war.

Now a junior officer with the U.S. Army's Third Infantry Division, Anthony Ardley is deployed to Southern Italy. He follows his unit to Sicily and Salerno until they arrive at the treacherous mountains at the Gustav line. When the Army wages an attack on Anzio to break the impenetrable front, he is thrown into the epicenter of one of the Allies' most disastrous WWII campaigns.

Determined to follow Anthony to war, Tessa Graham secretly enrolls in a training program for military nurses. Here, she meets a veteran suffering from severe battle fatigue that is destroying his mind. She may be his last hope for help. Meanwhile, her petitions to join the medical unit in Anthony's division are ignored. Her chance of joining him diminishes with every turn. All hope is gone.

Will the two young lovers find their ways to surmount their separation and the atrocities of war ahead?

The Rose of Anzio Series
by Alexa Kang

Book One – Moonlight

Book Two – Jalousie

Book Three – Desire

Book Four – Remembrance

Available now on Amazon

Also by Author

Christmas Eve in the City of Dreams, in the anthology
Pearl Harbor and More: Stories of WWII – December, 1941

Subscribe to
Alexa Kang's
Email List

Enjoyed my story? Sign up for my email list
and receive news, artworks, and updates
on the next book release:

http://bit.ly/RoAMailingList

Contact the Author

I would love to hear from you.
You can always contact me or follow me at:

Website:
www.alexakang.com

Facebook:
http://bit.ly/roseofanzio

Twitter:
http://twitter.com/Alexa_Kang

Email:
alexa@alexakang.com

<<<<>>>>

ABOUT THE AUTHOR

Alexa Kang's writing career began in 2014. She grew up in New York City and is a graduate of the University of Pennsylvania. She has travelled to more than 123 cities, and she loves to explore new places and different cultures. When not at work, she lives a secret second life as a novelist. She loves epic loves stories and hopes to bring you many more.